PARALLEL LIVES
A 60's Love Story

MARTHA ALDERSON

WITH BOBBY RAY ALDERSON

PARALLEL LIVES A 60's Love Story by Martha Alderson

Published by Illusion Press, Santa Cruz, CA

ISBN- 13: 978-0-9790596-6-7
ISBN- 10: 0-9790596-6-6
e-Book ISBN- 978-0-9790596-7-4
Library of Congress Control Number: 2020906590

Cover designed by Michelle Fairbanks of Fresh Design
Interior designed by Paula Chinick of Russian Hill Press

Second Edition
First Printing
August 2020

BILLY

ALONG A FORSAKEN stretch in the San Joaquin Valley, a dusty trail hugged Route 99. Railroad tracks ran along the opposite side of the highway, where hobos made camp near enough for train hopping and the mental hospital if help were needed. Two miles outside of town, not a breeze blew. Miles of cotton fields and reeking cattle dung added to the oppressive summer heat. Even the tumbleweeds seemed to sag under the boiling sun. A solitary jackrabbit looked up at Billy's approach.

What with the racket the freight trains made whizzing by every ten minutes, honking car horns on the highway, and his heart pounding in his ears, Billy couldn't think straight. Sweat stung his eyes. Unless he did something quick, his loot was going to end up in the dirt. Puffing hard, he checked behind him. No one was in sight, but that didn't mean he was safe.

Pausing only long enough to rip off his torn shirt, the boy emptied the bulging pockets of his dungarees and placed the food he'd stolen on top of the shirt. Wiping the sweat from his eyes, he tied the arms and tail of the shirt together into a package, slung the bundle over his shoulder, and took off running the last half-mile as fast as he could. The breeze he created felt good against his bare chest.

Coming up on the bleached backside of Grandma's house, Billy sneaked through the kitchen garden like the thief he was, crushing what was left of the garlic and puny green beans, now shriveled and dead.

A thump sounded at regular intervals. Billy's eyes narrowed. He ran around the side of the house reckless for a fight, if truth been told. Grandma sat in the old washtub smack in the middle of the front yard. Her knees stuck up, mostly covering her nakedness.

"What's all the racket?" Billy tried to catch his breath.

"Hey, Running Wolf. Workmen are digging a trench alongside the highway."

At two hundred pounds, Grandma spilled out over the sides of the tub. Her long black braid was sopping wet. Past the peeling paint and rotted porch, Billy spotted the empty screen door. He tensed, expecting the worst.

"Where's Ginger?"

"Huckleebuck, Billy," Grandma said. "That dog of yours is in heat. I got her tied up in the side yard."

No dust clouds down the dirt road signaled an outsider's arrival. The all clear didn't mean nothing, though. The law had come screaming out of nowhere for him plenty of times before.

"You about done here?"

Grandma looked up with a big smile. She had her mother's, Martha-the-Gobbler's, wide nose and round face. Her hands clutched the washtub's rusted siding. She shook her head no; she wasn't finished. Billy scowled. His empty stomach weakened him.

"Look here, Grandma," he said, untying his shirt bundle. "I got us some sugar and flour, all the fixings for—"

"Billy, I got something to tell you."

The sunlight caught Grandma's hair and turned the pitch-black mass nearly blue. She rubbed the wolf hanging from her neck, opened her mouth, and gulped like she was thirsty. Billy had never seen her act like that. And, why wasn't she scolding him for stealing? She was all the time scolding him. His heart froze over.

"You sick or something, Grandma?" he shouted over the noise of an incoming train. The ground shook beneath his feet.

"I got something to tell you, and I'd like to get out of this here tub first. I do believe I'm stuck."

"You are?" A grin pushed against Billy's fear and hunger and loathing.

"You better not laugh at me, Billy-boy. You best come up with a way to get me out of here."

Relieved to get things moving, Billy took both her hands and yanked. She didn't budge. He spat in his palms and rubbed them together.

"Try tipping me over instead."

Billy hauled up on one side of the tub as Grandma leaned over, and she slid out naked in the dirt. Seeing her as dirty as a grave-digger, Billy couldn't help laughing. He wrapped his arms around his head, but she didn't swipe at him. She broke out laughing, too. He flopped down next to her, rubbing mud across his bare chest, both of them laughing their heads off and both a muddy mess. Grandma caught her breath and nodded toward the kitchen.

"I forgot the drying cloth. Go look in the *wajandawgemek.*"

When Billy got back from the kitchen, Grandma had sloshed herself with what water was left in the tub. Drying herself didn't make her less dirty just spread the mud around. No sign of the law. They better not let up on him on account of feeling sorry for him. Still, things were looking up. He thrust out her housedress and walked toward the kitchen, imagining a tall stack of hotcakes. His mouth watered like a hound dog.

Grandma stayed right where she was, straightening the apron bow around her waist for what seemed like forever. All the good feelings building inside of Billy drained right back out again.

"Your ma's coming," Grandma whispered.

So, Ma wasn't dead after all. As his heart dropped

to darkness, Billy stared at a smudge of mud across Grandma's forehead.

"She found herself a new man. They're coming to take you back with them."

Wincing like he'd been stabbed, Billy swallowed wrong and ended up coughing. He turned away and tried to picture Ma in his mind, but he couldn't anymore. He remembered the day she left when he was five. She had just come back, and he sensed she was planning on leaving again, without him. All day long he planted himself as near to her as he could get. He wanted to be real close, ready in case she needed to hug him. She never did. And now, as much as he wanted to get out of the valley, he didn't need her either.

"Don't make me go," he pleaded, straining to get past the lump in his throat. "I promise you won't have to worry about me no more. I'll keep my mouth shut. Do what I'm told. Go to school. Pick cotton. And lots more, too. I promise."

Grandma wrapped herself around him. "Now, Billy. Don't get to fussin'. I do believe it's for the best. You have two little brothers you've never even met. You should be with your family."

"You're my family." His voice was as flat as an old tire as he gouged a hole in the ground, blooding his big toe. "When's she coming?"

"Soon."

He ran a palm over his damp cheek. "You coming with me?"

"This is my home."

"Then, I ain't going neither." Billy pushed away from her with tears burning the back of his throat. "Who's going to see you've got food to eat? And who's going to make you eat it before you give it all away to a tramp at the back door?" He crossed his arms, causing the hardened mud to crack across his chest. He glared at her.

Grandma looked away and swung his shirt bundle over her shoulder. She started toward the house. Though he should be drooling at the thought of her making biscuits and white gravy with squaw bread and honey, he wasn't hungry anymore. He spat on the ground and watched the dust rise.

"I never told you this, Billy. A vision came to me a few nights ago."

"Ah, Grandma."

"You listen to me and listen real good, Running Wolf. You're *Bodewadmi gdaw*."

"Speak English," Billy growled.

"You are *Potawatomi*, the true people of great warriors." She smiled in the aggravated way she had when she'd stopped listening; it was as if she stepped into a dream.

"Your spirit is too big for this place. One day you'll find the woman of your other half, and you'll become a *wkamek*, a chief of big medicine. I've been expecting this. They got good schools up there in the city. We'll put down tobacco for your journey. Whenever anything bothers you, you'll have that tobacco to depend upon the way our ancestors always have. Offer your *sema* to the fire, pray, and you'll do just fine. *Iwkshiye'tuk.*"

Billy suddenly wondered if any half-breeds like him were where Ma lived, and immediately convinced himself that no one there walked like Grandma did, toe-heel, to lessen the noise of her step. Down to the wrinkles across her face, she was all Potawatomi.

"I don't need me no damn Indian ghost to tell me what's going to happen. I can tell you straightaway right here and now. Me going with Ma is gonna end up like shit."

"Watch that mouth of yours," snapped Grandma as she slipped the necklace from her neck. "You ain't never going to get the life you deserve if you can't learn to think before you act out. Your greatest challenge will be to get control over yourself and that mouth of yours. Here, I want you to have this."

She touched the wooden carving gently with her fingertips and lifted the wolf to her lips. Then, she slung the rawhide cord over Billy's head. As she positioned the wolf at his sternum, the words she spoke were drowned out by a piercing freight train-whistle.

Billy yanked away. And then he ran.

"*Ni pi je ezhyayen?*" shouted Grandma.

Anywhere, he thought. Always running toward the highway. The further his legs stretched, the better he felt. The second he cleared the side yard, Ginger set to barking. She yanked herself free and made a beeline for him, the frayed rope hanging around her neck.

Racing together down the path he'd bushwhacked tromping back and forth to hitch Grandma a ride into town, he stubbed his toe. His heart jerked. Cringing, he refused to cry.

Ginger surged ahead. Billy followed the sound in his mind of thundering hooves from a herd of wild ponies. Ponies turned to tires slapping against asphalt and the sound of gear changes from Route 99. He always believed the highway led to escape and would one day reconnect the lost sections of his life that had been washed away.

Snatches of music from a car radio reached him. Through the trees he spotted the fender of a brand new '55 Hudson as it sped past on the highway. A '53 Studebaker, '49 Chevy, and a '51 Ford whizzed by.

Far south in the distance, sunlight glinted off the grill of a car he had never seen before. He turned and headed for the light with one hope: that someday was today.

MAJA

ON ROUTE 99, seven-year-old Maja Hawthorne sat next to her grandmother in the corner of a long black limousine. The two of them faced forward while Maja's mother and father sat opposite them in a seat facing backward. Their driver, behind a glass divider, was chauffeuring them home to the San Francisco Bay Area.

Maja whispered garble, meaningless to anyone else, nonetheless comforting to the young girl. Fussing, she still didn't have a plan how to delay their homecoming—preferably long enough to miss all of first grade next month. She shuddered, well aware she was heading toward a snarl even Mormor might not be able to untangle. She slung an arm across her grandmother's shoulder.

"Once upon a time," Mormor began, patting Maja's cheek as if reading her mind, and then picked up her knitting.

As much as Maja had loved Disneyland

yesterday, she liked even better Mormor's stories of princes and princesses that reigned in all the land. Mormor always included a reminder to be a good girl or suffer the fury of *Loki*, but Maja wasn't afraid of the handsome and evil fire-giant. She was brave.

Straightening the Minnie Mouse hat that Daddy had crowned her with at the opening ceremonies of Mr. Disney's make-believe park, Maja studied Mormor's mouth as she spoke. A buzzing masked a chant from deep inside. Rather than listen to the comfort that told her when best to keep to herself and turn invisible, Maja flicked off the distraction. She was determined to learn how to make sounds come out of her mouth right so people understood her. Mormor said Maja was unable to speak because Mother stood under an elder tree when she was pregnant. Mother said the reason was from listening to too many Swedish fairytales.

Mormor continued, "A little princess lived in a faraway county." Mormor's accent, like a lullaby, turned the story into a dancing rhyme. Her voice lifted at the end of each sentence, helping Maja follow the story.

"Olle-the-Loyal watched over the princess, for she was as delicate and pale as a lily."

Imitating the movements of Mormor's lips as she told the tale, Maja turned dizzy from the kaleidoscope of speeding changes. Her lips fell out of beat, and her tongue knotted in on itself—her breathing troubled and hot. Mormor knew the answer to everything, like where to dig for the firmest and tastiest wild mushrooms and how to steer clear of troll forests. Whispering to herself, Maja wondered why her grandmother didn't just invent a magic spell and fix her.

Mormor unraveled a row of her knitting. "It was not her beauty people admired. The princess was most renowned for her wondrous blue eyes, which spoke of things without words." Her story kept time with the click-clacking of her knitting needles.

Mother leaned forward from the seat facing them. Maja shifted as Mother rearranged the ruffles of her white ankle socks just so.

"Mor, not that story." Mother raised an eyebrow.

"*Fem, sex, sju, atta, nio, tio.*" Mormor counted her stitches in Swedish.

Barely swiveling her head, Maja snuck a look from the corner of her eye. Mother's fierce face spun Maja's attention straight ahead. Silent and still, she willed herself invisible.

"Maja must learn to use her words," said Mother. "In this country, a woman's beauty counts more than her brains. It's our duty to teach her to use that to her advantage. She could be in movies someday. Like Greta Garbo. I still think it was unfair of you, Richard, not to let me look up Greta. Walter's Disneyland is right next door to Hollywood."

Mother's voice floated faraway and wispy. She pulled a perfumed handkerchief from the cuff of her glove and dabbed behind Maja's ears.

Maja stared out the window for a sign of a prince or fairy godmother dressed in gold. Movies were big and loud and confusing.

"You shared the same ship to America," said Daddy. "That doesn't mean Greta Garbo would remember you, Birgit." Daddy changed to his happy voice, and Maja knew he was talking to her. "Kiddo, do you know what all those little puffs of white are on the plants outside—"

"Why not?" Mother said. "Because I wasn't allowed on the upper deck? She was waiting every morning when I snuck upstairs. She asked me to call her Greta, you know. And she was lovely to me, not at all withdrawn and private like the newspapers said."

The longer Mother spoke about the days of her great crossing, the cooler the air in the car turned, and the more relaxed Maja felt. Mormor's knitting needles stopped talking, and her breathing turned noisy. She was asleep. Now she would never finish the story.

"After killing more than 700 people and destroying half of Long Island, the Hurricane of '38 headed straight toward us," said Mother. "The waves were giant. The wind horrible. Greta and I stood side-by-side and clutched the railing for dear life. You don't just forget the person you shared a voyage like that with.

"Greta started out modeling for newspaper advertisements," Mother continued. "You have eyes just like her, Maja. I told you that. Remember? But to be in the motion pictures, you must first learn to speak. Try saying something for me now."

Maja called to the words. *Hurry, hurry. Quick, quick.* Words giggled and hid from her, shy about telling Mother that Maja did not want to be in the motion pictures.

"Maja's only seven years old, and already you've decided she's going to be a movie star?" said Daddy. "Really, Birgit. Don't worry that sweet little head of yours about being famous," Daddy said, using his happy voice again. "All you have to concentrate on is how swell first grade is going to be. You're excited, aren't you?"

Maja nodded, and smiled, too, but mostly because when Daddy leaned forward to speak to her, he slid off the edge of the low seat facing her. Squatted in front her, he patted down his wavy hair, curls Maja had inherited from him, and Mother turned into springy Shirley Temple hair. He pushed his fingers across his Clark Gable mustache and winked. Ripples of love swept against Maja's heart. She laughed into his brown eyes. He slid back in his seat.

That wasn't the first time Daddy had talked about school. Like the other times, his voice tried too hard to win her over.

Mormor snorted and woke herself up. "The princess' eyes spoke a language all people and every animal understood." Her voice was sleepy but stubborn.

"Not her eyes, Mor, her words. If our princess can't learn to speak up for herself, she'll be crushed at the s-c-h-o-o-l. You know that as well as I do," said Mother. "Maja, close your mouth. You're gaping."

Mother said Maja must learn to pay attention, but words crowded into everything. They droned on and on, shouted and whispered, hollow and confused. Without words, she could hear a mournful car horn from somewhere up ahead.

As the car horn blared louder, Mother crossed her legs and smoothed a hand down the back seam of her silk stockings.

Their limousine driver slowed behind a car pulling off the road. Wearisome cotton fields snapped into a stand of trees. As if she were following a pointing finger, Maja craned her neck for a better view. A car, its front end smashed against a tree on the side of the highway, flew into flames. Startled but strangely unafraid of the explosion, Maja threw her hands over her ears. To one side of the burning car, a man leaned over a woman with blood on her forehead. Two other men held something long and furry between them, the color of dusted brick. A dog.

Maja rolled down the window and poked out her head. A rush of summer heat slapped her face and smoky air burned her eyes.

Beneath the sound of the car horn, trees whispered and bushes sighed with a chant from one of Mormor's fairy tales.

He is coming.
For he is here.

The words came from deep inside of her and

sent popping bubbles through her bones just as an odd trilling flickered in her throat. She immediately opened her mouth for her pure and perfect speech to magically emerge.

"Maja, shut your mouth," scolded Mother. "Robert, knock on the driver's window. I don't want him stopping."

Ripped from the sound of the chant and all possibility of speech, Maja writhed against Mother's impatience. This time, however, her harsh words didn't shrivel her in anticipation of being stomped flat like a sow bug. And, this time, the sequins in her eyes weren't tears. They were embers of light, like tiny spinning fireworks.

Daddy cleared his throat.

"Now, now, Birgit," he said in a low voice with a smile on his face and his jaw twitching.

A shirtless boy appeared as if from the flames of the burning car. Confused about what was happening in real life and what the chant was, Maja grabbed hold of the window frame so as not to topple out of the car.

The men dropped the dog in an open trench. Running to the ditch, the boy set his jaw, his lips pressed into a little line. Maja's heart slumped. The dog was his. The boy raised his chin, pooling tears in his eyes from running down his face. Even with both her hands stuck out like a shield, loneliness crushed hard against her. The dog was dead.

"For heaven's sake, Richard, the driver is

stopping. Maja, stop mumbling, and roll up your window." Mother yanked Maja's foot and spoke so loudly that even if Maja were deaf, which she wasn't in the least, she'd still be able to hear.

"Your father will take care of this."

Daring to disobey, Maja thrust her head out the window, holding tight to her hat. The boy was tall and skinny and proud. Even with layers of dirt and a thick ribbon of hair hiding most of his face, he appeared strangely familiar to her. He also looked as if he could shout his name out in school and make himself understood. If they took him home with them, he could teach her how too.

An old woman with a long black braid and sad eyes held the boy against her to stop him from jumping in the trench with his beloved dog. Somehow Maja also knew her. The woman was like a tap from the other side of a covered window.

The driver stopped the car on the side of the road. The boy turned his head, and Maja's heart leapt like a rabbit springing over a hedge. In the boy's eyes, lines of trees and the shapes of bushes sharpened. His face glowed like a crown of peacock feathers on a sunny day.

Whispering to herself, Maja yanked open the door lever, tumbled out of the car, and ran to the boy who controlled the sun and the moon. Just short of him, she tripped over trampled weeds. He reached out. Clutching his hand, she felt the world sway back and forth like rocking in a cradle. Unlike Daddy's velvety and soft skin, the boy's hands were scratchy and rough.

Warmed to her toes and suddenly shy, she bowed her head. Through her eyelashes, she stared up at shiny tears that now gushed down his cheeks like a rainstorm. She lifted her head and looked fully at him. She wanted her eyes to speak without words like the princess in Mormor's story and bring comfort to the boy.

Around his neck hung a small wooden carving. Maja stepped forward. She lifted a hand to touch it. The boy stood still staring at her as if under a spell like in one of Mormor's fairytales. The wood under her fingers seemed to jump. Sure that the little carving was magical and could grant her clear speech, she looked for guidance from the boy.

His eyes flashed and the spell broke. With a miserable smile, he squeezed her hand. In that breath-snatching moment, they were inseparable. In the next, they parted.

And then Daddy was there. He put a hand on the boy's shoulder.

"Are you going to be all right, son?" Daddy asked in his low and serious voice.

The boy nodded and thrust his hands deep in his pockets without looking up.

Holding Daddy's hand on the way back to the limousine, Maja looked over her shoulder. She eyed the boy as her fingertips tingled like chimes on the wind.

AGAIN

DUE TO THE UNCOMMONLY hot fall days they'd been having, Billy woke with sweat in his ears. Even after two months of rubbing reality into gritty eyes, he still found himself in the middle of a hellhole. Damn. If he hadn't been proved right.

He rolled his eyes thinking about how living with Ma and her new man was a disaster. Then, remembering what day it was, he leapt off the couch that also served as his bed in the middle of Ma's front room. Unlike back home in the central valley with Grandma, the air in Oakland hung heavy, like a cloud of sticky blue exhaust. Ma's tiny, two-bedroom flat above The Drop-In Club—a neighborhood bar that also served as a Pentecostal church on Sundays—locked in the heat, even with all the windows open.

Torn and rumpled as it was, Billy slipped on the one shirt he owned and felt for the wolf necklace Grandma had given him. With his neck empty, he searched his pockets and thrust his hands between the couch cushions. If those two little brothers of his got their hands on it …

Billy burrowed deeper. Crumbs stuck in his nubby fingernails as he bumped into a lump. He lifted the wolf carving in the air like a trophy, and the lid clanked shut on his anger. He hung the necklace where it belonged without bothering to button up his shirt. It was too hot for that.

Howls came from the bedroom of the two pains-in-the-neck, slowing his getaway. Billy yanked open the icebox. Punching the top of it, he swore. As usual, Ma had forgotten to buy food. He missed Grandma's cooking. Hell, he missed everything about Grandma. If Ma knew how to cook, she hadn't shown any sign of it.

With the howling intensifying, Billy scrabbled under the couch for the scrawny orange he'd grabbed from a street vendor and hidden for when hunger scrapped his gut. He peeled the orange, the aroma teasing his nose. Fighting his own need, he gave half to each boy, tousled their hair, and dried their eyes.

Just as he was at the screen door, Ma stumbled from her bedroom wearing her ratty pink robe. Billy froze while Patti Page wailed from the jukebox at the club downstairs.

Ma sang along with the song, one side of her face swollen nearly twice its normal size. He swore under his breath. He didn't need her. Never had. Never would. He turned to sneak out of the apartment, nearly knocking over the rifle leaning up against the doorframe, the weapon Ma used to scare off the repo man. He steadied the gun, about to bust a gut, and eased the door shut behind him.

Her voice echoed in the stairwell.

"Billy Wayman Wolfe. You get back here."

He flew over the railing and hit the ground running.

"Goddammit, Billy. I need your help."

She might say that, but Ma didn't need him, not now that Ray was gone. Only good thing about Billy's birthday so far was his stepfather driving off in his moving van to pick up a full load for the Phoenix-Tucson run. Ray had snuck out before Billy had a chance to see what he'd done to Ma. She was safe for now. Trouble was, Ray would come back, and she'd let him in. Billy shook his head and clenched both fists.

Sopping sweat off his face, he stopped at the cracked and broken sidewalk and spit, wishing he could spew Ray out of their lives for good. Billy's balled-up knuckles throbbed, but he resisted the urge to unknot them, sure that his rigid spine and ready fists held him up.

"Tell me, Ma," Billy shouted back at her. "Why does Ray always beat you right before he leaves, anyways? So you don't forget him?"

"Billy Wayman, you best get up here. D'you hear me? I'll take the strap to you. This time I will. Truly, I will." She shouted from the open window. The pointy silver sunglasses at least sat on her battered face right. Billy had bought her the glasses after the last time Ray left. Time before that her nose was too broken and they would have hung crooked astride it. He could take Ray's aggression, his shoves and pushes, but to bully the little boys—his own sons— and beat Ma … Billy imagined aiming the rifle at Ray and pulling the trigger. Now that he understood Ray's pattern, he planned on being around to guarantee there wasn't never going to be a next time.

With the hair out of his eyes, he shouted back, not caring he was standing in front of the club with all the doors and windows open.

"Or, does he make you ugly on purpose so no one wants to look at you?"

Mister Sanchez stuck his head out of the bar. Billy took off running.

Ma screeched at him.

He pushed out his chest and pumped his arms. The air lifted the hair off his forehead, cooling his agitation. He ran through the parking lot, happy to cut, if only temporarily, the knot she'd made of his life, of all of their lives. The pavement burned his feet but not so much that he needed shoes. Didn't matter anyways. Never owned him a pair of shoes that fit. Today was going to change all that.

He jerked the bicycle he'd stolen when he first got to town out of its hiding place, jumped aboard, and mad-pedaled down the sidewalk. Old Miss Jenkins and her ma out on their morning stroll were dead center in his path. He steered hard to the right, pulled up on the handlebars, and rushed onto San Pablo Street. Tires squealed behind him, as he darted through two lanes of traffic. He ducked into an alleyway and shot into a blast of sunlight in the middle of the bustling world of commerce.

All along Broadway, everything blazed shiny and new, making his clothes look all the rattier and the bicycle rustier. Grim, he considered the scene: fancy jewelry and made-to-order clothes looked back from behind plate-glass windows. The latest cars— glistening new—glided along the street. He pushed away his self-pity and summoned up a picture of the keenest car, hands down, he'd ever seen. When he got to Oakland, he'd visited a library for the first time and looked up the car he'd spotted on Route 99—a Cadillac Fleetwood, Seventy-Five series. That car had become a symbol, a dream of getting for himself, and for Grandma and Ma, the sort of life that man had. Today marked his first step in that direction.

At 10th and Franklin, Hanes department store loomed into view. Grinning with excitement in his chest, Billy pulled to a stop next to a newspaper stand where his buddy Webb waited on his bicycle. Though he'd picked the meeting place, now Billy regretted not taking into account the nearness to the Open Market.

Webb stood in front of Toccoli's Delicatessen with hanging deep-fried piglets gaunt with dried up eyes still in their heads; turkeys and hams for

Thanksgiving; wine barrels overflowing with briny, sour pickles; and what must be the most mouthwatering baked bread he had ever smelled.

Billy breathed deep, almost keeling over with hunger. He made a mental note to swing by on their get-away and steal him a sausage and one for his brothers, too—none of the high-priced ones behind the long glass counter, but the tastiest one hanging from the awning above his head. His stomach bellowed.

"Why you got on that old Indian charm? I thought you weren't going to let people see it," said Webb.

Soon after Billy moved to Oakland, he'd met Webb. When Webb learned that Billy was also part Indian, though from a different tribe, Webb had made him promise to keep quiet about it. As well as part African American, Webb said that being poor and Negro was hard enough. Billy was proud of his Indian heritage, but he'd promised anyway. That promise had sealed their friendship.

"I need the good luck," said Billy, fumbling with his shirt buttons. His fingers were slick with sweat and wouldn't cooperate. He gave up. "I aim to steal me an alligator wallet in Hanes."

Webb scowled. "You don't need you a wallet."

Billy almost told Webb the wallet was for all the money he planned on making from his very first store job, sweeping up and doing odd jobs for the jeweler. He'd sent Grandma every quarter he made weeding and hauling trash since he got to Oakland, every quarter Ma didn't steal from him first. He worried about Grandma all by herself, and he was done with being poor. Work hard, fill the wallet, and he'd have him plenty to buy a house for Grandma with an inside bathroom and a yard with a fence so a dog could be safe. He might even let his little brothers come live with them. Ma, too—provided she didn't bring Ray along.

"Hold my bicycle in the ready," Billy said, keeping his voice low. "When you see me split from Hanes, I'll be hauling ass straight for you."

Billy's heart thumped in his chest as he left a dubious-looking Webb holding their bikes at the newspaper stand. He crossed the street, dodging traffic and nearly getting run over by a police car, and arrived in front of the giant double glass doors of the department store that took up much of the entire block.

His legs started shaking so hard that to get over the threshold he had to march locked-kneed. Even with all the practice he'd had stealing food in the valley for him and Grandma, he knew full-well that Oakland was no one-sheriff, backwater town. Poor kid at the counter with the most expensive items in the store; he was bound to stick out like a lightning bolt. He had to get in, grab the wallets—one for him and one to surprise Webb—and get out without the weekend security guard spotting him.

Then he remembered. He was twelve years old

today, a man. Couldn't very well go out and kill him a buffalo to mark the shift from boy to grown-up, not that he ever could. By way of celebrating his birthday and his newfound resolve to work his way to success—stealing the wallet was his ceremonial declaration out of poverty.

As customers milled around, Billy turned his back on his boyhood and marched into manhood.

THE CANDY STORE SAT in a small stone shop dwarfed on one side by the giant Hanes' building and, on the other, the clock tower. As much as Maja looked forward to her favorite candy—Rocky Road fudge—she kept from following Mormor, her parents, and their neighbor Clay inside. She wanted to hold onto the warmth she'd felt during the entire drive into Oakland from Great Oaks, the family estate in the sprawling foothills of Diablo.

The happiness inside was the same sensation she'd felt all throughout the bright summer days and into the nights after mysteriously connecting with the boy on the side of a forgotten highway. She'd relived those few golden minutes until the memory was as tattered and worn as her beloved picture books. Maja *still* couldn't talk right, but the boy's noble heart that demanded no words had made her wish to see him again. And so, everywhere she went with her parents, she searched for him. With hope in her heart that today was the day, she peered up and down the broad street and tree-lined sidewalk filled with busy shoppers and fussy baby carriages.

"Come on, Maja," said Clay, interrupting her search.

Maja smiled at Clay, her nearest neighbor and best friend. Their two families shared deep roots in the area and a friendship that spanned generations. Clay spent most of his time at Maja's house because his parents were rarely home, and he liked playing tennis with Daddy. Maja had always idolized Clay like an older brother and felt special when he didn't mind helping with her speech practice.

"Time for your favorite fudge," he said.

In the middle of talking, his voice squeaked to a high note and then dropped back to normal. Mother had warned Maja more than once not to laugh when Clay's voice went funny, that he was growing up and soon his voice would always be low and deep. Still, Maja couldn't help smiling; she wasn't the only one who couldn't speak right.

After choosing their favorite candies, Maja was the first one outside. A shout sounded and the sky turned brighter.

In a fit of unexpected confidence, she decided to speak. She formed the sounds just like Miss Sally, her speech therapist at school, was teaching her.

"Did you hear that?" Maja watched for a sign that her parents understood her.

Daddy pushed back his felt hat with its wide brim, grinning like the first time she dived off the deep end of the country club swimming pool. He offered her a piece of candy from a crumpled, white sack.

"Clay?" Mother always turned to Clay when she couldn't understand Maja. He was the only one besides Mormor who could untangle what Maja was trying to say.

"Gee, Maja. Hear what?" Clay's voice broke and cracked like a duck.

Maja did her best to keep a grin off her face at Clay's disobedient voice.

"I don't hear anything, Maja. Where?" he asked, his voice back to regular.

"Those people. There," tried Maja.

Daddy ran his fingers across his skinny mustache. He winked as they waited for a tight group of people to pass and the view to clear.

"Could it be any hotter?" complained Mother. Looking wilted and bedraggled, she had a preoccupied expression on her face as she twisted open the little metal latch on her willow-basket purse.

Vibrating with excitement, Maja craned to watch people scatter on the sidewalk. Daddy shook her arm like rattling her awake.

"There." He pointed.

A crowd parted, and a boy with wild hair darted across the street. Even so great a distance from where they'd first met, it was *him*—the boy with the magic carving. With her mouth open, Maja turned to share her parent's surprise. If they recognized the boy, they didn't show it. Beginning with a smile, she giggled and then outright laughed at the joy of seeing him again.

A dark-skinned boy held out a bicycle to the boy. The two of them leaned across their handlebars and pedaled like a blur.

Maja imagined ripping off her white gloves and yellow belt and double-collared little jacket with long, narrow cuffs that matched Mother's outfit down to the polka-dot dress. Mother went to a lot of trouble buying look-alike clothes. She said it would attract attention. When Mother was Maja's age, she'd wanted to be a model, and Mormor refused to help her.

More interested in turning invisible than showing off clothes in front of strangers, Maja imagined zooming on the back of the boy's bike, holding tight to his waist. She'd much rather travel the world with the two boys than do what Mother told her she must.

The boys disappeared. Not wanting to lose the undemanding freedom they stirred in her, Maja sensed they were still near.

"Those are bad boys," said Daddy.

Ready to stick up for them, Maja didn't bother as Mother laughed and kissed Daddy on the lips. Together with Mormor, her parents strolled to the car. In a dreamy mood, Maja hummed a happy tune and wrapped herself in a warm hug of excitement.

Clay came up behind her and pushed her forward.

"I've got a secret," he said, his voice lower than usual.

Me, too, crowed Maja to herself. She thought of the boy and wished Clay would just tell her instead of always having to tease her first.

Clay snickered.

Maja tilted her head to the side in question and raised her eyebrows. Distracted and unusually quiet, Clay didn't answer. She put a hand on his arm.

"Not now. Tonight, after your parents leave for the opera."

Clay sounded serious. His eyes were glassy and unfocused.

"Please." She formed the sounds with great care and using her very best manners. She wondered if his grown-up voice was making Clay act so strangely.

"You'll like it," he said, more to himself than to her.

He stared up at the old clock tower at the end of the block. Peering into his face, she sensed he wasn't looking at anything at all. Heat flowed from him as if something inside was about to boil over.

Maja trembled, suddenly frightened. It was as if an evil twin had replaced Clay. She searched up and down the sidewalk for the real him.

Breathing heavily, his voice rose. "Let's go, silly goose." Clay pushed Maja toward the car, sliding his hot and clammy hand down the small of her back.

CONFIDENT THAT THE HANES security guard didn't stand a chance of catching him, Billy pulled his bicycle to a stop several blocks away from the department store. He clapped Webb on the back.

"Thanks for your help, Daddy-O." Billy peeled away one of the wallets he stole and offered it to Webb.

Together, they smelled the genuine leather and grinned.

"I'm going back," said Billy, slipping his wallet in his back pocket.

Webb looked up, his eyes wide. "Are you nuts?"

"Only as far as the delicatessen," said Billy. "I want to grab me one of those hanging sausages."

"Someone recognizes you and you're dust."

"I'll be okay. See you later." Billy circled back the way they had come.

As he waited for a chance to snatch a sausage, his eyes came to rest on a two-tone, turquoise and white, Ford Fairlane Sunliner convertible with whitewall tires. The car was parked across the street not far from the entrance to the candy store. Billy whistled low. Now, not only in anticipation of eating the sausage, he salivated over the expensive car.

A man standing next to the car looked dimly familiar to Billy. Then he remembered the day Ginger died. This was the same man who had come for a yellow-haired girl who wouldn't let go of his hand. Seeing the man again, Billy felt the warmth of his hand on his shoulder and heard the echo of what Billy wanted to believe was sincere concern in his voice—

the kindest two gestures any man had ever shown him, especially on the saddest day of his life.

Not far away from the car stood the same yellow-haired girl from the side of the highway. Startled, Billy blinked his eyes. Then he stared at her, confused. Overcome by the shocker of seeing the two of them again, lonely without his dog, and missing Grandma, Billy gripped the handlebars to keep from falling over.

Grandma had called her *kwe wisaw ninsesen*—girl with the yellow hair. Now, Billy nicknamed her Wisaw.

A boy around his age had a hand low on her back. Billy recognized the look the boy gave Wisaw and immediately disliked it and him.

As Billy watched, the boy spanked Wisaw, causing her to lurch forward. Instead of moving his hand away, the boy, now red-faced, seemed to press his fingertips into her skin, as if probing for something. Wisaw slapped the boy's hand away, her face blazing.

The clock in the clock tower chimed.

Back at the car, a woman wind-milled her arm like a crossing guard. As the other boy slunk toward them, the woman turned away and tied a scarf around her head while the man helped an older woman— about Billy's grandmother's age—into the backseat. Even as they prepared to leave, Wisaw didn't move. Jostled by passing shoppers, she stuck her tongue out at the retreating figure. Billy couldn't tell if she was crying or ready to beat up the kid.

Guessing she was the man's daughter, Billy grabbed the chance to pay back the man's kindness. He crossed the street and stopped his bicycle steps away from her. She was trembling and whispering to herself though he couldn't make out what she was saying.

Wisaw turned her head. Upon seeing him, she gasped. The furrows between her eyes softened, and her trembling stopped. Oblivious of the people around them and with her mouth still in a surprised tiny O, she giggled. Billy's concern turned to a hesitant grin. Together they laughed in recognition.

She leaned toward him just as a passing man gestured and knocked into her. Billy held his bicycle with one hand and reached out to steady her with the other. As his fingers closed over hers, her breath seemed to catch.

Forgotten heart-skipping dreams swept over Billy. Trunks of jewels like treasure chests, snowy white skin, and huge eyes that turned into an owl. Then, just as it had been the last time they met, as if spellbound, Wisaw smiled and wouldn't let go of his hand.

Searching for something to say to protect her, Billy cleared his throat. "Did that other kid hurt you?"

She shook her head, though he spotted her hesitation.

"Keep away from him."

With her hand still in his, Billy headed toward the Fairlane threading through the people coming and going on either side of them.

"Hey there," Wisaw's father shouted. "What do you think you're doing?"

Her father's candy sack fell, scattering chocolates on the sidewalk. The other boy surged toward them low, hunched and glaring. Billy pushed out his chest and locked eyes with him, slowing the boy's forward progress. Billy anticipated smashing into each other. Hurting him wasn't everything—it was the only thing.

At the sound of another shout, both Billy and Wisaw turned. Someone pointed at Billy. The Hanes security guard shot from the double doors toward him.

Wisaw tugged on his shirt. He peered down at her.

"Go," she said.

Startled by the garbled word, Billy wondered if she was a foreigner.

"You sure?" he asked.

She nodded. Billy gave the other kid one last warning glare. Then, with his eyes flashing, he smiled an invisible cloak around her shoulders. She grinned and cupped her hands together, like holding a butterfly.

Billy hopped on his bicycle and sped away.

CLAY

SOON AFTER MAJA'S PARENTS' car disappeared from Great Oaks over the rumbling wooden bridge on their way to the opera, Maja's stomach fluttered. As if ten thousand butterflies lifted her off the ground, she'd floated through the afternoon reliving every moment with the same boy who had filled her dreams at night and who had occupied her thoughts while she learned to speak and knit with Mormor. From her surprise at finding him not halfway around the world but steps away from her, to the expression of longing on his face, she believed he too had thought of her every day as she thought of him.

Somehow the first time she hadn't noticed his large, blue-gray eyes. Then she had only noticed his wild brown hair, the glowing face of a crown prince, and his rough and scratchy magic hands. He'd seemed the shy one this time as she noticed his too-short trousers and bare feet and his wrinkled and torn shirt. Around his neck hung the same tiny wood carving that looked like a wolf. Curious, she'd peered it at. The wolf winked as if knowing something about her she didn't know about herself. If she hadn't been so surprised and wasn't so self-conscious about the way she talked, she would have asked him about it. There were so many things she longed to know about him.

The chance meeting felt as if it had lasted her entire life.

Lost in a waking dream of taking adventures with the boy on the back of his bike, Maja imagined the next time she'd see him again. The doorbell rang. Her skin jumped.

"That will be Clay," said Mormor.

Clay lurched into the living room, hunched over and hairy. Could be *Loki* the handsome fire-giant of mischief crouched beyond the big black windows that sent Clay's face into shadow. A movement in the giant oak tree out front made Maja flinch. Instead of making the night disappear, Clay's looks brought on mad and wicked fears of things she couldn't see. Whatever his secret was and why he had wrongly touched her, she didn't care anymore. She wanted her friend back.

Settling into her favorite chair in the family room off the kitchen, Mormor pulled out her knitting.

"Maja, you're shivering. Go get a sweater," she ordered.

Alarmed, Maja nodded, unwilling to travel alone down the long dark hallway for some silly old sweater. Without meeting Mormor's eyes, and even though the mystery boy on the bicycle had warned her to stay away, she followed Clay into the kitchen to help him prepare dinner—this being Carmen and Ramon's night off. He turned on the oven and took three TV dinners from the freezer, a special treat saved for her parents' nights out.

Maja sat at the table, waiting for Clay to turn around and fearful of who she'd see. Dreading that he'd say something nasty about the boy and wreck everything for her, she rose to her feet, set on keeping the boy her secret. Before she could escape, Clay spun around.

"What has a neck and no head?" he asked, his voice back to normal and kidding as usual.

Maja let out a relieved sigh.

"I don't know," she answered, and in the way they'd practiced together a thousand times. The words flowed off her tongue, knowing Clay would understand whatever she said. "What?" she asked.

"A bottle, stupid." He laughed, pulled back the foil from the potatoes, and continued cooking them.

As slow as she was with her speech and backward with her writing, no one had ever called her stupid. The word shrank her to the size of a thimble and shoved her into a tiny box. A lump of misery, she didn't know what she had done wrong and couldn't think of anything to say.

In the other room, Mormor's knitting needles fell silent.

Clay copied Mormor's snoring and ended up snorting like a pig. Instead of big and broad, his smile twisted as if he hurt inside from eating too much candy. *Loki* had put a curse on him.

Even as tears stung her eyes, concern for her friend tugged Maja toward him, though she had no idea what to do. Ignoring her, he turned his back and arranged the television trays.

"You can at least do the silverware and napkins, can't you?" he said, ending in his high voice—irritated or cross, Maja couldn't tell which.

Feeling miserable, she hurried to the living room and set up three tray tables. Mormor sputtered and pulled herself up in her chair. Clay turned on the television and sat down beside Maja on the sofa. Together, they watched *The Ed Sullivan Show*, the only television program Maja's parents deemed suitable for her.

"You're muttering and not eating, Maja," warned Mormor.

Startled, Maja scooped a forkful of mashed potatoes and forced herself to swallow.

Mormor moved her tray table to the side. Using her cane, she got to her feet and turned up the volume of the television. When Mormor's back was turned, Clay speared the piece of ham on Maja's tray and dropped the meat on his. His knee jiggled with his foot tapping the floor about a hundred miles a second. Maja smiled at him. His smile was normal this time. Relieved, she mushed her food into a little wad on her plate. Even before the television program ended, Mormor insisted Maja go for her sweater.

"I'm not telling you again," she said.

"I'll dump these in the garbage." Clay's voice hit a high note as he gathered up their empty dinner trays.

Maja froze, wondering if his evil twin had taken over again. Not giving Clay time to come back, she tiptoed to the hallway.

Whispering the name of Tomete, the good-luck gnome Mormor said looked after the house, Maja peered around the archway to the hall. Tomete was nowhere in sight. She wasn't surprised. The only actual sighting she'd had of his gray smock and red tasseled cap was late one night when her bedroom was the darkest. He'd danced a jig in the middle of her bed. After he disappeared, the night wasn't as scary, and she'd been able to sleep.

Laughter broke from the television behind her.

"Go," commanded Mormor.

The highboy towered on one side next to Mother's newest oil painting, dark and murky and smelling of fresh paint. On the opposite side of the hall, French doors uncovered against the twilight hour revealed the time when the curtain between the regular world and the invisible world thinned to expose trolls and giants and magic. Soon it would be pitch-black outside. Fear stabbed the back of Maja's neck.

Careful not to awaken an imp or sprite or an elf, Maja stepped into the hallway. She looked neither left nor right or even where she was going, staring down—conscious of her heart cringing, her step echoing down the long, darkened hallway, and her big feet plodding. The heavy stillness made her wish she hadn't started.

At the end of the hall, she peeked inside her bedroom. Hunched where her bureau should be swayed an evil old troll with craggy eyebrows, a nose as thick as a turnip, and massive hairy hands. She wrenched her eyes away and flung herself up against the hallway wall. Breathless, her legs went weak.

When nothing bad happened and her heart slowed enough for steady breathing, she poked her head back inside her bedroom. Her familiar chest of drawers stood like a watchman in a puddle of icy blue mist. Her relief at finding the troll gone and her bedroom safe sent her giggling. The sound came out as a squeak.

Whispering assurances that her sweater was on the hook just inside her closet, Maja slid open the door. A hand slapped over her mouth. Unable to breathe, she squirmed to free herself.

"Don't say a word," Clay whispered, and he pushed himself into her body.

MODELING

THIRTEEN, TALL FOR HER age, slender and quiet, Maja stood high on a ladder and reached for an orange. A breath of air trembled, blowing the sunrise away. Leaves on the trees shuddered.

"The elves have arrived," said Mormor from where she sat in a wicker lawn chair in the shade of the citrus grove behind Great Oaks.

Pine trees framed the orange trees near and silent on three sides. Mormor's fairies pulled at Maja like a lullaby, but she was grown up now—too old for such nonsense. She'd stopped asking for Mormor's tales the same day she turned her vengeance on Clay for hurting her. More sad than angry, she flicked her long blond hair, keeping back the tears. The pain of the past burned into the present as the never-ending threat continued.

"You're not invisible," said Mormor, knitting as usual.

Stung that Mormor could read her mind, Maja said nothing.

"There!"

Maja started at the sudden shout and grabbed the sides of the ladder to keep from listing backward. Her heart pounded.

Mormor dropped her knitting needles and pointed to a bird squawking like a scrub jay in a nearby pine tree. In almost the same breath, the bird trilled like a songbird.

Its tweets mingled with Mormor's voice. "The great communicator."

The excitement in Mormor's voice made Maja look down.

"The white of the mockingbird wing is your sign to speak up," exclaimed Mormor.

"I talk." Maja defended herself and then withered under Mormor's deliberate stare. "I do," Maja insisted.

With more important things on her mind than birds and words, Maja filled the basket with oranges, careful not to offend the buzzing bees tumbling into the orange blossoms around her head. Mother was due home any minute, and Maja wasn't dressed for their trip to San Francisco.

Maja snapped one last plump orange from the tree's interior. "Ouch," she cried, pricked by a thorn. A spot of blood mushroomed on the meaty part of her finger.

"All things beautiful have thorns to protect

them," said Mormor. "Orange trees. Rose bushes."

People would like the beautiful things better if they didn't have thorns, Maja thought and stuck her finger in her mouth. The blood tasted foreign and forbidden.

"Learn to speak up, or you'll be destined to live by your looks alone," Mormor continued. "Your words will protect you, but you must use them. Your teacher wants you to speak in class. You must promise you'll try."

Maja rolled her eyes and started down the ladder, not bothering to explain that she wasn't the least bit interested in taking part in school. She was still pulled out of her class for speech therapy. She still jumbled her sounds and talked funny. And, the kids at school still laughed at her. All she'd ever gotten out of talking in grammar school was teasing. Junior high school was proving to be more of the same. Humiliation belonged hidden away, not pointed out, explained, and reorganized.

"You mustn't let this idea of your mother's interfere with your school work," Mormor cautioned.

"I won't," said Maja, but the truth was that school was difficult for her. Unlike Mormor's old fairy tales that had invited her to live in the story, stirred her fancy, and made her feel more alive, her teachers' way of speaking exhausted her.

"You have a lot to learn," said Mormor. "When the time comes for you to meet the one true and precious someone destined for you and you alone, threshold guardians will demand a demonstration of your readiness. You can't have others speak for you. You must learn to become whole and complete by yourself."

Whole and complete? Maja frowned and waited for Mormor to say it again, this time in plain words. When she didn't, Maja remembered the boy. There was a time when she believed he was her one wild and precious someone, destined for her and her alone. He was the reason she'd worked so hard to learn to talk. She'd been so sure they'd meet again, and she had so many questions she wanted to ask him. Once upon a time, she would have done anything for him.

Descending the ladder, Maja missed a rung and took a giant step backward, landing hard. Her jaw hammered together, and she bit her tongue. Oranges scattered everywhere. Maja closed her eyes and cleared her mind of thinking and breathing and feeling, in the exact same way she closed herself off during the terrifying times Clay caught her off-guard.

"Stop daydreaming and listen to me."

Maja jerked at the harshness in Mormor's voice. She peered into milky white eyes that glowed like opals.

"You're a woman now. It's time you know. Your words are your thorns. You must use them."

Maja ignored Mormor as she gathered the oranges. The smell of smoke from a fire Ramon tended behind the line of garages mixed with the scent of oranges.

Maja picked up Mormor's cane from the lawn beside her chair, collected Mormor's knitting, and helped her to her feet. All the while, anxiety pulsed at Maja's temples at how slow Mormor was to unfold her body. Finally, she straightened into a standing position. Cane in hand, Mormor slipped an arm through Maja's and leaned on her.

Tires crunched on the long gravel driveway. Mother's green station wagon with wooden side panels appeared from around the entrance to Great Oaks.

"If you're nervous about going, use this opportunity to practice speaking up for yourself," said Mormor, as a cloud of dust caught and sank over the car. "Tell her."

"I'm not nerv—" Maja started as Mother emerged from the car, looking radiant in her flared white tennis dress. Maja's stomach flip-flopped at the thought of what lay ahead.

"Then why are you whispering?" asked Mormor.

Maja glanced at Mormor's certain face, surprised and frightened. She'd practiced hard to stop whispering to herself, not wanting to give away her hiding places to Clay.

"Cover your shoulders and put on a hat, Maja," called Mother. "Mustn't have a sunburn for today's shoot."

Maja sucked in her breath and answered quickly. "Yes, Mother."

The white straw hat Mother wore and her

oversized dark sunglasses made her look secretive, like Greta Garbo. Tennis racket in hand, Mother entered the house with a spring in her step. Maja could see that the prospects of her daughter following in the great Garbo's footsteps filled Mother with joy—more than Maja had ever seen.

Daddy had argued against Mother's idea.

"Now, now, Birgit." Maja had overheard Daddy say and imagined his jaw twitching.

"She's always going to talk funny and learn backward," Mother cried. "The right kind of man will never marry her."

"She's not even thirteen years old," Daddy had said.

"Modeling will help her get what she wants with her looks."

Double-parked at the photographer's studio, Mother opened the car door for Maja's clothes. At home Maja had liked the clothes Mother picked out for today and imitating the poses in Mother's Swedish fashion magazines. Now Maja felt dizzy and had to concentrate not to trip over her own feet.

"Hold this for me," said Mother, producing a hand mirror from an unfamiliar bag in the back seat.

Maja positioned the mirror, following Mother's instructions up, down, over, and tilted ever so much.

"Hold still," Mother said, lifting the mirror to the right height.

Watching Mother carefully reapply her lipstick,

Maja didn't remember Mother's eyes ever burning so brightly. Unlike her characteristically cool manner, Mother seemed nervous or excited. Maja couldn't tell which one.

"I expect you to do your best today," Mother said, rubbing a finger across her teeth.

Though Mother's words weren't a scolding, Maja nonetheless felt as if she was in trouble. "Yes, Mother," she said.

Mother leaned in for a closer view, peeled back her lips, and checked for lipstick smudges.

"Grace and poise will go a long way in helping you snag a great husband when you're older. Every man loves a pretty girl on his arm."

Maja shrugged. "Yes, Mother."

"Do I look all right?" Mother strained to see her side-view.

Nodding, Maja answered with her best speech, "A movie star."

An unmarked door swung open, and a dog the size of a pony trotted out and sniffed her. Maja recognized the man who followed as Jimmy, her agent. He was dressed in the same red jacket, red plaid tie, and red oxfords as the first time she met him. His oversized glasses with big, red frames made him look like a gaudy librarian. He held open the door with his cigarette hand and greeted Mother with a peck on each cheek. He took a puff from a cigarette stuck in a long red lacquered cigarette holder and wagged his fingers at Maja.

"Come along inside, darling. I want you to meet my friend, Ned."

Maja puzzled how to pass the dog. Then a man joined Jimmy in the doorway and called the dog to him.

"Birgit, this is Ned the photographer. Ned, Maja's mother," Jimmy said.

Mother stuck out a gloved hand to Ned. Usually stately and formal when meeting new people, Mother's eyelids fluttered as fast as bumblebee wings, and she sighed as if she were breathless.

"Maja, meet Ned," said Jimmy, throwing his cigarette on the sidewalk and slipping the cigarette holder in his jacket pocket.

Not knowing why Mother acted so strangely, Maja turned to meet the man who would take her pictures.

"Do you like dogs?" asked Ned, ruffling the dog behind its ears. "Charlie won't hurt you."

Maja hesitated, believing she did like dogs, but having never encountered one before, she wasn't sure. Zooming through her mind for the right words, she struggled to form an answer when Mother took Ned's arm and pointed out the clothes to take into his studio. Then, she pinched Maja's arm.

Sinking her voice to a hoarse and furious whisper, Mother insisted, "Stop mumbling."

With tears in her eyes, Maja snapped her mouth shut.

Mother disappeared inside with Jimmy.

Maja rubbed her arm and followed more slowly. The light in the studio was so dim that she couldn't tell where the ceiling ended and the walls began. Jimmy and Ned and Mother walked together to a piece of white fabric hanging in the middle of an open room. A solitary light bulb hung from overhead, illuminating a stool sitting in the middle of the backdrop.

Ned's hair hung over the collar of a yellowing long-sleeved shirt opened at the top.

"Ned is going to take lots of pictures today," explained Jimmy, as Ned walked around Maja, his eyes roaming over her the same way Daddy considered a new car—with Mother chattering along beside him.

Maja's cheeks burned. With her eyes on Ned, she stood very still. Daddy tested car tires by kicking them. She was ready to kick back if Ned tried that with her.

"That way when I hear about jobs I think are right for you," continued Jimmy, "I'll have your composite to show the client, so they know what to expect."

Mother, still sighing and blinking, interrupted with a question about modeling jobs, her hands fluttering. Surprisingly, her flightiness made Maja feel calmer.

Maja watched as Ned positioned spotlights running along the length of two ceiling-to-floor poles on either side of the draped white cloth. Then he moved behind a black camera on stilts, a cigarette burning between his lips. His legs spread, one foot on either side of the long legs of a camera stand, and he bent over as if taming a skinny, black flamingo. In her nervousness, Maja found comfort in the idea of a flamingo in the room with her. She named it Flame, which made her think of the boy who had appeared that long ago summer as if from the flaming car. Thinking of Flame boy and his magic touch sparked a surge of confidence.

The door flung open, and Mother suddenly appeared. Her cheeks pink, and clutching her purse, she flitted onto the white cloth and jutted out her chin. She put a hand on her hip, turned her face sideways, looked down and then up, and ended fully facing the camera.

Maja clapped as Mother held the pose, in awe of her beauty and grace and poise. If only Maja could do as well. Her clapping sounded hollow; no one else moved. Suddenly confused whether Mother was posing for a photograph or showing her how, Maja stared at the photographer helplessly. She wished Ned would snap a picture of Mother, knowing she'd swoon with joy.

Mother took a breath and seemed to come out a trance. She looked muddled, so Maja joined her on the little stage and reached for her hand. Mother slapped her away, scanned the room, and sauntered out with her head held high.

Barely breathing, Maja watched her go.

A skinny Asian man, carrying a huge suitcase, broke the tension.

"This is Tyrell," stammered Ned, looking toward the door where Mother disappeared. He lit a cigarette. "He'll do your make-up."

Tyrell applied the same make-up Mother used before a party: foundation, blush-on, mascara, eye-liner, and lipstick. Mother reentered the room, and then she tried advising Tyrell with her back as straight as usual, her breathing back to normal, and her eyes calm. While Tyrell went about his business, she left to discuss something with Jimmy.

Tyrell was gentle, and before long, his touch put Maja in a daze. She was nearly asleep when he positioned a mirror in front of her face. She didn't recognize herself, giggled, and felt safe in her disguise.

Ned stubbed out a cigarette in a rusty Folgers coffee can. Spotlights snapped on. The air heated up. Music started.

Maja didn't understand the words, but the slow, sad melody felt like church—but from somewhere deeper. Ned was speaking. She couldn't hear him because the same thing happened that often happened when she was scared—scared of finding herself called on in class, scared of the kids who laughed at her, scared of Clay catching her off-guard—she found herself transported back in time standing with the mysterious boy on the sidewalk by the candy store when she was young. Delighted at seeing him again, she gasped and put her hand to her mouth. The amusement in his eyes made her grin. Spotting the wolf around his neck, she reached out. Before she had a chance to touch the tiny carving, she was knocked off balance. The boy reached out a hand. At his touch, a bright and wondrous sensation rushed through her. As the feeling entered her heart, the world around her disappeared.

The overhead light snapped on, and the pole lighting clicked off. Ned returned. Flame, the winking flamingo, turned back into a camera on stilts.

Instead of Ned shaking his head and declaring her a failure, he was grinning like a teenager. Maja's confusion turned to worry. She must have given him something she wished she hadn't, something that was hers alone, not in a photograph for others to see. Mother had taught her that she could communicate with a pose, like finding the right words to say. She worried the pictures revealed her shame for strangers to judge.

"Enough here," said Ned. "I want to take some shots in Golden Gate Park before we lose the light."

More? Maja felt dizzy; she couldn't remember the last time she'd eaten.

"So, what do you think?" asked Mother, her voice tense as she pulled up her gloves and touched her hair.

"To be perfectly honest, I had real doubts when you arrived," said Ned, stuffing film rolls and cameras in a duffle bag.

"Doubts?" Mother asked, jerking her face around like a challenge.

Ned stopped what he was doing. "Let me see … How do I say this?" he started. "When you first arrived, your daughter's eyes were …"

"What?" Mother demanded. "What about her eyes?"

"Your daughter's eyes were vacant, empty. Lifeless almost."

Ready to jump for joy that her plan had worked, Maja looked down so Mother wouldn't see the smile on her face. Now they could go home.

"But …" Ned continued. "Once the makeup went on, and the lights dimmed, and the music started playing, her eyes started flickering. I just hope I captured the transformation in the photos. It was dramatic how they brightened and eventually even sparkled. You can't teach what your daughter has. She's raw, and she's got something out of this world. The public is going to love her."

Maja's skin vibrated. She shook chilled to the bone.

"No, no, no," she muttered.

"What's wrong?" asked Ned, eying her.

Unaware she'd spoken aloud, Maja shook her head. "I—"

With everyone's eyes on her, Maja couldn't remember how to speak. Even wearing the mask of makeup, her face burned hotter and hotter until she was sure she'd catch fire.

"Well that's a relief," said Mother, turning back to Ned. "So next? Shoot outside?"

"That's right," said Ned. Then he turned to Maja. "There's no turning back now, baby. From here on out, it's straight to the top."

Ned tweaked Maja's cheek and smiled at her. Maja flinched and lurched into the dressing room, locking the door behind her.

1962 – 1964

When my kind chooses a mate for life, our bonding is instinctive. But first, an internal union must be formed between our instinct and the Self. Two-legged ones without such a unity? Joining together becomes much more precarious.

The Grandson discounts Wisaw because of her age. Even so, now that he's met her he can't shake her from his mind

And, her? She knows without knowing how that the Grandson is destined for her. What she doesn't know is how much work will be required to prove she is emotionally ready to take him into her life. She is young and prone to get ahead of herself, especially when it comes to the Grandson.

Tasked with seeing their potential realized, I've lived long enough with the Grandson to know all I need to about him. To learn more about our young heroine, I must find a way to land in her hands. Just the thought of such a transfer makes me feel young again.

THE FACTORY

COME MONDAY MORNING, Billy woke before dawn and tried to get his bearings. The smell of coffee brewing and bacon frying confused him into thinking he was still a kid at Grandma's after a good day of stealing.

Brenda walked in, and Billy returned to the here and now. A cigarette dangled from her lips, and she carried a steaming cup of coffee. She was wearing a little pink flimsy thing with fuzz around the bottom. Their wedding night the day before last was mostly a blur. Still, Billy was pretty certain she wore the same thing that night, too. Underneath, her body glistened.

She set the coffee cup on a lug box next to his side of the bed. Only other thing on the box was an ashtray full of butts.

"Morning, Billy," Brenda said. She kissed him on the lips and then gave him her cigarette.

Billy stuck the cigarette in the ashtray and pulled her to him. She fell against his chest. The silky feel of her breasts on his bare skin gave him a hard-on. She kissed his neck and then his shoulder, finding her way to his chest, doing with her tongue what only she knew how to do. Billy lifted her away by her shoulders.

"You don't like it?" The look of surprise on Brenda's face made him laugh.

"What do you think?" He gave her a kiss and pushed off the bed for the bathroom.

Billy didn't want to worry Brenda, with her being pregnant and all, so he'd said nothing about the bills from the wedding. They weren't supposed to have shelled out money seeing as her ma promised to pay for everything.

Brenda slid her hands around his waist from behind. "What's the big deal?"

"Things are different now."

All the while he was shaving, Brenda rested her head on his back. When he was done, Billy pulled her around in front of him. As much as he wanted her, he shook his head and kissed her hard. From the bedroom, he asked her to use something besides the old lug box for a bedside table.

"Picked more peaches in the Valley and packed more boxes just like that one, than I care to remember."

"Sure thing, Billy. Anything you say."

Billy hurried through a shower and dressed,

slipping the carving Grandma gave him in his pocket and rubbing it for luck.

In the kitchen, two pieces of toast popped up in the toaster. Bacon lay in a pool of fat on a napkin next to the drainboard. Brenda flipped through a True Confessions magazine at the kitchen table, smoking a cigarette and singing along with a '45 spinning on the record player about a rebel who never does what everyone else does.

Brenda's makeup was smudged under her eyes, and she looked a little peaked around the edges.

"You all right?" Billy asked as he poured a cup of coffee.

"It's just morning sickness. My sisters had it a lot worse than me." Brenda sat up at that and put out her cigarette, pleased at the thought she might be doing something better than her three older sisters.

"I'm going to do my best for us, baby." Billy's breath came out as a wheeze. He shook his head, wondering what the hell was going on and remembered the same thing happened during the wedding. He coughed. "You know that, right?"

"Sure, Billy. Anything you say."

"Remember the vision I told you about? The one for our future?"

"What's not to remember? A fancy new Cadillac. You wearing a hat. Me in white gloves. Kids walking hand-in-hand on the way to the candy store."

"Kid, one kid." Billy coughed again though what came out was more like a bark.

"You're not alone anymore, Billy. You're married now. You take care of the money. I take care of you and, when they come, the ki—" She gagged and slapped a hand over her mouth and ran to the bathroom and threw up.

A car horn sounded out front.

"You okay?" Billy asked at the closed bathroom door.

"Go on," she said. "I'll have something good waiting for you when you get home."

The car horn blasted again.

Billy hesitated. "You sure?"

"Go."

Outside, Billy's cousin Jack waited in his Olds Delta, just like every other weekday. Except today, instead of walking out of Ma's basement, he strutted from his own rental apartment, a man of work and action, married with a baby on the way. Jack took a swig of Everclear from his hip flask.

John Law drove up beside them in a black and white. Jack lowered the flask. The copper passed them and kept going.

"You can't tell me he's five-ten," Jack snorted. He still stung from the police department's rejection for not meeting the height requirement.

Jack was sensitive about his lack of inches. For nearly as long as Billy had known him, Jack had worn lifters in his cowboy boots, and though he wouldn't admit why, Billy knew he also jacked up the seat of his car with bricks to make him sit taller.

"Ready for your first day?" Jack asked.

Billy answered by reaching for the flask. With a moment's hesitation, Billy took a swig and screwed up his face against the vile 180 proof liquor as it burned his throat. He passed back the container. Jack swallowed more and stashed the flask in his jacket pocket for later at the foundry.

Jack didn't mention the wedding though he'd been there, plastered as usual. When Jack was married, he'd sit drunk at the bar, telephone his wife, and yell about where the hell was she and accuse her of all sorts of nasty things, even though she was home all along. After he'd sobered up, he'd say it wasn't his fault—that women could just about drive a man crazy if you let them.

"I read in the newspaper this morning there's a pill that can stop a woman from getting pregnant," said Jack, one arm stretched across the length of the bench seat, the other resting in the open window with his index finger hooked in a spoke of the steering wheel.

"That so?" Billy said, thinking to himself: *medical miracle*.

"Yup. A doctor gives them to you. Pretty expensive, I hear."

Rather than drive straight to the foundry as usual, today Jack drove to 71st Avenue and MacArthur Boulevard. A blown furnace at the cast-iron foundry convinced Billy that his time working with molten iron was over.

None of the guys from the foundry had been invited to the wedding. Brenda's mother didn't think any of them qualified as family or friends. Billy did stand up about Webb. Against all her objections about inviting a Negro to the wedding, he insisted Webb was his best man and had to be there. Then Webb went and joined the Marines and didn't come after all. A week ago, he'd shipped off to Vietnam.

Jack stopped at the cyclone gate to General Motor's Fisher Body automobile factory, the same plant Billy had driven past all his adult life. A bit breathless in anticipation of what was coming, he got out of the car.

"Ain't going to make the kind of money you're used to making at the foundry."

"I plan to do double shifts at first. Two bucks forty an hour ain't much. But the pay is a lot better than the office jobs I looked into. The guy who hired me said my hourly goes up in ninety days. Then I'll be doing better."

Inside, the factory noise slapped against the supervisor's words as Billy followed him, squeezing past moving cars, dodging welding sparks, and ducking under automated machinery. Cars never stopped moving on the assembly line.

Some jobs appeared a lot harder than others. They passed a heavy-set guy hustling to pick up parts, set down tools, climb on and off the car, and then start all over again. He had a sad look on his face and was sweating heavily.

The supervisor left Billy at his station with a cold look and a warning.

"Doing your job at the right pace without any mistakes," he said as if he was asking a question. "Not easy."

Six thousand men worked two separate shifts. Three in the afternoon to midnight suited Billy just fine. With those hours, he should be able to spend some time with Brenda, too, though he wasn't holding his breath. She'd taken real good care of him the first few days after the explosion, tending to his wounds. Then, once he was up and about, she made it clear she was happier when he wasn't at her apartment. The bigger the baby grew inside her, the more she pushed him away. Seemed she preferred discussing baby clothes with her sisters than to be with him.

Two-thirty the next morning, Billy stumbled home and into the bathroom. Not wanting to wake Brenda, he closed the door before turning on the light. Glare off the white walls blinded him, and he fell against the toilet seat.

Brenda moaned in her sleep. Billy untied his shoelaces and, taking his time and trying to be gentle, he struggled to yank off his socks. A guy on the line next to him advised him to get some rubber-soled shoes. He figured that out on his own after the first few rotations of squatting and jumping in Corvairs and Chevy IIs, what with all the twisting and turning that came with installing carpet and screwing in the trim around the headliners, and jumping out again. His white socks were stained black from popped blood blisters.

He filled the bottom of the bathtub with warm water and eased in his feet, socks and all. As he sat on the side watching the water turn pink, he decided Jack was right. First thing in the morning, he'd see about getting his job back at the foundry.

When he woke up, he felt differently. The guys were all right; their storytelling and jokes made the monotony bearable, and there was room for advancement.

At three o'clock Billy was back on the line, except today he wore rubber-soled canvas shoes with a little give. He had to borrow money from Jack to pay for the new shoes. All of their money was going toward getting ready for the baby.

The auto parts for the assembly plant were made in Detroit, shipped to San Pablo, and assembled at the factory into finished General Motors' cars. A conveyer belt pulled a line of partially built automobiles through a long tunnel, bringing the work to him. At the foundry he'd had to cross back and forth. The factory was stifling, but compared to working next to the roaring foundry furnaces the temperature was downright balmy. Even so, all day long, with his feet throbbing and his back aching, he imagined walking out. The only thing stopping him was not wanting to mess things up for the guys he worked with on the line. Somehow, he made it to quitting time.

The next morning, Billy was back at it again. It was for the money. If he could last ninety days and keep his eyes open, he'd earn an hourly rate higher than at the foundry. The earplugs he'd bought blocked most of the shrillness of the drill and the machine gun racket from air-pressured wrenches.

While he was planning his life, Billy became aware that his stomach grumbled. The lunch break whistle sounded.

Malakaton, a giant of a man who worked beside Billy installing the package tray in the back window, lumbered up next to him, humming one of the Hawaiian songs he sang all the time. Up close, Malakaton—or Mal as the guys called him—was even bigger than he first appeared. Not that he was much taller than Billy, maybe six feet, two inches, but he weighed at least three hundred pounds. How he got in and out of the cars to do his job was a mystery.

"Find a way to turn the routine into a song. Hypnotize yourself to it. Work as hard and as fast as you can and keep your mouth shut. Survive for ninety days and Local 1550 will take you. With the union behind you, you protest this job of yours."

"Protest," Billy repeated, trying to keep up.

"You're doing the work of two men. You know that, don't you?"

Billy shook his head no.

"Work standards are a contractual issue," Mal continued, rooting around in his breast pocket. "It's between you and your committeeman. He'll take care of you, but you're going to have to ride him to get anything done. Union reps aren't what they used to be."

Mal flipped him a tiny white pill.

"What's this?" Billy asked, catching it. As he looked from the pile growing in his hand to Mal, he paused to nod at the fellas gathering around them.

"They give you energy and make you feel good," said Mal. "You better get yourself a load of Benzedrine because if you want to be taken seriously by the workers in here, you're going to have to work twice as hard."

"Why's that?"

"Because you're white, you're young, and you got you a good-looking face."

"Hey, kid. Want to work a double?" Shouting over the noise of the factory, the supervisor kicked the heel of Billy's shoe.

On his knees, Billy nodded without stopping his work.

After that, he worked every bit of overtime he could get and filled in for guys who failed to show up the day after payday. Seven in the morning to three-thirty and then double back from four in the afternoon to one in the morning earned him more than twice his regular salary.

While he was keeping his mouth shut and working his tail off, life outside the factory speeded up. Brenda gave birth to a tiny baby girl they named Lisa May Wolfe. Right after, he convinced Brenda to take the pill, pleading for time to practice this father business with one. She wanted more kids badly, so watching her swallow that first pill made him feel like she understood their money situation, and they were working together. For good luck, he carried Grandma's carving in his pocket. His breathing even got a little better.

On the other side of the country, Joan Baez and Bob Dylan sang "Only A Pawn In Their Game" at the foot of the Lincoln Memorial during Martin Luther King's march on Washington. Eighteen days later, a bomb went off at a Sunday school in Birmingham, Alabama. Four little Negro girls were killed.

On November 22, 1963, Billy crammed a bent piece of trim around the headliner of a Chevy II. The more frustrated he grew, the more fiercely he prayed for a break.

Words boomed across the loudspeaker system.

"President John Fitzgerald Kennedy is dead."

Shouts ricocheted across the factory.

"I repeat. President Kennedy has been shot and killed."

They walked off the line in a show of respect.

After four months, Brenda still wasn't over Kennedy dying. Even with his assassination, she hadn't stopped believing that life could be like *Leave It To Beaver*. For Billy, though the ambition he'd been following faded a little bit more every day, he hadn't entirely lost the vision of how things were supposed to look. But deep inside he knew that if the days Brenda longed for had ever existed, they just might be over now forever. And not just because Kennedy was dead but because of how he died.

Lyndon Johnson took office, giving speeches about "building a great society, a place where the meaning of man's life matched the marvels of man's labor," whatever the hell that meant. A year later, President Johnson signed the Civil Rights Act. After that a few women were hired on at the factory. Soon after, the factory moved to a new plant out in the Fremont sticks.

Billy bought a little two-bedroom house that nightly, when he walked through the door to his wife and daughter, softened his cynical heart. The bills kept piling up as Brenda bought plates and sheets and things she said were necessary. He went on working every bit of overtime and all the double shifts he could get.

At least the job was getting a little better. He joined the United Auto Workers union, and just like Mal told him to, Billy complained to his commit-teeman about his job. With only the vaguest idea how things ran, he made a point every day to go to the glassed-in office where everyone in the factory saw him harass his committeeman to stand up for his contractual rights. The last time he stalked by, his reflection in the windows looked like an Indian staring back at him. The next day, Billy got a crew cut.

Finally, management hired another guy to install carpet. Now all Billy had to do was screw in headliners morning, noon, and night. This was the first union he'd ever known. Thanks to them, his pay didn't go down. That and the protective gloves and goggles, medical benefits, and bathroom breaks, all thanks to the union—but still the grind was grueling.

As he did most days, Billy didn't wake up until noon. He rested a hand on either side of the bathroom sink and leaned straight-armed over the basin, dropped his head between his shoulders and closed his eyes. His breathing deepened and his arms turned to upholstery stuffing. He jerked, listed backward and clutched the medicine cabinet to steady himself. On his way out as always, he pulled Grandma's carving from his pocket.

He drove to the factory with one hand on the steering wheel, the other hand rubbing the carving between his fingers. With his head in a fog, he couldn't remember what day it was. Taking in the cherry trees blooming and green wrapping the east foothills, he assumed it must be spring. Stuck in the windowless factory, he missed the days with Grandma and how their entire lives revolved around the outdoors—her rituals and the little kitchen garden, hunting and fishing, and getting by. With the schedule he was keeping, Billy worried how he was going to be able to give the good parts to his daughter.

At work, he ran goop along the inside of the headliner and screwed it in just like he did the one before that and the one before that and all of them he'd done last week and the months before. Today, he didn't even notice the drill of the screwdriver and the pump of the goop, his mind crowded with dreams. He planned to buy a station wagon and was trying to estimate when he'd have enough money saved up to give Grandma a new roof.

"Billy. Billy Wayman. That was the break whistle."

He leaned back on his haunches and blinked up at Malakaton.

"You all right?"

Mal put a hand under Billy's arm and boosted him to his feet in a shot. Mal shook him a little as if to help straighten out his joints.

A guy with red hair and a freckled face stepped over from the next line and leaned in on Billy until he was pressed against the car he'd been working on and couldn't go any farther. He smelled stale coffee on the guy's breath. Billy cleared his throat and felt for the carving in his pocket. He hoped this wasn't going to turn out bad.

"Billy, Red. Red, Billy," said Mal.

Everyone was on a break, and the line was off.

Still, guys on either side ran drills without stopping. The pattern was different than what they usually followed and could almost be used as a cover for any bloodshed these guys had planned for him. A dull ache bruised Billy's chest, making it tough to breathe.

"We're walking out today. What do you think of that?"

Red spoke so low that Billy had trouble hearing him over the drilling. He glanced at Mal, hoping for a clue. Mal scanned the factory.

"Where're you going?" Billy slumped suddenly weary.

"On strike."

The word sent a chill across Billy's neck, and he coughed.

"A new facility means a new contract," said Mal. "Management is threatening to take away benefits, things we fought for and won just a few years ago. One way to get them to listen—strike. We had to keep it from everyone until today. If the board finds out before we pull off the strike, they'll stop us cold."

Billy remembered reading something in the union manual when he first joined about the membership voting to strike.

"Hell, that's if it's sanctioned," said Red.

"Then there'd be ballots and everything would be certified all neat and tidy," said Mal.

"This one ain't going be like that. Hell, this one's going to be real messy," said Red. "A wildcat."

Billy tried to understand what was happening

and keep his breathing steady at the same time. As fast as Mal and Red threw the conversation back and forth, he felt like he was watching a ping-pong tournament.

"The entire membership walks out at the same time. It's the only way we can show our opposition to the factory officials and our elected union officials. They're as bad as management."

"What about our pay?"

"Strike benefits," said Mal.

"I'm not saying all of us don't pay the price," said Red. "But hell, it's our duty. The union committeemen and board ain't doing what we elected them to do. So, we give them a wildcat strike."

Billy licked his lips and shook his head.

"Illegal," said Mal, looking over their heads again. "Unsanctioned. And there's only one way it's going to work. Everyone's got to be with us on this. Do you understand?"

"Hell, sure he does," said Red. "So, you with us?"

Stalling for time, Billy hesitated. His breathing wheezed. At least, if they walked out, he'd have time to find out what the hell was wrong with his breathing, though without enough money to pay for the doctor's visit.

"I got a new baby. I'm barely making it as it is," Billy said, surprising himself.

"Didn't figure you for a family man, you being so young and all. Sure, it'll be hard. You don't have to tell us that."

All the other guys with families were in for this. Billy had two options: Play it safe, which meant he was a broken man and might as well give up on life right then. Or, feeling reckless, he could follow the path of the wolf and act.

"What do we do?"

At five fifteen the factory official handed Billy his check. Billy avoided looking the official in the eye. Mal had only talked about what happened if the UAW officers learned what they aimed to do. Billy didn't even want to imagine what the guards and company men would do to them after firing them first. Then, there was Brenda. She was going to have a wall-eyed fit when she found out this was his last full paycheck for a while. He was going to have to get another job, maybe two, until the strike was over.

He slipped the check in his pocket and glanced at Mal. The two of them looked at Red, who nodded. Billy walked in silence, following the line of yellow paint running down the aisle to three guys adding windshield wipers, the battery, and front bumper to the same car. When they saw him, they nodded and kept working. In the pit beneath the car, three guys kept attaching the gasoline tank and greasing the chassis. Everyone knew to wait until Billy reached the end of the line and started back. Then they'd throw down their tools and scramble out of the pit. All together they'd meet up with the rest of the guys in the middle and walk out, just like Red said.

Rubbing the carving for luck must be working because all the guys in line were raring to go. Getting hotter by the minute and trying to breathe, Billy marched straight past the guys who tested the headlights and turn signals and put gasoline in the tank. He'd never given much thought to the three-foot shadows encircling the guys on the line. Except now, up-close he saw they weren't shadows. Each guy stood in his own puddle of sweat.

Harvey—the very last guy on the line—had the nickname Skypiece, because of the felt hat he wore off-duty. He was an old Negro and liked nothing better than telling Billy how he'd been working on the line longer than Billy had been alive.

The little pouch on Skypiece's belt for his punch tool was open as he punched the final inspection card for the bright orange GTO without acknowledging Billy. Skypiece was a loyal guy, and knowing how he felt about the factory, Billy thought he should go slow though with sweat pouring off his face, and his shirt sticking to his back, and steam clouding his eyes, he'd have to be careful not to boil over.

"Nice car," Billy said, wiping an arm across his forehead.

"Custom job for some kid's birthday," said Skypiece.

Through the open car door, Billy smoothed a hand over the leather seat, watching Skypiece circle chalk around a ding Billy couldn't even see. Usually, repairs were made after the car left the line, custom cars always first. With everyone walking out, he wondered how long before the dent got fixed. An impossible question, just like how to convince Skypiece to lead the guys out. Billy's breathing was so bad pain hammered his chest.

"My daddy lined up every morning at the factory gate in the thirties," Skypiece said, testing the door by swinging it back and forth. "Company prizefighters and goons enforced the rules and were always a lot harder on the Negro workers than whites. If Walter Reuther hadn't come along, there wouldn't be a union. And without the UAW, we wouldn't have the benefits we've got now. They protect all of us. A wildcat strike messes with the order of things."

Pushing Billy aside, Skypiece thrust out a grease can to hold, and he smeared a dab of the black lubricant across the door hinge.

"You okay, kid? You look a little pale," said Skypiece, still working.

Unable to restrain himself any longer, Billy dropped the can. With sticky fingers he rubbed his good-luck piece with a vengeance and asked for Skypiece's decision by raising his eyebrows, like *now or never.*

Skypiece tossed the inspection card on the dashboard and pulled his favorite hat from his back pocket.

"Surprised, huh?" he asked. "Look kid. Someday a moment will present itself to you. When that moment comes, don't turn your back on it because you're scared of losing what little you got. If you do, you'll spend every day after regretting it. Every man is best suited for one job. This one's mine. You still have yours to find."

Skypiece turned up the felt edges of his hat. "Let's go," he exclaimed and slapped Billy on the back.

The wolf carving popped out of Billy's hand. He reached for it as it sailed through the car window, and missed. It landed in the gap of the passenger bucket seat.

"Let's get out of here," cautioned Skypiece

Leaning through the window, Billy stretched for the carving. Just out of his reach, he grimaced at the time he'd lose opening the door and grabbing it. Refusing to look back, he hustled to join forces with the rest of the guys—rubbing black goo that was stuck to his fingers across both his cheeks. A rush of adrenaline shot straight up his spine.

War paint.

GTO

A MONTH AFTER MAJA'S sixteenth birthday, Daddy turned into the brand-new—and nearly empty—high school parking lot driving a bright orange GTO. From where Maja stood on the sidewalk with her friends, the car looked like a sleek and powerful wolf.

Jumping up and down, her friend Linda waved her arms over her head. "It's here," she shouted.

Standing behind Linda, Dana caught her arms. With her arms pinned at her sides, Linda chewed her gum a hundred miles an hour. The three of them had been smoking pot together, and when Linda got high, she tended toward overexcitement.

The car roared. Gravel spat. Sweeping her hair from her face with a wide cloth headband, Maja took a better look at the car Mother believed would teach her assertiveness and confidence. It was huge compared to the tiny brochure picture and appeared as if it could crush anyone who tried to hurt her. Maja imagined mowing down mean people and making the world a safe place. The car looked equally capable of devouring her, as well.

Daddy steered toward them. The engine slowed from a deafening growl to a gentle purr. He turned off the key. The car leaped forward. Maja shuddered at the thought of taming this beast.

Cool and spring-like in a blue seersucker suit, Daddy pushed up his black-rimmed glasses and held open the car door.

"Happy birthday, kiddo."

Six different things she wanted to say became one simple smile. After years of speech therapy, she spoke well enough to be understood. The difficulty now was deciding which were the right words to pluck out of a mob of confusing feelings. She recognized fear and didn't know how to ask for help.

At the sweep of Daddy's arm, Maja slipped into the driver's seat, hoping he wouldn't smell the pot. Then again, if he knew she was loaded, he'd insist on knowing where she'd gotten it—Brad, star quarterback and her boyfriend dressed in color-coordinated golfing attire. One day all purple like a grape, another all green or yellow or red, strutting around school like a peacock. Daddy would make sure she never saw Brad again, and he wouldn't let her drive. The very last thing she wanted was to disappoint Daddy, but ... she also wouldn't mind an excuse to get out of driving this brute.

Inside, the car was close and intimate like the cockpits of Daddy's friends' private airplanes. The leather smelled like a new doll, and the familiar scent made her giggle. She wrapped a hand around the wooden gearshift knob and practiced flicking it from side-to-side. Her smile faded at the car keys dangling from Daddy's fingers as he stood by her door.

He looked as doubtful as she felt. "Ready?"

Maja nodded.

"We'll cruise the strip in style." Linda pushed past Daddy and hopped in the back seat wild-eyed. She licked the leather and scrunched up her face.

Daddy gave Maja a reassuring smile and shut the door. When he made his way around the car to the passenger side and spotted Dana, he stopped. She had been standing there all along, but with the car hiding most of her, this was his first real look. Dana wore a two-piece bathing suit.

"Hello, Mr. Hawthorne," said Dana.

Maja held her breath. Linda slid to the side window, watching for his reaction. His eyebrows shot up. He stuck his hands in his pockets and stared steadily into Dana's face, not once dropping his gaze to the rest of her. Dana's laugh was deep like a man, her body curved like a woman. She could never be a high-fashion model with a figure like that. Not that she'd want to anyway.

"Challenging the system, sir," said Dana.

Dana's act of defiance in wearing a bikini to school came out of a committee Maja and her friends

85

served on together the summer before their freshman year. As a group, they decided things about their new school, like the colors, red and gold; mascot, mustangs; motto, freedom means responsibility; and the rules, none. If they wanted to, students went to class. If not, they didn't. Mother's influence had assured Maja a spot on the committee. She wasn't expected to say anything, and she liked serving. At the time, she and the others believed the principal and their parents would never agree to their no-rules policy. Now, their freedoms seemed natural, and having a car of her own added to the possibilities.

Daddy cleared his throat. "Does your father know about this?"

Dana raised her eyebrows. "I'm sure he will," she said and joined Linda in the back seat.

Still standing outside the car, Daddy glanced at Maja's friends. His eyes traveled more slowly to Maja.

She flushed. Avoided his gaze, she switched on the car radio and spun on high Bob Dylan singing "The Times They Are A-Changin'". Motioning to Daddy, she smoothing a hand across the soft brown leather passenger seat. Bumping up against something buried in the gap, Maja wrapped her fingers around a tiny piece of wood no larger than a postage stamp.

Daddy slipped into the car. With eyes glittering, Maja handed him the small carving.

He held up to sunlight a howling wolf. "You found it in the car?" He looked at her oddly and thrust out his chin as if nudging her awake.

With her heart pulsing in her ears, Maja barely heard him. After a pause, she nodded.

Pinching her thumb and forefinger together, a vision flashed like a mirror in the sunlight. Maja smelled a faint hint of grease on her fingers as she tried to recover from the unexpected thrill of finding the carving.

The tip of the wolf's tail was missing, and a tiny crack ran from snout to forehead. The wood inside the split was redder than the polished patina covering the rest of the piece. Her ears were plastered back, worn and smooth and tiny. Her front stance was solid, one foot a bit in front of the other.

Daddy wiped the carving with his handkerchief and dropped it in her outstretched hand. A feeling of hope warmed her loneliness. Two months ago, a month before Maja's sixteenth birthday, Mormor died in her sleep. Mother retreated to her bedroom, leaving Maja to grieve on her own. Great Oaks withered inside.

"Your mother wanted to be here, but there was a last-minute cancellation for that painting retreat in Spain she wished to attend. She flies out tomorrow. The trip will do her good. Take her mind off Mormor. She's packing now and said to be sure to tell you she'll be at dinner tonight."

Daddy was composed, straightening his long, narrow tie and positioning the tie clasp just so, in the constrained way he always acted when he was uncomfortable and had to face Maja with disappointment.

Maja was so startled at the news of Mother leaving the country that her mind went blank. She pushed back tears, then wondered why she cared. Other than Carmen and Ramon, Mother hadn't been around to greet her home from school in a long, long time.

The school bell echoed off the hill behind the parking lot. In seconds, kids would parade out of temporary classrooms for recess. Brad's debate class was near enough to the parking lot that, if he were looking, he was likely frowning. He wasn't keen about Maja having her own car; he preferred she depend on him to drive her.

She slipped the wolf in the pocket of her Capri pants and, not feeling so all-alone anymore, turned the key and punched the accelerator. The engine roared. Linda screamed.

Daddy grabbed the dashboard and pushed up his glasses. "All right now, kiddo. Remember what I taught yo—"

Maja rammed the gearshift into first.

"Ease out on the clutch," Daddy said quickly. "Slo—"

Maja jerked her foot off the clutch and pressed down on the gas. The car stalled. On her third try, with patient help from Daddy, she got the car going. Tires squealed all the way out of the parking lot.

Two days later, the weather was cool and windy. Before dressing for school, Maja gently pushed a rawhide cord through a tiny hole at the top of the wolf carving. As she worked, she thought about what Mormor once said about how in Sweden, the spirit of growing crops took the form of a wolf. When the wind rippled like waves across the ripened fields, a wolf passed through. The story gave Maja a sweet feeling that the carving came to her as a gift from her grandmother, and that Mormor lived on in the wolf. By wearing the necklace, Maja had access to Mormor's power and strength.

Before slinging it over her head, Maja held the carving up to the sunlight, unable to shake an even deeper feeling that she'd seen the carving before and somehow, if only she could remember, she knew who the rightful owner was.

Over the necklace, she wore the sort of shirtwaist dress, buttoned all the way up, that Mother liked but where Mother's dresses were monochromatic pastels, the dresses Maja wore were shorter and richer in color. She threw a ribbed cardigan over her shoulders.

Feeling confident with the wolf around her neck and her newfound independence, she trotted down the hallway to breakfast to find Daddy had already left for work. Distracted by the thought driving her new car to school, she scooped strawberries picked from their garden and served from the sideboard, barely smelling Carmen's fresh corn tortillas. She should have just let Brad drive her to school.

Seated at the table, she tucked her hair behind her ears and stared at her bowl of strawberries, as if they could remind her how to coordinate the gearshift and the clutch at the same time.

"*Hola, mija,*" Carmen placed a covered soft-boiled eggcup in front of Maja.

Startled, she watched as Carmen whacked off the top of the egg. Carmen raised her eyebrows, requesting to know what was wrong.

Not wanting to worry her childhood nanny, Maja touched Carmen's arm to say she was fine, though she didn't feel at all fine about driving the GTO.

Carmen crumpled the little egg hat in a napkin.

Beyond the French doors, a turkey buzzard soared over the greening hillside. The giant bird swerved, caught a wind current, and disappeared into the haze.

On the wooden bridge, leaving the ancient and rambling Great Oaks estate, the car jerked and came to a stop. Maja drew a deep breath. She found strength in the badger and beaver and bear totem pole faces grinning at her from either side of the entrance to the bridge. She got the GTO started. Traveled inches and stalled again. She squished her left foot against the clutch, shoved the car in gear, and let up on the pedal. The car died. She thought about leaving the car and hitchhiking to school. She nailed her foot against the clutch, restarted the car, and pushed down on the accelerator. The louder the engine screamed, the hotter her face turned.

Daddy's voice came to her from a long tunnel. "Ease out on the clutch. Slooowly." Her neck snapped back and she was off like a shot.

At school, Maja cut third period with her friends, and together they hiked up the hill behind the school. The others tossed their books and binders under a giant oak tree and sprawled in the field of wild mustard flowers. From out of the pocket of her shorts, Linda pulled a long, slender package of marijuana and rolling papers. Her latest hairstyle—an asymmetric, five-point cut—swung forward, covering an eye.

Maja sank to her knees in the crushed wild mustard meadow, with her chemistry binder clutched to her chest. Not studying last night—having modeled in San Francisco so late she nearly missed Brad's entire football game—she was behind. Just as Mormor had warned, Maja had lost her way in school. Modeling was to blame. Maja had hoped to please Mother with modeling. But if Mother couldn't even be bothered to stick around for the big fashion show yesterday, Maja was done with her agent and with Mother's insistence that she model.

She let her hair fall forward and hide her face.

"I'm quitting," Maja said, without raising her head. Her words came out raw and choppy.

"You're quitting school so you can model

fulltime?" asked Linda.

Maja shook her head. "I shouldn't have had to," she said, faltering.

"What, Maja? You shouldn't have had to do what?" asked Dana.

"They were all staring at me." Maja shuddered. "She lied."

"Who? Your mother?" probed Dana.

Maja nodded.

"You walked in the show in the city yesterday?" asked Linda, leaning forward.

Maja nodded again, feeling dejected.

"That's so boss," Linda exclaimed. "I heard about it last night on television. Designers from all over the world. A fundraiser, right?"

Linda kept talking without waiting for her to answer, which was just fine with Maja.

"The Palace of Fine Arts is being torn down and a permanent copy built," Linda explained, sounding like an expert. "The one that's there now hosted the 1915 Panama-Pacific International Exposition as a symbol of the city's resurrection from the great earthquake of 1906. Now everyone wants it preserved."

On days like today, when Maja didn't know what to say, words drifted like dust without substance.

"Driving took forever," Maja blurted after a quiet moment. "And then ... I don't want to talk about it."

"So you want to quit modeling, not school,"

said Dana. "Is that right?"

Maja nodded, wondering how she'd ever get up enough nerve to tell Mother. Clasping her cold and clammy hands together, Maja drew up her shoulders and sighed. Her friends looked at her uneasily, and Linda passed her the joint.

Smoke filled Maja's lungs, and blood beat against her eyelids. She drew again and then again until her mind stilled. The past melted, and the future vanished. She tilted her face to the sun and felt its warmth on her shoulders. She touched the wolf carving at her neck. An instantaneous release of tension sent her floating.

"You sure you're okay?" asked Dana.

"I want to go to college," said Maja, careful to make the words come out right.

"Forget college. Brad will marry you right now," pressed Linda.

Maja shook her head. She was grateful when they didn't discuss it any further.

As her friends smoked pot and messed with their hair, Maja fiddled with the wolf carving, embarrassed by her tears and show of emotion. At least when she modeled, she hid behind layers of makeup, and no one could see her blush.

Waiting for her face to cool, Maja tucked her hair behind her ears and pulled out her notes, hoping for last-minute help. Down the hill the football team scrimmaged on a muddy field. Brad was easy to spot.

After his game last night, he took her home and

parked on the street side of the bridge to Great Oaks to smoke pot and make out. He kept saying he wouldn't do anything she didn't want him to, but every time she pushed his hand away, he clawed his way back, pinching and clutching and kneading her skin. It took her nearly an hour to get out of the car, and today she felt beat-up, sore, and aching all over. She was beginning to wonder if all guys were untrustworthy.

Dana flicked a match, and Maja watched her light another joint. Hoping the wolf carving helped her do well on her chemistry test today, she retied the rawhide cord like a choker with the excess cord falling down her back. Instead of bringing her peace, the wolf trembled, making Maja feel like she was standing on shaky ground.

"None of the teachers fell over themselves yesterday about my bathing suit like your dad. I think it's sweet he's such a prude," said Dana. "Your dad's the coolest, Maja."

Today being too chilly for something as skimpy as a bikini, Dana wore a traditional cardigan twin set. Having borrowed her mother's cat's-eye sunglasses, she pushed back a bob haircut.

With her friends' conversation playing in the background, Maja had trouble making out her chemistry notes. The letters flipped, turning their backs on her as words somersaulted across the page.

"I know why Amy's not in school anymore," said Dana. She took a long drag off the joint and let out her breath all in a rush. A wispy cloud settled over them. She coughed and handed the joint to Maja.

"Amy's pregnant," said Linda, smacking her gum. Linda was obsessed with the idea of going all the way with her boyfriend and terrified of getting pregnant.

Maja flipped through her notes, her fingers leaving sweaty streaks on the pages.

"Amy's dad thinks all our teachers are communists and out to corrupt us," said Dana.

"Really?" exclaimed Linda. "So does my dad, but he says he'll let me stay as long as I'm a good girl. A communist is someone who's brainwashed, right?" Her eyes were glassy, and her face shiny in the bubble she blew. The bubble popped.

Their experimental high school was radically different than the more established high school across town. Mother had fought John Birchers when they wanted to shut down their new high school.

One teacher transferred from the old school. The rest of the teachers were recent graduates from the University of California at Berkeley, the university Maja dreamed of attending in a couple of years. Knowing Mother viewed college as a prime location to snag a rich husband, Maja would use that to argue her case about quitting modeling so she could concentrate on school.

"Are you going to let Brad do it, Maja?"

Rather than answer Linda's question, Maja watched the scrimmage break up below, and the football team head for the locker room.

Dana eyed her through the smoke. "How was dinner with your mother before she flew off for Spain?"

Maja thought before answering, gazing off into the mass of oak tree branches above her.

"Brad was furious she invited Clay instead of him," Maja said in the silence that followed.

"It's weird the way Clay is always hanging around your house," said Linda.

Maja had spent years hating how everyone, Mother and Daddy especially, was taken in by Clay's transparent act: charming to Mother, forthcoming and polite to Daddy, and sweet and inviting to her friends. Maja was relieved that someone else saw what she already knew was weird and creepy, very, very cruel, and wrong.

"I mean he's out of school," said Linda. "He has his own parents."

"Yes," Maja said with much bitterness.

"Weird?" Dana chimed in. "Maja's got the coolest parents ever."

"Did Clay ever try to do it with you?" asked Linda, on her knees.

A buzzing sounded in Maja's ear.

"I'm telling you straight out," Linda cried, not waiting for Maja's answer and continuing in a whispery voice. "This weekend I'm going all the way with Ronnie." She leapt to her feet and danced the twist.

"It's not all you think it is," cautioned Dana.

As the sun crept across the long green football field, and the time for the test neared, Maja's stomach curdled.

The recess bell reached them. Nothing happened below for a moment, and then their classmates streamed from buildings like busy ants.

"I've got to ace the test," Maja said, collecting her papers in her binder and getting to her feet.

"We're coming too," said Dana.

The three of them hiked down the hill together.

"Why don't you like going all the way, Dana?" Linda was nothing if not single-minded. Not waiting for Dana's answer, Linda continued. "My mom says if I want to marry wearing the white of the Virgin Mary, I have to save myself for my husband but—"

"The white of a virgin," Maja repeated, the buzzing in her ears now a pulsing beat.

"If you want to wear white on your wedding day, then you have to be a virgin, silly," explained Linda.

"Says who?" probed Dana.

Linda spit out her gum and peeled a fresh piece. "Father Frances."

Maja blushed and took a step back, tripping on a dirt clod. Dana steadied her.

"You and Ronnie do everything else. What's the difference?" said Dana.

"My hymen isn't broken. In case you don't know that either, Maja, the first time your boyfriend enters you, he breaks your hymen. The spot of blood is a sign to him of your virginity. My mother says that in some countries, people parade the bloody sheets down the center of town for everyone to see."

Linda's words jolted Maja. The white of a virgin. The first time he entered you. Ruby-red blood. The smell of burnt metallic. Clay had buried dirty feelings of shame and humiliation deep inside Maja. Mormor had told her that before she could have the one true wild and precious someone, destined for her and her alone, Maja had to become whole and complete by herself. She'd never considered that Clay robbed her of that chance by damaging her beyond repair and making her unworthy of love. Maja touched the wolf carving at her neck so she would not cry.

Linda looped an arm in hers. Maja's body, stiff as an ironing board, relaxed.

Brad broke from the crowd with a wave. In his yellow sports shirt and yellow slacks and loafers, he resembled a banana.

"Dana told us when she did it," said Linda, with a sideways glance at Dana. "I'm telling you I'm doing it this weekend. You're still a virgin. Right, Maja?"

Startled, Maja looked up and winced. After thinking about it for a second, she disengaged from Linda. Taking a long breath, Maja glanced over her shoulder with an expression a photographer had once called coy.

"Wouldn't you like to know?" Maja said, speaking so easily, she surprised herself.

Then she whirled around and ran from her

friends. What happened was a long time ago.

She reached Brad and kissed him hard on the lips.

His face shifted, and he roamed her body before linking eyes with her.

"What was that for?" he asked, holding her tight.

"Still want to go out tonight?" she asked.

"I thought you couldn't."

"Now I can."

Walking arm-in-arm with him to chemistry class, Maja smiled sadly. Now that she thought about it, there was no reason not to give Brad what he wanted. The pressure of the rawhide cord around her neck made it difficult to swallow.

1968

These two, as with all two-legged ones, have been written upon by life and heavily burdened with short-comings and flaws. Until they turn inward and resolve their weaknesses, poor choices will spin them apart.

This is the time to discover who they are alone and of the pursuit. Not the pursuit of each other, but the pursuit of themselves.

For the Grandson? His task is to find and listen to the still-point at the center of his spirit.

And for Wisaw? Her greatest challenge will be moving from silence to a liberated voice, from object to the main subject of her own life.

CHALLENGES

THE WILDCAT STRIKE AT the automobile factory taught Billy one thing. Never underestimate management. The workers had gotten so fired up that if their guys had known they were being filmed, even more of them would've jumped on car hoods hollering and screaming. As it was, ten union men were fired for the illegal strike, and not one of the changes they wanted from the wildcat came even close to happening.

Now three years later, Billy was the father of three and in worse financial shape than he had been then. Except that now he was a union representative and carried the added responsibility of taking care of, not only his family, but the guys too. The decision he was expected to make today could break him.

He flicked his cigarette out the car window. The wind sent an ash back into his eye. Squinting, he rolled up the window against a cold February morning. His foot on the accelerator and steering with his knees, he cupped his hands against his mouth, hoping to warm up his blood. Could be the cold making his hands shake or could be the six cups of coffee and fistful of Bennies he'd taken to wake up and get on the road well before dawn and his family stirred.

The idea of tracking down the wolf carving Grandma gave him hadn't occurred to Billy until lately. The more the pressure mounted, the more desperate he grew for the reminder of his dreams. And, if there was ever a time he needed the power to unleash the wolf inside of him, today was that time.

The special order GTO could have come from anywhere in the western states; to find the buyer so near had Billy speeding.

Brake lights of the car ahead of him blazed, forcing Billy to slow down, and then come to a complete stop. Road construction ahead. He drummed his fingers on the steering wheel, waiting behind a long line of traffic.

After fifteen minutes of waiting and with no sign that the flagman planned on waving them through anytime soon, Billy turned around. As tempting as it was to wait as long as it took, just knowing that the answer to what happened to the carving could be within driving distance lightened his mood. The decision he had to deliver at work pulled him back to Fremont. He'd try again another day.

Aware that the GTO could drive up right beside him at any time, Billy found himself looking for it.

On the other side of the street up ahead, a guy walking a dog stopped and yanked the leash hard enough to knock the dog off its feet.

"Hey," Billy shouted.

The guy was an asshole. A quick and mean one, too. Billy slowed down the car.

The guy yanked the leash again and hauled up the shepherd so it was hanging there, strangled by the collar. The longer he held the dog in the air, the redder the guy's face turned, and the madder Billy got. The dog had a pathetic look on its face.

Fuming, Billy stopped the car in the middle of the road and rolled down his window.

"Hey, man, what's the point of that?" Billy worked to keep his voice neutral and spoke only loud enough to be heard. Not in his usual neighborhood, he didn't want to cross any lines, visible or otherwise.

The guy dropped the dog to the ground. "What's it to you?" he said and stomped away, dragging the dog behind him.

The guy was right. The dog was none of Billy's business. Besides, he couldn't afford to be late to his meeting with management this morning.

In his rearview mirror, Billy saw the guy yank the dog in the air again.

Billy threw the car in reverse, tires squealing, and turned the wheel into a skidding stop—cutting off the guy. Billy jumped out of his car.

"Maybe you didn't hear me before." Billy made his voice louder and tried not to wheeze. "I asked you, what's the point of that?"

Now that Billy was standing outside his car, the guy didn't look so tough. As a matter of fact, he looked scared. Billy stood his ground, waiting for the guy to let down the dog, not much older than a puppy. Ready to hit someone, instead, Billy dug his hands in his pockets where he wished for the millionth time he'd find the carving.

The guy lowered his arms until the dog was back on its feet again. He put both hands in the air and backed up.

"I don't want any trouble, man. You want this piece of shit, take it." The guy threw the leash at him and ran back the way he'd come.

Billy looked down at the dog. He could swear it smiled up at him.

"Shit," Billy said. "Me and my big mouth. When am I going to learn?"

The dog jumped in the front seat of his '58 Chevy without being invited, and together they raced to work.

The automobile factory looked like a prison, just how management intended. Security guarded the gates in and out. The guys even marked their time working inside according to prison time given for crimes. He wasn't planning on being a lifer, hoping to get out in ten to twenty—grand theft.

Billy drove to the front of the three-mile parking lot, found a spot about a half a mile away from the factory's front entrance, parked, and opened the door.

"Go, Sister Wolf," Billy said. "Be free."

The dog didn't budge.

"Out," Billy growled. "Git."

The dog still didn't budge, so Billy rolled down his window for her to escape. He reached to roll down the other window, too. The dog slapped a wet tongue across his ear, leapt over the front seat, and landed squarely on the back seat. Not wanting any more dog slobber, Billy left the back windows up. Partway to the guard shack, he looked back. Sister Wolf had her face smashed up against the rearview window. Billy groaned.

Inside, Webb met Billy on the catwalk, and together they entered the union office set in the middle of the plant.

When his buddy from the old neighbor returned the previous year after two tours of duty in Vietnam, Billy had convinced Webb to hire on here. As kids, they'd taken to each other right off, and time had done nothing to change that. When union elections came up, damned if Webb didn't get elected union rep himself.

Billy shouted over the noise of the factory. "Where is everyone?"

"Meeting's off," said Webb. "Word has it Alabama's looking for you."

Billy groaned and steeled himself.

The all-glass room felt like swimming in a god-dammed fish bowl. Windows on either side looked out at hanging air guns and metal crossbars, welders and wires. Lines of cars and trucks and men stretched all the way around the shop floor in a circle. The rank and file went about their business, some scowling and others grimacing. Most of them had an eye on him and Webb. Billy spat in the trashcan and missed.

"Here he is now," Webb spoke under his breath.

Billy's heart stopped in the time it took him to breathe and then sped zero to sixty in a tenth of a second. He lit a cigarette. Seeing his hands shake slapped sense into him. He sat down so as not to pace. With all expression wiped off his face, Billy swiveled and faced the guy responsible for making his life miserable.

As a matter of prejudice, Alabama would never enter the office with Webb inside. Or so Billy hoped. With the door open, factory noise hammered his ears but didn't interfere with Billy watching for the knife he was sure Alabama managed to smuggle past the guards, just like he'd slipped inside the factory.

"Being here is going to make things worse for you, Alabama," warned Billy.

Alabama nodded toward Webb, his eyes darting from one corner of the factory to the other. "Make him leave."

"We can talk from here," replied Billy, as calmly as he could muster.

Alabama was a painter and a white supremacist. Every faction in here had their supremacists—whites, blacks, and Chicanos alike. The rank and file Alabama controlled were a group of white conservatives, outlaw biker gangs, rednecks and hillbillies from the valley. Most of the guys Billy represented were part of the two hundred men on the frame line, trim line, and the body shop. As Alabama's committeeman, Billy's job was to negotiate the man's suspension—when what Billy really wanted and what Alabama deserved was to be terminated.

"I ain't got time for your squawkin' an' talkin'. I want every one of my past suspensions wiped out, this one lifted, an' my job back." Alabama stuck his hand in his pocket.

Angry now, Billy scooted to the edge of his seat.

"I know what I'm doing. Now, leave the property before you make a fool of yourself for the second time with that fucking switchblade of yours."

The break whistle blew. Alabama's men gathered on either side of the office.

"You got no call to speak to me like that after what me and my boys did to get you elected, okie-boy," said Alabama. "You forget what color you are?"

"I appreciate all you did for me in the election," said Billy. "Don't get to thinking that means I'm going kiss your ass. Theirs neither. I ain't."

Alabama's eyes turned dark as he stepped over the threshold. A lead weight slammed against Billy's lungs. Webb didn't move.

Billy spoke as lackadaisically as he could with his heart racing and no breath. "The hall. An hour." Billy wondered if that gave him enough time to investigate the whereabouts of his carving and make it back in time for the confrontation he dreaded.

"You best be careful, okie-boy," said Alabama. "Real careful."

Alabama left and Billy wondered how much more messed up his life could get.

IN BERKELEY, A HALF an hour north of Billy, Maja vaguely heard the telephone ring. Lost in her studies, she didn't bother getting up to answer it.

"It's for you, Maja," shouted Dana.

Maja shouted over *Jimmy Mack* by Martha and the Vandellas on her stereo. "Take a message."

"Maja."

Maja threw down her pencil and left the Greek mythology report, due in a couple of hours, with crumpled papers spread haphazardly across her desk. Refusing to look at or acknowledge the poison letter from her academic advisor she'd pinned to her bulletin board, Maja started out of her bedroom and tripped over a pile of books.

The hallway was long with ceilings that soared into darkness in a house once grand and historic and now old and rundown. The upstairs telephone hung on the wall across from Maja's high school friend's bedroom in the Victorian they shared with two other university roommates. Having never had sisters or brothers, Maja hadn't experienced living with anyone her age, and she rather liked it.

But at that moment, Maja wasn't thinking about her roommates' hustle and bustle, their laughter and drama. As she walked towards the telephone, she formulated her demand that Mother limit her calling. A call every single morning for a year and a half in order to nag her about moving back to the Great Oaks was too much.

Angry now, Maja cautioned herself not to slip or give away a clue that she was still in school. So far, she'd been successful at keeping that fact from Mother. Besides, Maja loved living in Berkeley. Driving into town for the first time, far from the threat of Clay, Maja felt as if she was coming home.

Everybody in Berkeley was into creating excitement. A sense of expectancy hummed—even at night—after seven o'clock at Great Oaks, only the crickets chirped. The Fates, three goddesses she'd chosen for her class paper, demonstrated that Maja had some say in her future by the choices she made.

By the time Maja reached the end of the hall, she'd practiced in her mind the choice she planned to make.

Maja grasped the phone and blurted out, "Mother, you ca—"

"I've arranged for a car brought around to the photographer's studio at exactly six-thirty," said Mother.

Maja groaned. Jimmy must have heard her message that she planned to bail on the photo shoot that afternoon. This car, or whatever Mother had planned, was her insurance that Maja would be at the studio—doing precisely what Mother wanted, as usual.

Cautious now, Maja spoke before Mother hung up. "I need ... I have to—" Nearly using the excuse of needing to study, she stopped and steadied herself. And then, with a pumping heart and hot face, she told Mother the truth about tonight.

"I have a date."

Even in her state of uncertainty, the words spoken aloud surged a flutter of excitement through her.

"I thought you weren't seeing anyone," said Mother.

Maja twisted the telephone cord between her fingers. "Well, not really a ... It's more—"

"I was going to tell you tonight in person."

Maja stopped fidgeting. "What? Is Daddy ...?"

There was silence on the other end of the phone.

On a European holiday with Mother, Daddy had suffered a head injury when their tour bus hit a bump in the road. Though able to protect Mother, Daddy flew from his seat and slammed his head against the bus ceiling. Now he had negligible spoken language and no sense of smell. For a year and a half, he'd been steadily losing weight.

Mother assumed when Maja helped bring Daddy

home that she'd put off attending the university. Maja stayed on to help at Great Oaks until the fall. Then, without telling Mother any differently, she went ahead with the classes she'd signed up for toward an undergraduate degree. Maja was ashamed of lying, but one lie forced another, and before long, leaving out the lectures, labs, homework, and volunteering at Napa State Hospital on the weekends became easier than admitting her dishonesty. Mother knew that Maja modeled. And Maja modeled so she could afford to secretly stay in college and fulfill her promise to Mormor and graduate.

"Mother? Is it Daddy?"

"The last of your father's investments are gone," said Mother.

"But Daddy's okay? He hasn't worsened?"

"Listen to me, Maja. We have no money left."

"No money."

"All that's left is the house, the silver, and the cars," said Mother.

At nineteen years old, Maja was intent on becoming a speech therapist to help Daddy. At times like this, when she didn't know what to say, words drifted in slow motion like the dust motes floating on a single ray of sunlight through the transom.

"For heaven's sake, Maja. This is no time to clam up."

Walking until the telephone cord was stretched all the way out, Maja paced back the way she had come. Her stomach rumbled. She wanted a cigarette.

A glimmer of hope broke through the landslide.

"My modeling money," Maja said in a rush. "Samuel can—"

"We've already used that. I regret having to put such a burden on you and at such a young age. Your father's future depends on you."

Maja fell against the wall. Suddenly cold, she hugged herself, wishing she'd thrown on a robe.

"We'll discuss it tonight," said Mother.

"I have a date." Maja held firm to the one thing she was sure of.

Heat from standing up to Mother rose off her pajama collar, turning Maja from cold to hot as she untangled herself from Mother's words.

"For heaven's sake. The opera is *Beauty and the Beast*," said Mother. "You simply must see it. First production in the city since before you were born."

Carmen must have entered the study where Mother was on the telephone. She reminded Carmen to take care of watering the violets, as if by now Carmen didn't know that violets disliked getting their leaves wet. Mother ended her instruction with what Maja was sure had been Mother's intended message.

"Whatever you used in the foyer has turned the tiles into a skating rink. Clean them again, this time with water. We must be careful Mister Hawthorne does not fall," Mother finished.

Mother turned her full attention back to Maja. "Everyone who is anyone will be there tonight."

Her tone sounded incredulous that anyone

could possibly get along without her guidance. "Jimmy guarantees your picture will run on the society page tomorrow. You know what that could mean to your future."

Today's scheme to catch her a rich husband, Maja thought, was intended to divert her attention from the real message: Model to support the family. The realization that school would be out this time, for real, spread over Maja like a straightjacket. Academic probation wasn't going to stop her. Neither would this. She'd just have to find a way around having to give up everything she wanted for the good of everyone else.

"I'm sorry, Mother," Maja said, feeling sorry for herself, too.

"Jimmy hands you an opportunity for good money and a little fame and you refuse it," said Mother. "But you should do what's best for you. I told Samuel we should just sell the house. It's mortgaged, of course, but we'll gain enough money to pay your father's medical bills, at least for a few months, so long as we find a way to live cheaply. Of course, we'll have to let Carmen and Ramon go."

Words fell over Maja like a net. "You wouldn't do that."

"We have no choice," said Mother. "You do. Model, or find a rich husband. For heaven's sake, we can't support you. We couldn't afford a new dress for you tonight, so I borrowed one from Mimi. She wore it once to a private party, and none of our friends were there. Your father is expecting you to come. We'll pick you up at six thirty. Do your best at the shoot today. All of our futures depend on it. *Hej då.*"

BILLY FOUND HIMSELF STANDING in front of the file cabinet in the factory union office without a clue what he was looking for. Webb rifled through a stack of complaints piled up in front of him, making him look busy.

"The Panthers are lining up behind Skypiece," Webb said.

Billy stared out the windows—on the lookout now not only for Alabama showing up with even more of his guys, but also watching for Black Panthers. Billy had two cases. He could get one guy's case through, and that was if he fought hard and was real lucky. Skypiece or Alabama? Smothered, Billy looked for something to smash.

"The guys are here." Webb nodded out the window to where Mal and Red headed down the walkway.

If Alabama's guys made any trouble now, Billy would have three of his own men beside him. The two of them stopped at the bulletin board, where Red crumpled a paper in his fist. He tripped over a loose board and yelled about the safety hazard. After the wildcat strike, and Mal and Red and Billy and Webb were elected union officials, Red started strutting around like a goddamned bantam rooster. Mal dragged Red into the office.

Similar to the few women who had hired on at the factory, Mal didn't fit neatly into any of the one-third white, one-third black, and one-third Chicano factory male divisions. Hawaiian and Chinese, Mal was nearly eighty pounds heavier than when Billy had first met him five years ago. Billy recognized the Hawaiian tune Mal hummed as a joyful one, a pretty good sign.

"You two seen this?" snapped Red.

Webb smoothed out the latest hand-drawn cartoon posted by the other side in the ongoing battle of the brown-nosers, management lackeys, milk toasts, and yes-men in opposition to Billy's dope-smoking revolutionaries, druggies, and alcoholics. The bulletin showed a guy with his eyes bugged out, a joint in one hand, a beer mug in the other, and a slew of electrical wires strung up behind him—most of them connected to his ass. Anyone could tell it was Red by all the freckles.

The caption on the cartoon read: "Wired tighter than P.G.&E."

Ready to laugh, Billy pulled away from the desk, not wanting to piss off Red.

"We're talking about the Panthers," said Webb, dragging Mal and Red into Billy's problem.

"And ..." prompted Red, hanging his pea coat over the back of his chair.

"Skypiece lost a finger, brother," said Webb. "Every part in that entire bin is defective. More men

117

are going to get hurt. If the company had confiscated them and ordered new, the accident never would have happened. The Panthers want the company to pay all his hospital bills and time off."

Billy waited, knowing there had to be more.

"The Panthers want the company to take full responsibility for his accident, in writing," said Webb.

Billy groaned.

"And, they want Alabama gone," finished Webb.

"How am I supposed to do that?" Billy demanded.

"Alabama's agitating for every last Black in here to be maimed or killed."

If Webb hadn't been so firm about protecting their childhood promise to keep their shared Indian background a secret, Billy thought, right about now Webb would remind him that if Alabama even suspected that Grandma was a full-blood, he would turn on Billy in less time it took to blink an eye. Later Alabama would explain he wanted to see the color of a half-breed's blood. And Webb would be right.

Billy squashed out his cigarette butt. The ashtray was too full. He dumped the ashes in the can and watched a paper fire flicker out.

"Can you get the Panthers to back off?" asked Mal.

Billy stared at Webb, who was filing a complaint in one stack and turning the next form on a second pile.

"Not if Billy rolls over."

Billy kept his eyes trained on him.

"Maybe I can," said Webb after a hesitation. "But that ain't the point."

"What is the point?" snapped Billy.

"Point is you're white," said Webb. "You never take a dime of the money you're offered under the table. Never affiliated with any one group in particular. You could have had a supervisory position, but you turned it down. The guys respect you. Management fears you."

Red and Mal nodded with that, Red with a begrudging frown on his face.

"You're the only one who can do this, Billy," urged Webb. "Skypiece has a legitimate grievance. Alabama deserves to be terminated. The Panthers want you to prove you're the man they think you are by doing the right thing by Skypiece and get Alabama fired."

Avoiding Billy's eyes, Webb traced a finger from the middle of the table to the wooden edge and back. Red and Mal said he was crazy, but Billy swore that ever since Webb got back from 'Nam he hadn't once looked Billy straight in the eye. Billy was spared the draft, so far anyway. Five years ago, the birth of Lisa classified him with a 2A deferment from being drafted. One year later, with two kids, he qualified for a severe hardship deferment. Then came Melissa last year. Problem was Billy didn't come from money, and he wasn't a college boy. He was twenty-three years old, and this war seemed destined to drag on forever.

Webb pushed away from the table and walked to the windows, a Green Beret with a cruel streak he never had before Vietnam and just couldn't seem to shake. He wiped away his breath on the glass and stared out into the factory. Webb might be seeing the men. Or, he could just as easily see a jungle full of enemy fire and burning bodies.

"The election's right around the corner," said Red.

"Gee, thanks, Red. I nearly forgot," Billy growled.

"Take it easy," said Red. "You weren't the only one Alabama helped get elected. We owe him, too."

"This is Billy's decision," said Webb. "Let him do what he thinks is best."

Red crossed his arms and stared down Billy.

"Election or no election, we're here to give fair representation to all the men equally," said Mal. "It's your job to negotiate for Alabama. Get enough of his past infractions removed from his record, and he won't get fired for being drunk and disorderly this time."

Outside the windows, a line of base frames moved down the conveyer belt from overhead hoists. A workman dropped a dressed engine into place. Another guy hooked up the drive shaft. By the time the first guy took his hoist back to the line of engines, another chassis waited. Neither worker had been issued gloves or protective eye gear.

"Company's not going to replace the universal

joints that hurt Skypiece. On or off the record," Billy said.

"That's why the neglect's got to be documented in writing," said Mal. "Same shit happens again, and we've got us an even deeper pattern of collapse recorded. Setting precedent is what we do."

Buried in the belly of this beast, Billy's body felt like a vibrating riveter and his breathing wheezed. A couple of years ago, after he couldn't stand Brenda hounding him about his poor breathing, he went to the doctor. The damned guy told Billy he had asthma and then turned around and said that it was psychosomatic.

"What the hell does that mean?" Billy had demanded.

"Your poor breathing is all in your head from stress," answered the doctor.

Billy had stomped out of the office as the doctor shouted after him to quit smoking and learn how to calm down.

"I'd like to see you try dealing with workers who don't give a damn about your job and management who doesn't give a flying shit about its workers," Billy had shouted over his shoulder.

Billy sat still and tried taking long slow breaths. Then, still wheezing, he said, "I'm going to the hall. Alabama with another day with no pay ..."

Despite saying that, Billy stayed in the chair.

"Before you go," said Red, reaching in his chest pocket. "A rep from the United Farm Workers dropped these at the hall as we were leaving." He spread four tickets out on the desk like playing cards. "Their thanks for the check we sent them. It's a benefit for the farmworkers. Tonight. The Fillmore. Us four are going to listen to this here Carlos Santana and his blues band."

Proud of himself, Red settled in the chair with his hands behind his head. The freckles across his face looked like scattered jigsaw puzzle pieces.

"We are, are we?" said Webb, picking up a ticket and looking it over.

"Hell, you want to support Cesar Chavez and the farm workers, don't you?" Red said.

"We found out real quick during the wildcat strike what it's like when strike funds run low," Mal said, sliding two chairs together, and sat down. "Morale suffers. The cause falls short. The UAW standing in solidarity with our fellow UFW brothers. The concert tonight will be good for you, Webb. It'll be good for all of us."

Webb opened his mouth to answer back. Billy stood up first.

"The four of us are going," insisted Red, stopping Billy and slipping the tickets back in his shirt pocket. "Tell them why, Mal."

"I scored."

The furnace kicked on. Stale cigarette smoke rode in on a wave of dry heat.

"Scored what?" Billy asked in the silence.

"Four hits of Ozly's Blue," Mal answered.

"Jimmy Hendrix's acid of choice. Made by a San Francisco chemist."

"Count me out," Billy said and left.

"Billy, wait," called Mal. "You know you have a dog in the back seat of your car?"

Billy groaned.

THE FILLMORE

BEFORE MAJA LEFT FOR the photographer's studio, first she stopped off at the end of the hallway. She stood looking at the telephone for a long time. Nodding to herself, she picked up the handset. She returned it to its cradle. After a couple of minutes, she sighed, picked up the phone again, and put it to her ear. At hearing the dial tone, she felt her face flush.

She stuck her finger in the first number to dial and, as she rotated the dial clockwise until her finger touched the metal stop, she turned light-headed. By the last number, she was dizzy, and her vision turned gray.

Just as Maja was about to hang up, Carmen answered.

"Hola," Maja gushed.

"Hola, mija," said Carmen. "Let me get Mrs. Hawthorne for you."

"No." Maja didn't mean to shout. She took a deep breath. When she spoke, her words jumbled and stuck in her throat.

"Qué?" asked Carmen.

"A message."

"You want me to give Mrs. Hawthorne a message?"

Grateful for Carmen's understanding, Maja nodded, even knowing Carmen couldn't see her.

"Por favor, tell Mother …" Maja knew she was mumbling and hoped Carmen understood her. "Tonight. I'm not going."

There was silence on the other end of the telephone. Then Carmen said, "You're not planning to attend the opera?"

"Correct." Maja nodded. As a compromise, she had decided to go to the modeling job.

"Okay, I'll give Mrs. Hawthorne the message … Oh. Here she is now."

Maja slammed down the telephone. Panting, she fell against the wall and slid to the floor. She put her head between her legs and concentrated on breathing.

"Thank you," she murmured, after the fact.

After her heart slowed down, and her vision returned, Maja wondered how much money she'd make from the shoot today and even if it was a paid gig. Jimmy had always given the money she earned to Daddy's attorney who then sent Maja an allowance every month.

Maja called the attorney. As she left a message

with his secretary, her voice quivered, and her words balked. After she spoke to Jimmy's secretary, Maja hurried to her bedroom for her purse and car keys. Feeling a wave of unfamiliar confidence, she pulled a velvet pouch from the bottom of her sock drawer and stuck it in her purse.

At the photographer's studio, Maja lit yet another in a long line of cigarettes, hoping to quiet her rumbling stomach. Last year, Twiggy, a British waif-like girl with big eyes and a flat chest, dominated the cover of every major fashion magazine. Since then, Jimmy wanted Maja skinny and said cigarettes would curb her appetite. He was right. If she quit smoking pot and didn't go on any more fooders, cigarettes would work a lot better at keeping her—as Jimmy said—all eyelashes and legs. Maja liked the way she looked, though. She didn't want to look like a twig.

Neil messed with Maja's hair. Squirming as the minutes ticked faster, she wished he would hurry. Otis Redding's voice filled the empty studio, telling everyone how good his girl made him feel.

Suddenly, Maja knew Mother would show up even in spite of Maja's message. On edge and ready to burst like an overfilled water balloon, Maja pointed at the clock, her hands damp.

"Loosen up," complained Neil.

Maja tilted her head to the side and then up, her face always looking for the light, and her heart searching for meaning.

Modeling to put herself through college honored Mormor. Modeling to pay for Daddy's treatments would be difficult, but Maja believed she could do it. Thinking about it, she wasn't entirely surprised about his lack of money. Great Oaks was vast and the house massive.

Deep down she doubted her ability to work enough to pay for both school and Daddy's doctors while also managing to attend classes. Grimacing, she acknowledged that next week's formal meeting with her academic advisor could mark the end of her college career, though why she had no idea.

The collar of the starched white blouse tightened around her neck. Modeling to support Mother's lifestyle was something else entirely. One thing she was sure of, she wasn't going to devote her life to work she didn't love, nor would she quit school just so Mother could hire a limousine for the night. How dare Mother take her money without first asking her permission.

"Anger. I like it," said Neil.

Maja rolled her eyes, imagining Mother's revelation as a trick to manipulate Maja into opening up for the camera again. Mother was crazy if she thought using fear and coercion would crack the lock. Still, if there truly was no money left, giving only enough to get by wasn't going to work anymore.

In the tiny bathroom at the photographer's

studio, Maja sped through changing into street clothes. Then she opened her purse and withdrew the velvet pouch. She loosened the drawstring and lifted out a silk scarf. Taking great care, she unwrapped the silk. Sitting in her hand was the little wooden carving. The wolf's eyes peered up at her as if asking why it had been tucked away for so long. She teared at the sight of it.

"I'm sorry," said Maja. She had placed the carving in the pouch after Daddy's accident, though now she couldn't remember why.

She lifted the wolf to her lips. With its eyes still on her, the wolf seemed to see something in her she had yet to discover. Wondering what that might be, Maja draped the necklace around her neck and tucked it under her turtleneck sweater. A tingling raced through her bloodstream.

When she ditched the studio, it was six twenty-five, and the next thing she knew, she was catching her breath as Raul's truck lurched toward San Francisco. She was proud she'd said no to Mother, but she also knew that relaying her opposition in a message didn't count as much progress.

Trucks and cars and cabs streaked past them in the slow lane.

"I hope I didn't make us late." Maja concentrated on speaking clearly. Anymore, most people were unaware of her speech problems. As much as she didn't want Raul to suspect, trying made her self-conscious.

"Dolores Huerta speaks after the first set," Raul said, his voice thoughtful. Without much differentiation between s, z, c, his speech sounded soft and exotic. "You'll like her. Carlos Santana plays before and after her speech. You'll like him, too."

Over the noise of the wind rose his excitement. She and Raul had met a few months ago at Napa State Hospital on Maja's first day volunteering with autistic kids. Raul interned on weekends as a social worker. Other than the hospital and a philosophy class they shared, this was their first time out and their first time together at night. Maja smelled open skies and dusty trails when she was with Raul.

Raul kept his eyes on the downtown traffic as they exited the Bay Bridge. Dusk, the time when the real world intersected with the world of the trolls, turned the city foggy gray. At the bottom of the off-ramp, a red traffic light glowed. The truck came to a stop. A green Muni bus approached the cross-traffic signal. For a few seconds, the lights inside the bus fell on commuters hunched together like tired props in a raw photograph. And then, the bus swerved on its way.

"Professor Hicks' lecture." Embarrassed for speaking up, Maja looked away.

Raul touched her arm. The kerchief tied across his forehead Indian-style sent a shadow over his eyes. Headlights from an oncoming car found them and made them shine.

"Nietzsche's parable," he said.

"I missed something."

"How to slay the Dragon of Thou Shalt?" asked Raul.

Maja nodded.

"I was hoping for the answer myself," he said.

Raul grunted as he rolled down his window. The light changed, and he stuck out his arm to signal a right turn onto Van Ness Avenue. The Opera House came into view, lit in wavy, yellow lights with long tails floating from the square building. The thickening fog intensified the effect of the spotlight up close as it circled the sky, announcing the opera to the galaxies. Television crews and lines of limousines made Maja's stomach hurt. Suddenly remembering the required speech for tomorrow's class, she should have stayed home and practiced.

On the other side of the familiar landmark, Raul pulled onto a side street and into a parking lot and turned off the engine. Maja sank into herself, wishing she could magically slip through the seat cover and disappear.

"Why are you parking here?" she asked, scanning the lot.

"The Fillmore is over there." Raul pointed across the street where music blared from a two-story building.

A hole in one of the painted-black windows sent out a kaleidoscope of colors. I could have gone to the opera, she thought. *I could have snuck out and met Raul, too.*

She slid off the front seat, self-conscious in her faded jeans and bare belly under her favorite jacket, just as a Jaguar sedan parked beside Raul's dented Studebaker truck.

A man in a tuxedo offered his hand to a woman in a long gown of pink chiffon. In the dim light, the cotton-candy color set off the yellow in the woman's skin and made her look older than she probably was. He opened the back door and out swept a girl of about ten or twelve. In a gown that matched her mother's, she glided alongside her parents likely under the spell of her first opera.

A guy with long, frizzy-red hair strolled between them, whispering out of the side of his mouth. "Acid. Grass. Mescaline."

The crowd of concert-goers and opera-enthusiasts arrived together at an appliance store on the corner where Walter Cronkite's face spread across every television set lining the window shelves. Rice paddies filled the screens. A bomb exploded on the television—blurry images of the Vietnam War.

The two crowds split and went their separate ways.

At a poster-splattered door, Raul handed tickets to a guy with eyes spinning like pinwheels. Maja peered back at the bright lights of Van Ness Avenue and wondered how much Mother's limousine cost. And the opera tickets?

IN THE FACTORY PARKING lot, Billy convinced Mal he needed the dog and was relieved when Mal took Sister Wolf.

Billy spent the rest of the day unable to breathe, pacing the union hall, cringing at every other sound— sure Alabama was creeping up from behind him. After avoiding him, Billy finally accepted that he wasn't going to meet with the company men until morning. There was no comfort in the extra time. Thinking and planning and logic weren't going to get him out of this one. Someone was going to get hurt.

He drove down the quiet tree-lined street to his two-bedroom house in Fremont. When he found himself white-knuckled, he tried easing up on the grip he had on the steering wheel. The driveway was filled with tricycles and toys, so he parked on the street under a tree with no leaves.

The smell of meatloaf and potatoes and the whine of Elvis met him at the front door. Billy's shoulders relaxed, and he felt contented in this tiny bubble called home, far from the pressures at work.

Lisa saw him and screamed.

"Daddy, Daddy."

His little girl jumped into his arms. Billy held her close. Brenda walked in, beaming to beat the band. From the way she kissed him, right off he knew he was in trouble.

She prodded him with a smile and a nod. "What'd he say?"

He looked at her bleakly, sensing a trap.

"The job interview," she reminded him. "In Oakland."

With the sweetness of her kiss still fresh on his lips, Billy groaned.

"Oh, baby, I'm sorry," he said.

"You didn't go." Brenda anchored her fists to her hips and glared at him.

He sighed. "I know how much it meant to you."

"How much it means to us, Billy," she urged. "To us as a family." Frustration carved shadows under her eyes.

"You're right. I got caught up with things at the factory …" Billy stopped when he saw she wasn't interested.

"I'm sorry. Tomorrow," he promised.

Starving, he checked the kitchen. Overturned plates of food smashed all over the table showed the kids had eaten. There wasn't a plate set for him.

"Wash your hands. I'll fix you something."

Billy swung Lisa onto his back. Even with his troubled breathing, he galloped past Brenda to the stereo with his little girl kicking his sides. Winded, he leaned over the hi-fi, dipping farther than he needed. Lisa squealed and tightened her grip from sliding over his head. They laughed together as he lifted off Brenda's Elvis '45, put on The Doors, and cranked up the volume.

The little girls howled from their bedroom.

"Now look what you've done," snapped Brenda, storming out of the kitchen. "And just so you know, the kind of man you want to be doesn't listen to that kind of music." She stomped to the kids' bedroom.

The telephone rang. Hoping to catch his breath, Billy pried Lisa off his back, but she tightened her grip around his neck and dug her knees into his sides. She didn't say anything. Neither did he.

The silence between each ring was filled with the Doors imploring him to wake up. His stomach growled.

Summer Rose spotted him and zoomed his way. Brenda snatched the telephone as Summer leaped into his arms with Lisa still stuck to his back. The girls smelled clean. They were happy and well fed. Brenda was a good mom, Billy thought. Brenda called him a hothead and explained he was so hostile on account of Ma and how he'd been raised. He admitted he was impulsive sometimes but guessed Grandma's theory was closer to the truth. He had a wolf caught inside.

Brenda hung up the telephone and cleared her throat. "Now, don't go and get all upset. My sisters are stopping by after dinner."

"Not tonight," warned Billy.

"They're not planning on staying long."

"I'm not going through another night with Carol harping on me."

Billy's throat turned bitter as the two of them stared at each other. Lisa slid down his back, choking him. He snatched hold of her arm, and she let out a gasp. Aware of how skinny her arm was and how tight he gripped it, he put an arm under her and hoisted her higher. She leaned her head against his back. He felt her heartbeat, and he coughed.

"Let's don't do this," said Billy.

"What?" accused Brenda. "Talk about how you never keep your promises?"

"I said I was sorry."

A car horn blared from the street. Billy forced himself to move away from Brenda and stepped over Melissa. Out the front window, Red's car idled with Webb in the driver's seat and Mal in the back.

Lisa shouted right in his ear. "Daddy, Daddy. It's Malie."

"What are they doing here?" demanded Brenda.

Billy put down Summer and helped Lisa off his back. Lisa shoved her face up to the front window, waving both arms over her head.

"There's union business tonight," said Billy. "I told them I was staying home."

The doorbell rang.

"I'm going to see if Malie brought his ukulele, Daddy," squealed Lisa. She opened the door with both hands and streaked past Red at the doorway.

Summer took off behind Lisa. Red caught Summer and held her back. His face reddened when he saw Brenda.

"Brenda." Red nodded. "Hell, I'm sorry to bother you, Billy."

Melissa, who'd crawled to the window before her sisters ran off, started crying. Brenda picked her up and dragged shut the swinging kitchen door with such force it thumped back and forth.

"Hell, we thought we could do without you," said Red, loud enough for Brenda to hear in the kitchen. "Looks like we need a vote. You make a quorum," he finished.

"Daddy, Daddy," screamed Lisa from outside.

Billy pushed past Red and rushed outside. Mal had the damned Sister Wolf by a leash and was doing his best to keep the dog from jumping on Lisa.

"Look, Daddy, a dog. A dog," Lisa said, making a face that asked, *I believe in miracles, do you?* She sighed for emphasis and leaned forward with a fist on her heart.

Red raised his bushy red eyebrows and jerked his head toward the car, letting Billy know a vote was not what he had in mind at all.

Brenda shouted a warning as if reading Billy's mind. "Billy."

"What are you doing here with the dog, Mal?" Billy asked, trying to breathe.

Under one arm, Mal had a giant-sized sack of dog food and a pillow and clutched a kennel in his other hand.

Brenda came out of the kitchen.

"I'm sorry, Brenda, Billy," said Mal. "She only stopped barking when we got here. My roommates said no."

"Now what do I do?" asked Billy.

"Better put her out back." Mal gave Billy the leash and nodded at the girls rooted in place, wide eyes glued to the puppy as it reared up and fought against the leash to flatten them. "Let her sleep in the kennel next to your bed, or she'll bark all night."

Mal ducked his head and put the kennel in the hallway, then headed back to the car with Red.

"I'll find it a home tomorrow," Billy said to Brenda, who was as frozen in place as the kids were.

He took the dog out back, threw the dog bed on the ground, and slid the glass door shut. The girls plastered their faces to the glass, making the dog bark. Lisa rapped her knuckles against the glass. She shook her finger at the dog.

"No, no, Sadie," Lisa said.

The dog whimpered and settled down.

She looked over her shoulder. "I named him, Sadie, Daddy."

Billy glanced at Brenda. She turned away.

"Go," Brenda said. "Just go."

"Wait up," Billy called to Red.

INSIDE THE FILLMORE, Maja shook out her hair. Clusters of men mingled with a mass of college students. Raul grabbed her hand, and together they swept across a ruby-red carpet and went up the stairs as part of a huge wave ascending into a smoke-shrouded hall of flickering bright lights and loud music.

Maja slowed down and looked behind her. A girl overtook them and disappeared into a crowd of gyrating kids, mostly her age. Overstuffed chairs and velvet sofas lined the walls. Beneath Maja, the floor vibrated to the music.

Raul grinned. "I'm glad you came."

Colored lights keyed to the blues music flashed in his face.

"Me, too," said Maja, happy.

Raul pointed to the stage. "Carlos Santana."

Smoke hung above a man stooped over a guitar. Surrounding him were a keyboardist, a bassist, and a drummer behind a drum set like the Beatles. Another drummer—with his fingers taped white—sat off to the side of the stage with a long, narrow bongo drum between his legs.

Carlos Santana tilted his face. His ponytail fell between hunched shoulders. Furrows cut across his forehead like a fertile field. A black mustache winded down either side of his mouth and covered his chin as if a mask had slipped and landed there. He wore cowboy boots made of a patchwork of colors.

"I need to see some people backstage," Raul spoke close to her ear.

Maja cringed at the thought of meeting new people, preferring being surrounded by strangers.

"Is it all right if I stay here?" She spoke softly, not wanting to draw attention to herself.

Raul hesitated.

"That's okay." Maja shrugged, feeling guilty for putting Raul on the spot. Then speaking brightly, she said. "I'm happy to go if you think I should."

It was as if Mother stood right alongside Maja, armed with all her "Thou Shalts," all her better ways of doing things.

Raul motioned for Maja to follow. Instead of going backstage, he stopped at an empty sofa under a colossal banner ornamented in gold and United Auto Workers emblazoned with huge black letters. They were about twenty feet off to the side of the stage.

Raul nodded, encouraging her to sit. When she was settled, she looked up. To her amazement, Raul was walking away. Maja wasn't used to asking for what she wanted, especially since she was rarely given it, except by Daddy. An electric thrill sparked the air. She touched the carving at her neck, her fingers trembling. The smooth feel of the wood brushed aside her speech assignment tomorrow, her guilt for letting down Mother and Daddy, and the layer of shame always just beneath her skin.

As the wooden wolf wrapped her in a cocoon of throbbing lights and music, Maja's skin tingled, and her stomach fluttered. Dead from her neck down for far too long, she felt overcome by a sense of weightlessness, as if her body was beginning to awaken. Maja rose to her feet and swayed to the music.

ON THE DRIVE TO the Fillmore, Billy accepted the tiny blue pill Mal handed out. The others tossed theirs in their mouth and swallowed it with a swig of beer.

As they joked and laughed and nothing seemed out of the ordinary, Billy swallowed his.

By the time he was inside the Fillmore floating on a pillowy sofa up against the wall near the stage, Billy couldn't remember how he got there. A guy at the microphone whispered words of justice.

Feeling a nudge, Billy strained to open his eyes to blues and greens pulsating on the floor in front of him. He leaned forward and looked into an agitated lake. As he fell into the water, Webb steered Billy away. The water turned into a dance floor. Secret moves smoothed into quiet. Fins of turquoise and red bled into a girl with her back to him. Swaying back and forth, long yellow hair flowed like a river. Her movements slowed as the music slowed. The air turned sweet.

"She's his," said Webb, and nodded.

A Chicano walking away from the blonde girl wore faded blue jeans, and his long-sleeved snap-down shirt tapped at Billy. He'd picked cotton alongside Mexicans dressed in the same kind of cowboy clothes and work boots. The two biggest things Billy had learned from the Mexican workers was that as poor as he and Grandma were, they were poorer still, and that those with the least always seemed to give the most.

Light-headed, Billy leaned back. Sofa pillows wrapped themselves around him. Grandma and him. Mexicans and him. Autoworkers and farmworkers. All of them shared one thing: they got the crumbs

141

while others sat down at the table to eat.

A speck of red like a pinprick of blood flattened against the back of his eyes. It changed to the color of new brick, and then to the color of the tree bark where he grew up. The same color as the path his great-grandmother Martha turkey-gobbled on her drunken walk home. In the middle of the path glowed the wolf carving. Tears filled his eyes.

The path cleared.

PSYCHEDELIC COLORS TWIRLED AROUND the room. A man as huge as a house offered Maja a joint. She shrank from him until spotting the merry eyes and rosy cheeks of Olle-the-Loyal. Next to him stood a Negro who looked just like Tjovik-the-Wise from the same tale. The one missing from Mormor's fairytale was the queen's choice—the handsome prince. Maja looked for him without success.

Olle-the-Loyal blocked the crowd like a standing sentinel. Someone else was there, too. A presence Maja sensed but couldn't see. Loaded, behind her eyes stars grew brighter and seemed to multiply. An urgency shot through her. A lesson waited to be learned.

Giant speakers loomed from the stage like great black crows. The room turned hazy beneath cigarette and marijuana smoke.

Beneath her, the floor trembled. Vibrations shuddered. The colored lights clicked off into darkness. Music stopped. The stage turned black.

The shaking beneath Maja grew to a fevered pitch like a herd of wild ponies tramping, stamping, and panting across the floor. Heartache and happiness, fear and wisdom, sparks flew, and depths opened.

"Earthquake," someone yelled.

Maja listed to the side. She stumbled and stuck out both arms like a trapeze artist as the floor beneath her feet creaked and shifted erratically. No one ran from the room. No one breathed a word.

Someone clutched her elbow. Through his touch, Maja found her balance. Heat penetrated her skin and into her bloodstream, coursing up her arm and into her heart. Maja knew that touch, warm and steady on her elbow.

She turned and, blushing hard, drew in a sigh.

The boy from her childhood, now a man, concentrated on keeping her upright. Then he looked at her and turned from serious to amused. He chuckled softly.

His touch was all there was and all there ever would be.

SHAKING ENDED AND THE earth turned still.

Lights flashed on, then off and then on again, making Billy dizzy. It was as if he'd caught a glimpse of his entire life, watched it dissolve into nothingness, and come back from the void. The light show started

143

up. Music began as if it had never ended.

Startled, he realized he had hold of the blonde girl's elbow. Wisaw flashed in his mind. He blinked. He knew he was high. Billy looked at her again. He just didn't know he was this high. Impossible she was the same girl. He shook his head, struggling to make sense of their strange, improbable, unbelievable reunion.

They faced each other as if they'd arranged this meeting long ago, and every moment had steered them to this exact place and time.

He drew in his breath and took his time exhaling, enthralled by watching her eyes wake up. A flame burned, catching fire to a hanging iridescence behind her eyes. The blaze burned brighter.

All the blood rushed from her face, and she went from red to white.

Mesmerized by her, Billy watched her struggle to breathe properly with her hand at her neck. Silver confetti fell from her eyes. She'd changed since the last time they'd touched, but much of her was the same. Her face still radiated joy and was determinedly brave. She'd grown taller with the same matter-of-fact acceptance and surety that they belonged together. Her lips parted. Neither of them spoke.

She took his hands in hers as heat warmed and flattened and elongated their grasp. She started to raise his hands to her lips as she'd done when they were kids. Suddenly, she was reaching for him. Pulling him to her, she rewarded him a kiss.

The spark from his mouth turned her self-conscious. She ducked her head.

Billy lifted a hand to smooth back a strand of hair that had fallen in her face. Simultaneously seized by a fiery heat and an icy chill, he was no longer able to differentiate between what was real and what was the high. Billy did know, however, that a married man kissing a girl who wasn't his wife would only lead to trouble for both of them.

He dropped his hand.

"WHO ARE …" MAJA STARTED, as a rusty iron gate creaked open.

She watched the eyes of the boy-turned-man glaze over. Shutting her out, he looked over her head. As when they were young, and he saw Daddy coming for her, his eyes flashed. The grown-up prince backed away.

In a daze and without even knowing the man's name, Maja opened her mouth to beg him not to leave. Then, suddenly she was a girl of seven on the side of a forgotten highway staring at a wolf carving that seemed to be staring back at her.

Raul appeared beside Maja. The moment dissolved.

The grown-up prince disappeared into the mass of people like a puff of smoke, a magician's trick. The wolf was his.

"Sorry I was gone so long," said Raul. "Something came up backstage. You all right?" he asked, peering into her face.

Torn, Maja wanted to run to the man, return the wolf to him, find out who he was, and why he appeared in her life again. He was her earliest memory. Having replayed every detail of their two encounters in her imagination a million times or more, they were as fresh as if they had happened yesterday. She knew her side of the story. She wanted to know his.

"Quite an earthquake," said Raul, his hand on her arm. "Were you scared? Maja?"

It took all Maja's strength and attention to return to Raul. She shook her head and was silent. Raul stood so near she felt his breath. They did not touch. As the pressure of the man's lips glowed against her lips and settled into her heart, she tried to explain.

Raul stopped her by pointing to the stage.

Maja tucked what just happened in a secret vault in her mind for safekeeping until she had a chance to relive the moment and that kiss in peace and privacy. The man's lingering touch, like a magic wand, had rendered her whole and complete. She blushed, reliving his lined face and lean and muscular body. At least he no longer was shoeless. She grinned like a love-struck little girl.

As the song ended, clapping and hollering encircled Maja. She scanned the room, but it was too hazy to make out people in the dark. Instead, she turned to watch the furrows in Carlos Santana's forehead relax.

The applause faded, and Carlos breathed into the microphone. "Thank you."

A spotlight snapped on. Santana, near in age to the man from her past, shaded his eyes against smoky white light running from the stage to the ceiling, a stairway to heaven.

Grateful for the light, Maja let her eyes roam the crowd, searching for the man. Gigantic red flags hung from flagpoles on either side of the stage emblazed with the same black Aztec eagle that appeared on the bumper sticker on Raul's truck.

"*Viva la causa!*" shouted Santana, his black mustache twitching and patchwork boots glowing.

The crowd followed, their excitement coursing through Maja's body. "*Viva la causa.*"

Feeling as if the world were broadening and deepening before her, Maja shouted with abandon along with everyone else. Having never used her voice with such power behind it made her feel as if the louder her voice, the better chance for her to find the man in the crowd and their voices to join as one.

Overflowing with gratitude to Raul for bringing her here, she smiled at him. Raul showed no emotion. Maja went quiet, too.

Standing beyond Raul, a girl stared at Maja, her look dagger sharp. It was the girl who'd followed them earlier. Maja's stomach stung. She had the distinct feeling she wasn't wanted there.

She slouched, wishing she were invisible, and looked for the man. Did he belong here? Was this his cause? She spotted Olle-the-Loyal. No crowned prince.

Santana motioned to someone off to the side of the stage. Maja leaned forward slightly and, without moving her head, looked again. The girl still stared at her. Maja arched back. Uncomfortable and not knowing what else to do, she concentrated on what was happening on the stage.

"Cesar Chavez is too weak from his fast to be here tonight," said Santana. "From the beginning, he and Dolores Huerta have fought side-by-side for farmworkers' rights."

At the name of Cesar Chavez, a ripple of admiration flowed through the crowd. Maja had forgotten the exact date Raul told her Chavez started the grape pickers' strike. She did know that Chavez's cause had spread to a national strike and made the purchase of wine a political act. Before Daddy's accident when Mother still threw black-tie cocktail parties and dinner gatherings, the affairs ended with guests clutching wine glasses in a hot debate over table grapes and Mexican farm labor.

Santana adjusted down the height of the microphone for Dolores. She was tiny.

"Let's show Carlos and the guys how much we dig their music," Dolores shouted.

Everyone cheered. A chant went up. "We want Carlos. We want Carlos."

Alone on the stage, Dolores's eyes were soft and patient. Maja fidgeted, wishing Dolores would just ask Santana to speak for her. Instead, the woman wrapped both hands around the microphone stand and, even as the murmuring from most of the people in the crowd grew louder, she began speaking.

Maja shuddered. Raul wrapped his arm around her. At his touch, she tensed. To hide it, she moved a little closer.

"Pedro, put up your hand," started Dolores. "There, in the back. Pedro gives an honest day's work six days a week. So do his wife and children. We believe they deserve an honest day's pay. You believe that, too, don't you?"

Grunts of agreement tossed about here and there, low and reserved like a bass guitar. Maja's armpits were sticky as if she were standing up there in front of everyone. She imagined speaking in front of her entire class tomorrow.

"Would you call a one-room, dirt floor shack made of sheet metal where Pedro and his family live, fair?" asked Huerta. "No running water, no bathroom, no bed, fair? Pedro doesn't complain. He is one of the lucky *campesinos*; his family has one lone gas burner to cook on."

Huerta's speech pulled Maja out of herself. The woman spoke clearly and simply about men and women working toward a better life. People who picked this country's fruits and vegetables with callused hands and aching knees, broken dreams and lost hope deserved better. Learning that their kids breathed crop-dusted poisons kindled Maja's indignation and outrage. Surely, when everyone heard about this, the deplorable conditions would improve immediately.

Huerta's weariness gave way to strength, and she grew larger. Head erect, arms at her sides and feet planted shoulder-width apart, Huerta was not one to give away power or deflect it.

Imitating the woman's stance made Maja aware of how seldom she stood up straight in public. She was surprised to find she was taller than Raul.

"Cesar Chavez goes without food to remind workers of their pledge for nonviolence," continued Huerta. "He also reminds growers that we, at a mere eight thousand strong, are no match for the land-owners."

Olle-the-Loyal cupped his hands around his mouth. "The UAW stands in brotherhood with the UFW."

Startled, Maja hadn't realized Olle-the-Loyal was still so near. Goosebumps shivered across her arms. Her mystery man was in the same room with her. She could be patient. She didn't expect to see him again until he was ready. So far, the timing of their chance connections seemed fragile and awkwardly off, like coming in for a landing and missing the tarmac. A lesson seemed to be forming for Maja to learn that not only her mystery man but also Dolores Huetra had something important to teach her.

THE DECISION

BILLY AWAKENED, WISAW CURLED beside him, her breath warm against his chest. Before he opened his eyes, she vanished like vapor on hot asphalt. Awake and asleep, both at the same time, he was less confused than disoriented. Memories came in fragments. Last night, he was kissed whole and complete.

The alarm clock shrieked. Skin leapt off his bones. Billy snatched the clock and squeezed it with both hands, fingers fumbling for the turn-off button, his heart slamming against his chest. Even after it was off, the noise bounced in his skull, making him woozy. He felt next to him in bed, making sure Brenda hadn't left him yet. Relieved to find her there, he closed his eyes.

Brenda's breathing slowed. The little sucking noise she made in her sleep brought an old Wilson

Pickett song to mind and all the things Brenda used to do to him in the midnight hour.

Pre-dawn turned their bedroom dingy and small. Sadie whimpered as Billy stumbled out of bed. The dog looked out from the kennel and smiled.

In the bathroom, Billy crouched over the faucet and drank like a parched hyena. Then he chased Sadie outside and fed her.

At the guard booth at the auto plant, Billy pulled his identification from a plastic wallet Brenda gave him last Christmas. She said it was from the girls. The guard glared at him. Billy scrunched his eyes and flashed his badge. This morning, cold as a well digger's ass, wasn't entirely to blame for his shaky fingers. After frisked for knives and guns, Billy slipped his wallet in his pocket and wondered whatever happened to the genuine alligator wallet he stole. Twelfth birthday. Hanes Department store. The girl.

That day presented a future different than the tough, closed-off, pissed-off, son-of-a-bitch Billy had wrapped himself in. In those few fleeting moments with Wisaw, he had wanted to do better. Be better. More. Acid might be making him think in shorthand, but it wasn't responsible for conjuring up Wisaw last night. Her presence wasn't random. Three times. Meant something. Three times. No coincidence.

Billy shook off all thoughts of her as he walked as normally as possible inside the factory toward the stairway to management offices. Rising out of the bowels of the plant, the morning whistle was the saddest sound he ever heard. As he considered things now, the battle wasn't between Alabama and Skypiece or the Panthers and Whites and Chicanos inside. The true enemy was the establishment. They might not necessarily be out to *destroy* all union workers, their constituencies, customers, and even the country itself. Still, politicians and management were, and always would be out to protect themselves and their shareholders first and foremost.

On the second floor, Webb stepped out of the shadows. He'd changed his hair. Now it was so bushy that he seemed to have grown at least another two inches since last night. Seeing Webb's profile showed Billy his old friend again. No longer a guerilla fighter for Special Forces and part of the counterinsurgency. No longer responsible for burning down huts and poisoning the water of people he didn't know. Last night, colors from the light show flickered across Webb's face, and all the past that had been messing with his head was gone. The past vanished and Webb was pure again, like when they were kids together.

At the Fillmore, life had clicked into focus. Billy wasn't ever going to be a bank teller. That was what Brenda wanted, not him. The loss of Brenda's dream could change everything he had here and life as he knew it.

Webb was still in 'Nam during the wildcat strike, but the rest of them who served on the picket line had been given union history lessons from Skypiece, whether they wanted them or not. Daily, Skypiece would read aloud about Walter Reuther from a biography about the founder of the UAW that he'd checked out of the library. Billy memorized a quote of Reuther's: "There is no greater calling than to serve your fellow men. There is no greater contribution than to help the weak. There is no greater satisfaction than to have done it well."

The second whistle went off. From the third floor landing, it sounded more like a burp. Crowded and dirty, under-lit with broken and rusted equipment, fractured bones, and ten-hour shifts, sometimes up to six and seven days a week—none of it was visible from up here at the management level.

Billy pinched the filterless end of his cigarette, took a last hit, and cursed as he burned his fingers. He mashed out the butt under his boot heel on the catwalk's metal grating. Last night, Dolores Huerta reminded him of his grandmother's prophesy that one day he would lead men.

Today just might be that day.

Two hours later, Billy and Webb blasted out of the meeting room, nearly plowing into Mal. Billy's heart sped like a car engine with a stuck throttle. He had the urge to kick something. Mal lorded over the door with his arms folded like a sentinel, staring down guards who glared right back at him.

"Red's still tripping from last night," Mal spoke low and out of the side of his mouth, as the three of them made their way down the stairway. "He said he'd get here just as soon as he's able."

"Everyone's taking odds how much higher Webb's hair can get," Billy said in a light-hearted tone, trying to control the buzzing vibration through him and knowing hostile ears were listening.

Mal chuckled. Webb stared straight ahead. Webb and Mal moved as a unit, pulling Billy along between them. Wound tight and finding the feeling irresistible, Billy wondered if they could hear his heart popping.

One of the soft-trim guys shouted. "Way to go."

Already word of Billy's meeting was ground into the noise of the line starting up. As the guys turned back to their jobs, it seemed to Billy their spines were a little straighter.

Webb and Mal navigated Billy through the plant, his arms pinned in at his sides between them. He wasn't sure if they were trying to keep someone out or him in.

"I didn't give up anyone," said Billy.

"At the hour and a half mark, I figured you were holding tight," said Mal.

"It wasn't like that." Webb's voice was hoarse like he was talking in church. "You should have seen him, man. Billy Wayman stood them down. I can't believe it, and I saw it with my own two eyes."

Billy tried to look at Webb. Wedged between him and Mal like he was, it was easier for Billy if he kept his eyes on the guys straight ahead on the assembly line. Knowing Mal wasn't going to let him go until Webb and he told him everything that happened, Billy let himself be pulled out of the factory and into a light drizzle. The three of them walked past the guard shack to Billy's car, so he could break the news to Alabama.

An assembler raised a hand at them. "We're behind you, kid."

Even guys on the three-mile hike through the parking lot, who hadn't even been in the plant yet, already knew. The old guys didn't look as winded as usual.

At his car, Billy dislodged from Webb and Mal and dug out a ring of keys from his pants pocket. Taking his time, he flipped through the wad before picking out the key to his Chevy.

"I saved Alabama his job," Billy said.

Mal nodded.

"Skypiece will be paid for the time he was out," Billy continued. "That, and all his hospitalization. He gets his money, and we get it in writing."

"What'd you have to give up?" asked Mal.

Off in the distance, a line of haulers loaded brand-new cars fresh off the assembly line and ready for marketplace.

"Made me listen to a bunch of horseshit about getting along and keeping things calmed down," replied Billy. "The importance of keeping people in line."

Webb grabbed hold of both Billy and Mal.

"Don't you get it? Billy Wayman Wolfe is a

ghetto boy, fair-minded to Blacks and Chicanos alike. Even the Panthers and the parolees like you. Sure, Billy's part in the '64 strike played into it, and it was brilliant the way you slipped that in as a reminder. But that's not why the company caved. You show'd 'em there might be all-out war inside. Management is scared. They believe you're the one with the rank and file behind you. They're hoping you can keep a lid on."

The thorn. Planted. Now. Keep it sharp and stuck firmly in management's side, Billy thought to himself. That part wasn't going to be easy.

Napa State Hospital

THE FOLLOWING NIGHT, MAJA slipped the wolf necklace around her neck, knotted an orange kerchief behind her head, and returned to the Fillmore alone.

Unable to spot the boy-turned-man, she returned the next night, again wearing the wolf, the same scarf, and again holding-her-breath hopeful. Refusing to leave her alone, her heart kept whispering that their encounters were not coincidental. The tingling in her spine, a faint sensation of déjà vu, the two of them didn't just fall in the exact same place, at the exact same moment by chance … over and over again.

Unsuccessful at finding him at the Fillmore, Maja called the operator for help.

"There is a local UAW chapter in Fremont," said the operator.

Maja tried on several outfits before deciding on a simple cotton fitted dress with a wide lapel collar edged with lace and long sleeves. Grinning at the chance of learn something about the man—anything solid that made him real, Maja twirled around her bedroom.

Humming a little song, Maja pulled a floppy hat low over her eyebrows, like hiding behind a mask. Mother believed women were supposed to have eyebrows and, since Maja's were too blonde to show, she should paint them on. Mother didn't know Maja had stopped wearing a bra, and she wasn't around to complain about her daughter's dark circles.

Mother's morning calls had been absent for more than a week as if, so long as Maja said yes to every job Jimmy arranged for her, she'd earned her freedom. So far Maja was keeping up with both studying and modeling, but school demands and all the modeling jobs piling up had her worried.

Maja stuffed the map of the Bay Area into the green and yellow macramé purse she'd knotted herself. The map had her route to Fremont marked in red pen. Checking for the keys to the GTO, she opened the front door with a flourish. Coming face-to-face with her academic advisor, she stepped back, a cold chill running through her heart.

With Mr. Evans standing so near to the door, Maja smelled his stale cigarette breath.

"Well, well, well," he said, tapping his clipboard with the tip of his pen. "Time for your one required surprise visit." He lifted his voice at the end of the sentence, like a kindergarten teacher to a room of excited five-year-olds or a circus ringmaster to a rapt audience. Sweat covered his temples.

Maja took another step back. Uninvited, he followed her inside. His presence in her house made her skin itch as if something nasty crawled through the hairs on her arms.

This wasn't the first time her advisor had shown up unexpectedly. Soon after she received his letter about her probationary status, Mr. Evans had started calling the house. Then he showed up outside her house, revving his black Corvette Stingray just as she was leaving for class. Insisting he drive her to school, he would agitate Maja about her classes the entire time and not let her leave until he showered her with compliments about how fond he was of everything about her. Somehow the compliments made her feel worse. Her dislike for him deepened further when he started showing up after class. Though he never acknowledged her professors, Mr. Evans was quick to recount their below-average performance reports of her.

"Which," he often said, wagging his finger in front of her nose, "isn't going to get you off probation anytime soon."

Maja hated most when he made her sit with him while he showed her what she was doing wrong on her assignments. He leaned in a little too close and breathed just a little too hard.

This was the first time he'd been inside her house.

"I … I'm late … for an appointment," Maja said quickly, wishing her roommates were home.

Mr. Evans scanned the entry hall, and then peered into the parlor. His black-rimmed glasses, tweed jacket, button-down shirt, and loafers made him look scholarly. The sunlight told another story: yellowing at the collar, a frayed lapel, and glasses that appeared to have no lenses. He looked slovenly and rundown.

"I'm here to ensure your living environment is conducive to studying," he reported.

Confused as to what she'd done wrong and thinking how much pot was all over the place, Maja cringed.

"My roommates," she said. "I'd rather—"

He looked away abruptly, marking a paper on his clipboard. Maja tried looking over his shoulder, but he rotated away.

"A mark against you for this mess," he said.

A black knife twisted her heart as he motioned toward the parlor that reeked of wet wool socks and was cluttered with bicycles and jackets, random shoes, and an old bucket to catch rainwater. Dana's art project for her final leaned up against the wall.

"Oh, no, I study—" Maja started and then ripped off her hat and ran after him, disadvantaged by his abrupt and unpredictable shifts.

She caught him upstairs headed straight for her bedroom door. Lucky guess? Or, had he somehow already known where she slept?

She slipped in front of him.

"I've ... I've got to run," she said in a rush, fighting the urge to shove space between them.

He wrote on his clipboard and paused, his pen poised for more. "School related?"

"School related?" Maja repeated as the bottoms of her feet tingled.

Mr. Evans cocked his head with his eyebrows up as if amused by her discomfort.

"Why ... no ... no, not school related, really," she stuttered.

He walked around her into her bedroom. With sunlight flooding through the windows, she saw his thinning hair and dandruff on his shoulders. Before he spotted the ashtray with, not only cigarette butts, a joint or two, Maja blocked his view, trying to act natural and not show she was hiding something.

He glanced up at the word 'No' written in big, brash letters above her mirrored closet door. Dana had made her the sign when they'd moved into the house together. Dana knew, better than most, how incapable Maja was of standing up for herself, especially when it came to random men who were nice to her.

"Women make the same sound crying as they do cuming," Mr. Evans said in a low voice, smoothing a hand over her bedspread.

Maja's eyes flew open. Not wanting to let on that she'd heard him, she didn't breathe.

As he jotted yet another notation, she mouthed

the word 'no,' sad that the pressure of that tiny word still felt so foreign against the tip of her tongue.

"What's that you said?" Mr. Evan's voice came in a quick accusing tone.

"What? Oh, oh … nothing," Maja stuttered, surprised she'd said the word aloud and then wondered why not speak up.

Eying her suspiciously, he frowned and looked behind her.

When he rifled through papers strewn across her desk, Maja did speak.

"I'm going to be late," she repeated, motioning to the door to usher him out.

Ignoring her, he gave a little nod to his letter on Academic Advisory stationary pinned to her bulletin board. Then he picked up a green folder from her desk and jabbed her carefully researched and typed report at her.

"I assume this is a term paper?" he said.

"Yes," Maja said, her hand still outstretched.

"I'll want to check it over first before meeting with your teacher to discuss your progress." He put down the report and leafed through several pages on his clipboard.

His words hit squarely on her forehead.

"Check it over?" She snapped her arm to her side.

He didn't look at her, which was good because Maja didn't think she could look back at him.

Mr. Evans whirled around, clutching her green folder.

Confused, she reached out to snatch it back, as he hurried from the room. Missing her chance, she tripped down the stairs behind him.

"You're taking my paper?" she cried.

Without answering, he left the house. Maja slammed the door, turned the deadbolt, and then leaned against it, fighting back her rapidly building nausea.

Outside, her advisor revved his Corvette, giving Maja the distinct impression that he was not only showing off but that he also seemed to draw power from his car. She'd take him down with her GTO easy, she said to herself. Then she shook her head for having such a foolish thought.

Rather than drive to the UAW union hall in Fremont as she'd planned, Maja visited the Academic Advisory Center on campus to formally request a change in advisors.

"I'll have to research your case, dearie," the woman at the counter said. Visibly scattered, she checked first in one file drawer in the wall of file cabinets, and then another.

"But if he's not on your roster—"

"Happens all the time, especially to me." The counter woman sighed. "This new-fangled record-keeping system … You look like a nice girl. I'm sure everything will work out just fine."

"Is there someone else—"

The woman tilted her head with a pointed look

"Someone who knows the recor—" Maja followed.

The woman wrote Maja's name on a tablet of paper.

"Maja Hawthorne. Is that right?" the woman said.

Maja nodded.

"We're hiring all the time," the woman said. "The records just haven't been updated. I'll send you a letter with my findings later today."

"You will look into it?" stressed Maja.

"That's what I said, dearie," the woman repeated, sounding tired. Then she closed the frosted glass partition and disappeared.

Come Saturday morning, Maja still hadn't heard from the advisory office. Lying in bed, she spun in a panic of loneliness with no idea how to separate herself from her academic advisor. Until she was assigned another advisor, Mr. Evans was in control of her academic probation.

Gasping for air, Maja jumped out of bed, dressed, and packed for her final weekend volunteering at Napa State Hospital. If she'd let go of her dream of graduating, her advisor would be a problem in the past. Sticking around was prolonging what she knew she'd eventually have to do—drop out of school. But before she left, she had something to prove.

In the parking lot in front of the speech clinic at school, a ten-seater school bus idled. Raul stood in line to board, wearing the same red kerchief around his forehead he'd worn at the Fillmore. By the time Maja loaded her things and stepped aboard, all the seats in the back of the bus where Raul sat were taken.

A shadowy figure leaned over Maja. She opened her mouth to scream. Not a sound came out. She kept trying and trying and trying. She awoke as the van bumped off the main street of Napa. With her heart leaping out of her chest, she spotted the familiar wrought-iron lettering for Napa State Hospital.

The bus dropped all the volunteers outside the dormitories. Raul strode up to Maja, and her fears shrank. Light filled her eyes. The smell of earth mixed with the scent of hard work and sweet after-shave lotion.

"Spring." Raul pointed to a lone green shoot in a stark flowerbed.

Maja grinned. "A promise."

"I'll see you later at the Canteen."

Clutching her notebook to her chest, Maja checked in with the staffers, her heart beating fast, apprehensive and excited to see Kenny.

As she opened the door to Ward B, she braced herself for the stench of urine. Disinfectant stung her eyes. A slew of children as young as five years old and up to twelve, filled the dirty green playroom with their usual crying and screaming. No more than twenty-five kids were legally allowed, but there was always more than that. Most of them rocked in place, perched on the backs of sofas, sitting at tables or standing. Today, every child wore a football helmet. A new child banged his head against the wall. Plaster chipped away, leaving a dirty yellow pockmark.

Staffer Sara waved. She wore a wrinkled knit pullover shirt with no pockets or buttons and faded trousers that long ago had lost their crease. A stick-like contraption hung from a clip at her waist. Maja pointed to the child banging his head and lifted a hand in question.

Rushing to his side, Sara unclipped the stick and jammed it against him. There was the sound of an electrical discharge. The boy arched in agony. He stopped banging.

"Two new kids, both head-bangers," Sara shouted over the commotion, pointing to the helmets. "It's contagious."

Feeling the boy's pain and unable to speak, Maja looked back and forth between the stick and the little boy. Staffer Sara followed her gaze and lifted the stick in the air.

"A shock-stick," said Sara. "It's really just an adapted cattle prod, the latest technique in extinguishing inappropriate behavior. Two shocks for violent behavior."

"A violent solution for violent behavior?" said Maja, angry and shocked, though not surprised. She had learned about the new approach in class, but to witness such brutality against a child ...

Shaken, Maja left the chaos of the ward for the

cracked and abandoned playground, where Kenny marched in a wide circle just as he had every other Saturday. He jabbed a stick at a sky the color of the cement walls. The idea of him being hurt frightened her. Who would protect him from pain and abuse?

Maja leaned on the gate. Kenny looked top-heavy in his bulky green parka and black football helmet. His movements might be repetitive, but they were also slow and deliberate and full of grace.

Before long, Maja forgot all about cruelty, the past, the claustrophobic pressures, and dark thoughts cluttering her mind like a colony of flapping bats. In their place, an idea sparked a deep feeling. No one had protected her, but perhaps she could protect Kenny.

Kenny completed one circle and started on the next one. He hadn't moved his eyes from the tip of his stick or deviated from his exacting pattern, but Maja wanted to believe he knew she was there. Dana pitied kids like Kenny, preferring to work with the mentally retarded. Maja admired Kenny. He'd found a way to create an impenetrable protective wall around himself.

She stopped him with both hands on his shoulders. He kept his eyes on the stick, though now his tapping was more of a pattering. She searched his face under the football helmet for a sign. His eyes were averted, as usual. His little pink cheeks glowed. If he were content, who was she to assume she had anything better to offer?

"Does that big old helmet make your head hot?" she asked, not expecting an answer.

She did her best to tuck Kenny at her side, but it was like trying to bend a matchstick without breaking it. As they walked together, she reviewed the steps in the new approach she planned for today. She felt the crushing pressure of time running out and the fear of disappointment. That would *not* interfere with their time together. She wanted—*needed*—to provide clear data that proved Kenny's infinitesimal progress, which she hoped would better his chances for future therapy.

The deserted classroom crowded with empty tables and stacks of chairs fit the sanctity of a therapy room Maja's professor had stressed, a quiet place where the child felt safe. In a cleared-out corner at one end of the room, a one-foot-deep tray with six inches of sand sat on a table about waist-high to Kenny. His therapy centered on a three-story wooden dollhouse filled with furniture Daddy had bought for Maja's fifth birthday. She brought the house on the bus one weekend and told the staff they could use it, too. Everything was always as Maja had left it the week before.

The first time she showed the dollhouse to Kenny, she gave him a company of toy soldiers that he promptly buried in a far corner, where they probably still were. Exposed in the sand were little plastic dolls, with movable arms and legs, and dressed in light summer play clothes.

Every action Kenny took with the family and toy house meant something to him. The theory was that by Maja verbally relating his actions, he'd connect her words to those actions.

After Maja removed his helmet and jacket, Kenny faced the sand with his eyes straight ahead and his hands at his side.

"I brought you a little dog." Maja spoke the simple sentence carefully and clearly, going through the steps she was learning in school, and waiting to see what he did next.

Kenny had confirmed Maja's belief that a child as isolated as he was could externalize his inner self through play. However, she wasn't sure how to prove the subtleties of his change. Nuances weren't measurable. Non-verbal communication like the way he turned his shoulder, making sure she saw what he was doing in the sandbox couldn't be established. The straightening of his spine and tilt of his head when she spoke to him proved too delicate to transfer into hard numbers.

As seriously as Maja took the challenge to prove her time with him hadn't been useless, pointless, or a waste of time, Kenny had given her the far greater gift. The chance to practice her speech without fear of being lashed out against or given a funny look was building Maja's confidence, while also building her desperation to protect their time together.

Kenny snatched the toy Rin-Tin-Tin dog Maja offered and the little girl doll. His hand grazed hers, sending out warmth. Tempted to mark his act as deliberate social contact, she knew her professor wouldn't believe her.

Kenny arranged the girl on a kitchen chair in the dollhouse and placed the dog at her feet. Maja narrated Kenny's play as precisely and accurately as she could while jotting his actions in her notebook. She worked to keep her voice and expectations neutral.

He picked up the boy doll and buried his face in the sand. A spark shot through Maja. This was it. If he revealed why the boy was facedown, she could … what? Show he was opening up? She was leaving him. But if her findings encouraged another student to continue …

"Kenny buries the boy doll in the sand," Maja said, leaning in nearer to him.

She held her breath, knowing how key the boy doll was. It was important that he was not included in the sweet kitchen scene.

The classroom door opened. Panicked, Maja raised a hand to stop or at least silence the intruder. She kept her eyes trained on Kenny.

"Kenny turns the boy facedown," she repeated, tempted to urge him to go further and resigned that prompting was wrong.

Static filled the room. Kenny frowned.

Distracted, Maja looked up.

"Enough for eight," barked Staffer Sara into a walkie-talkie. "Send Jose. Over and out."

Sara picked up a child's chair, one in each hand, just as Kenny's face crumbled like Pepparkaker. He swept out an arm and toppled the playhouse with a crash. Twenty-two pieces of doll furniture flew across the room.

Maja squatted and wrapped her arms around Kenny, pinning his arms at his side.

Sara drew her cattle prod and started toward them.

"Just go," Maja said, sticking out a hand to stop her. "I've got everything under contro—"

Sara pressed the button.

"No," Maja shouted as tiny veins of lightening hit Kenny's chest. Holding him close, Maja's body snapped as his body did.

Sara leaned in for the second shock. Shaking all over. Maja rose to her feet.

"That's enough," Maja snapped. She stood guard over Kenny, who squatted on the floor rocking. Maja's face burned, and there was a choking feeling in her throat.

Sara tried to push past her. Maja shoved. Sara dropped her prod, stumbled, and fell backward.

"You're going to hear about this," was all she said as she retrieved her prod.

That night, Maja told Raul what had happened as they hiked up a trail to the top of a knoll behind the hospital, following the scent of fire. Darkened trees loomed in silhouette on the eastern rolling foothills. The flat middle of Napa County spread out

173

in acres and acres of plowed fields.

Off to the west, a fire burned near enough its smoke bothered Maja's eyes. Raul laid his jacket on the ground. She was happy to be with him as they sat in silence and watched the fire spread. Bats flew low over the tilled soil.

Wanting to drive away the incident with Staffer Sara, Maja wondered how to ask Raul about the girl at Fillmore without sounding nosy.

Raul broke the silence. "You're a volunteer. They can't fire you."

"I'm on academic probation," said Maja. "I wasn't thinking about how much I need these credits when Kenny got shocked."

The reality that credits no longer mattered injured her heart.

"You stood up for what you believe in," said Raul. "You protected him."

"His outburst ... it was progress," declared Maja. "He showed ... emotion. Then this afternoon ... at the Canteen ... he leaned next to me. After months of nothing ... and suddenly ... after the shock. I can't explain it. An opening. An honest-to-goodness first."

"You're meant to do this work, Maja," said Raul. "Compassionate. Encouraging. Positive."

Maja glowed in the silence that followed.

"What will happen to him ... all of them?"

"When the closures start?"

Maja nodded.

Raul shrugged. "Closing the hospital is just a part of Reagan's larger plan." He jerked a thumb over his shoulder. "He's out to pound all state-run institutions into the ground. Except, of course, prisons. Group homes will pop up all over the state in a year, two tops. The rest will likely end up on the street."

"Someday …" Maja hesitated.

"What? Someday, what?"

"I wonder if I couldn't open a home for autistic kids," she said.

Convert a wing of Great Oaks, she thought to herself. There was more than enough room on the estate for Mother and Daddy and a bunch of autistic kids. She could picture such a possibility in her mind's eye. She leaned back, excited and full of ideas.

A star streaked across the sky. The glow of the fire was too far away to block the ancient web of stars and the patterns they formed. Beneath the smell of smoke laid the scent of dusty books, wet dirt, and fat strawberries.

Raul's body was warm. Maja had given him no explanation about her connection to the man she kissed at the Fillmore. It would sound crazy. Still, that one kiss, no matter how confusing, opened up an urge to be touched and kissed—not fast and passionless like all the nameless and unexceptional boys she'd had sex with and didn't love. She longed to be held close by a man and be understood without saying a word.

Maja relaxed against Raul. She knew if anything

happened, it would come through her, not at her—
a first.

"What'd you think of Dolores Huerta?" Raul
asked.

"I'd never heard a woman strong like that … and
in front of men … out in the open."

"Do you want to hear her again?" asked Raul.

Maja nodded.

"Come to Delano with me tomorrow." Raul
leaned forward.

"The central valley?" said Maja.

"Cesar is breaking his fast with Bobby Kennedy.
Dolores will be there. Ten thousand people showed
when we marched to the state capitol. With Kennedy
there, who knows how many people will show. It will
be just the two of us in the truck."

Maja weighed the paper due on Monday with the
chance of seeing Dolores Huerta again … and Robert
Kennedy and Cesar Chavez.

"Before you answer," Raul said, sounding weary,
"you should know something. Papa came to this
country through the *Bracero* Program in the late fifties.
He never went back but he also never stopped being
Mexican. The girl at the Fillmore? When we were just
babies, my father gave her father his promise we'd
marry. It doesn't matter how many times I've told
him no. He's waiting for me to live up to my family
obligation, get a job, and marry her."

Disappointment dragged Maja's heart.

Raul rose to his feet and offered Maja his hand.

"I'm not going to marry her. I will choose my own bride."

Using his help, Maja got to her feet just as her high school friends surfaced in her mind bubbling on about the gift of a bride to her husband. Unbidden, the memory of Clay rose, and she breathed fast, gulping to ward off the wave of nausea that swept over her.

Raul led the way down the bluff. "We're lions, you and me, running off into the desert."

"The Dragon Of Thou Shalt," breathed Maja. "Can we ever really?"

"Free ourselves?"

Maja nodded, even knowing he couldn't see her.

"I sure hope so."

Then he turned around as if waiting for her answer. Her face felt warm as she looked into his sweet, dark eyes.

"I'd love to go with you tomorrow," Maja whispered.

DELANO

"TAKE A LESSON," Brenda yelled from the front door for Billy to tag along and play golf with her sisters' husbands.

Billy was well aware that Brenda was hosting a Tupperware party and didn't want him hanging around. Because he didn't play golf—and because his mind was on other, more important things—Billy passed on the golf.

Making that choice was easy. On the other hand, it proved harder to decide between driving to the East Bay to look for the man who bought the GTO and to find the wolf carving or going to Delano with the guys. In the end, Billy picked Delano. Holding out against management was the first real stand he'd ever taken in life. It made him feel good inside. He liked challenging the status quo in the company of Chicanos and Negroes, and the students, and workers, and women demanding cataclysmic change.

"I won't be home for dinner," Billy called and raised a hand as Webb drove up.

"Get a hair cut."

Billy slammed the car door, rode with Webb to the union hall, and boarded a rental bus along with Mal and Red and other Green Caucus members. Alabama would never get on a bus full of Chicanos and Webb. Still, Billy watched for his adversary and followers to appear as disgruntled as ever. Though Billy had saved his job, Alabama hadn't gotten over Billy standing up to him in front of his men.

When the doors finally squeaked shut and they were on their way to the Central Valley, Billy pulled his cowboy hat down over his eyes.

A siren shrieked in the distance, like someone caught by surprise. The sound built to a high-pitched wail. Reverberating in Billy's head, the siren split into a thousand colored fragments. He was still high all right.

All the guys turned silent as the ambulance screamed past. The bus creaked back onto the highway and talking and laughing started up, muted though, out of respect for guys trying to sleep. Billy sat up and pushed back his cowboy hat as someone fiddled with a transistor radio. Static lodged in Billy's head.

"Thought we lost you both there for a minute." Red pointed at Webb who sat rigid, staring straight ahead.

This wasn't the first time Webb had checked out. The darker the news turned in Vietnam, the more bewildered Webb grew. He'd joined the army out of honor and the desire to do something meaningful. At the Fillmore, he told Billy it wasn't the guilt that was killing him. It was his doubt that any of it meant anything. On the way home that night, Webb had sobbed and fought off screaming faces. Because of that, Billy kept quiet about the couple other times he'd dropped acid, not wanting to encourage Webb.

Billy probably shouldn't indulge either, but with the altered states of awareness, an entry point to the future and other planes of imagination became clear to him. Surrendering to the high and trusting what he was being shown, was helping him flow with everything that was expected of him at work and at home. Freed from the box he'd been living in his entire life, Billy wasn't ready to squeeze his way back in.

Red twisted in the seat in front of them, handing him a beer. "It's the siren. Flashback to 'Nam," Red said, stating the obvious.

Mal leaned back in his seat and hummed one of his favorite Hawaiian love songs. Webb's eyelids fluttered. His sagging skin hardened.

"What are you staring at, man?" demanded Webb.

Although he was relieved Webb had come out of it, Billy wasn't sure anymore what his friend would and would not do.

"Hell, we ain't looking at you," spat Red, piercing a can of beer with a church key and pushing it in Webb's hand.

"How much further?" A toothpick bobbed up and down in Mal's mouth.

"We'll be there when we get there," said Red.

Up ahead, a jacked-up pick-up truck sat cockeyed on the side of the highway. A young Chicano was changing a flat. A girl in a peasant blouse and jeans stood off to the side.

Billy took a swig of beer. As he spotted her long, yellow hair swaying on the breeze, he swallowed wrong and ended up coughing.

Still sputtering, Billy sat up in his seat and stared. Wisaw again. The air turned sweet. As Billy tried to convince himself that the chances of seeing her out here in the middle of nowhere were near impossible, all the guys started cat-calling, pounding their feet on the floor of the bus and crowding the windows.

The bus came alongside the girl. She looked up. Their eyes met. Billy's world turned silent. As the bus continued past her, Billy craned his neck, unwilling to break their connection. The girl stepped forward as if to follow him. Even when she was just a speck in the distance, Billy kept his eyes trained on her. Finally, he fell back in his seat. He shook his head in disbelief. Another unbelievable and far-out sighting.

The floor shook the night of the earthquake at the Fillmore with that girl. He hadn't been able to get that moment and the touch of her lips out of his mind. And here she was again. Beyond her face and those eyes, a familiar stand of trees swayed in the wind not far from where Grandma still lived. The ditch where workers threw Ginger's body was paved over now.

Webb nodded to the front of the bus. Strolling through the middle of the material handlers, assemblers, spot-welders, painters, hog ringers, and forklift handlers came two of the few women in the entire plant. Not surprised they'd joined the bus, Billy was surprised the girls headed toward them. The guys stomped and slapped the seat covers in front of them, calling attention to the girls as they passed.

Irritated and wanting to enjoy what little was left of last night's high in peace, Billy shifted in his seat. In the heat, his shirt stuck to the plastic seat and plastered against his back. His hat fused to his head.

Webb nudged Mal. The big guy snorted and fished the toothpick out of his mouth.

One of the girls was Janice, a recent graduate from New York University. Remi hailed from the University of California at Berkeley. Management didn't know the two girls were college graduates. Management also didn't know they were communists. Never would have hired them if they had, too afraid of what the girls would get management's factory peons to do in the name of Workers Unite as if the men hadn't long ago figured it out for themselves.

Not the types to be run off, the two girls continued down the bus aisle without falter. Why they joined the Green Caucus was a mystery. Sure they were liberals pushing for workers' rights, job safety and all, but the girls were downright radicals. Neither girl had pulled out a pamphlet, but Billy bet the farm that both girls could recite every word of the Central Committee of the Communist Party of China's "People's Voice" and the "Red Flag."

Janice stopped where Red's outstretched legs prevented her from going farther. Of the two girls, she was smaller and darker. She had a nice body, and long, black, curly hair. Behind the wire-rimed glasses, her black eyes were always serious.

"Uglier than a junkyard dog and dumber than a post," muttered Red.

"Why that's no way to talk about yourself, Red," said Remi, the taller and lighter of the two. "It doesn't become you."

"We want to talk," interrupted Janice, all business.

Billy kept his eyes hidden in the shadow of his cowboy hat.

Webb slid the Coleman beer cooler into the aisle to prevent the girls from getting any closer. Then Webb folded his arms across his chest with his fists clenched, giving his muscles the appearance of being bigger than they actually were. Webb didn't like the girls: they were too outspoken against the war.

Billy lit a cigarette. He took a long drag and coughed.

"We've got ideas about the next election," said Remi.

"A little early for that, ain't it?" Red threw a mock frown to each of the guys like he couldn't figure such a thing.

Billy grinned. Remi frowned.

"Why so quiet, Billy?" asked Janice.

Not bothering to answer, he pulled his hat lower and closed his eyes. He came to when he heard his name mentioned.

"… and Billy's name goes up for president," Janice was saying.

At that, the last of the leftover high Billy had been enjoying disappeared in a snap.

"That puts you, Red, at vice-president." Janice widened her eyes and shrugged as if she was lobbing a challenge to Red.

The girls were up to something. Billy just wasn't sure what or why it involved him.

"Hell, Billy's only twenty-four years old," said Red. "We ain't much on taking a pig in a poke."

"And that means?" said Remi, smirking.

"He hasn't been tested," answered Red.

"He handled the Skypiece case with management," said Janice. "The guys like him."

"It's true, man. Billy can win." Webb looked like he was waiting for Billy to say something.

A bee buzzed in Red's window. It found its way out again.

"He's the one who can win," urged Janice. "He's

got the Chicano vote."

No way could he win. The girls were using him.

"The Negroes will vote for him, too," said Janice. "Won't they, Webb?"

Webb hesitated. He blinked once and cleared his throat, speaking to Billy rather than to the girls. "The Panthers know you bailed out Mavericks at City Hall, man. And you did right by Skypiece."

"One thing. Billy's got to declare before the Negroes put up somebody else," said Janice.

Red's face turned red, and his freckles disappeared. He glared at Billy as if all this was his fault. Janice cocked her head, waiting for Red's answer.

Billy decided to relieve Janice of any further delay.

"You girls come into the factory thinking you're going to do something important," Billy said, starting at random. "You pass out subversive material, get the guys riled up, and you do it to advance your political agenda. The workers are the ones who end up out of a job if we act out or call a strike management breaks. Not you. You're off to fight for your next righteous cause. And by the way, Skypiece is not a case. He is a man who lost a finger because management didn't live up to their responsibility." Billy's breathing broke.

Guys from the middle of the bus had turned around listening. Billy flicked his cigarette out the window in a sharp, irritated gesture.

Janice stood up. "We do care about workers'

rights, and you, Billy, just happen to be our best bet."

She stared hard at Billy and returned to the front of the bus.

Route 99 took them smack dab through the center of Delano where it was hot and dry enough to turn the air hazy. Trucks and cars crowded the streets. Thousands of people streamed into a clearing where Mexican men in headbands, straw hats, and black armbands directed their bus into a parking lot filled with other buses—some from high schools, colleges, and some with church names, and many, like theirs, private rentals. All of them glittered, saturated in a rainbow of light.

Still vibrating from the twist the girls threw at him, Billy gazed over the heads of the people crowded in a town square lined with oak trees. Red United Farm Workers' flags, with the black Aztec eagle in the middle, flapped overhead. Banners with the UFW official motto, "*Viva la Causa*," and others with *HUELGA,* draped from taut wires.

Smoke billowed from barbecue pits. The smell of grilled hot dogs and hamburgers, mixed with hot tortillas, got the guys on the bus moving. Most of them were Chicano. Other than Webb, there were a couple of blacks. Red and him were the only whites.

The last ones off the bus, Billy and Webb, joined college boys in sports shirts and slacks, and men with stooped shoulders, lined faces and crippled hands.

They all melted under the oak trees' shady canopies, where Mal left with the local UAW banner tucked under his arm and an additional donation they'd brought.

Before long, the giant banner was suspended between a basketball hoop and a tree branch. In line for vats of beans and rice, Catholic priests in white collars and black short-sleeved shirts mingled with Mexican and white men, women, and children.

Mal bullied his way to the front of the line and stumbled back with a soggy paper plate piled high with food.

Thinking of going without eating and drinking only water for twenty-five days for a cause—like Cesar Chavez's spiritual hunger strike for non-violence—made Billy famished.

His cowboy hat broke the sun, but it wasn't until Billy sat at a picnic table in the shade, eating, that he started feeling better. Eating standing up, Mal spilled beans across the tabletop from a second plate of food.

Red mumbled around a hotdog in his mouth. "Hell, those girls have got a lot of nerve."

"They're up to something." Billy dismissed their proposal as ridiculous. Besides, any advancement in his life now felt like being thrown straight into a roaring fire.

"I know you don't want to hear it, Red," said Webb. "Janice is right about Billy." Webb watched most of the rice he shoved onto a plastic fork roll off.

Red pushed his plate aside. "Hell, so now just because they say different, our plan don't mean shit?"

"First off, 'our' plan is news to me," said Webb. "Second, the guys pay their dues and don't see what it's getting them. Chavez is fasting because farm-workers don't believe they can win without violence. Billy will fight so our guys don't have to."

Webb said all that while spooning rice and beans into a tortilla, as if concentrating on one thing helped him open up about something else.

An assembler came up and asked Red something.

"Those girls are bulldogs," Mal said. "They grab hold of something, and they're not letting go without a fight." Mal raised his eyebrows and headed off for more food.

Billy ignored Webb staring at him from the other side of the picnic table, and he lit a cigarette. Red kept talking to the assembler.

Webb spoke under his breath. "You'd win hands down."

"No way. Doesn't matter anyway, Brenda's yelling at me to quit. Besides, nothing is going to work unless we're all behind it," Billy said, looking at Red's back.

"Brenda wants you to quit the Executive Board?" said Webb.

"She hates the factory."

"Even after all it's given you guys?"

"She hasn't forgotten the strike," said Billy.

Though he'd hardly eaten, he pushed away his plate. "Most of us lost more money than we'll ever make back."

"President locally could get you noticed by the guys at national," urged Webb. "You could give your kids nice schools and a swimming pool."

Webb's mention of service at the national level caught Billy by surprise, and his mind ballooning out in all directions at once. National. Billy was only now starting to maneuver the challenge of living with one foot cemented in Brenda's conventional life and the other skating through the freedom in his mind. President and vice-president both demanded more time at work and less at home. He'd probably get a pay raise. Brenda would like that. Still, Billy didn't believe Janice was telling the truth. He put the girls' idea out of his mind.

A bullhorn sounded, and someone from up front yelled for silence. The message was repeated until the noise died away.

"Cesar Chavez waits for us at the UFW field office." The bullhorn went silent.

Everyone cheered at Chavez's name, and the crowd of people in the food line shifted. As they all moved out of the square and into the street, Billy thought about what Chavez had suffered and sacrificed for the sake of principle to have people cheer like that. Just hearing Chavez's name gave people hope, made them believe anything was possible—that size wasn't measured by inches and feet, money and assets, physical strength, but by one's actions.

Mal sang an upbeat Hawaiian song until they turned off the paved road and started up a dirt path. Dust, kicked up by thousands of feet, forced Billy to tie his handkerchief around his face like an old-time bank robber. Even so, the air was thick and hot. He had a hard time keeping his eyes from watering.

A crumbling, low rock wall meandered across green rolling hills, like a dragon in the San Francisco Chinese New Year's parade. A lizard slept on a stone, and a bird sang like falling water. Billy casually surveyed the crowd around him. He noticed there weren't many blondes around.

Up ahead, an old packing shed came into view with an upholstered easy chair, like what's in someone's front room, and instead was sitting on the front porch. A microphone stood in the center. Two giant speakers, the size of those at the Fillmore, flanked either side of the building. Everything was faded to the same dusty beige.

The bullhorn sounded again. This time the call for silence came from behind them. A hush moved from the back of the crowd, swept over Billy, and continued forward.

The crowd parted for a man with a face marked by the sun. He leaned his head on his shoulder as if unable to hold his head up, and half-walked between a priest on one side and a man with thick sandy hair, a sports jacket and tie on the other. Cesar Chavez.

Robert Kennedy. The priest was a stranger to Billy. Three men moved slowly across the trampled earth. When they passed him, Billy joined in the clapping.

Chavez had gone more than three weeks without food. There were carved gullies in his face. Holding him up, Kennedy, in comparison, looked so vigorous that he made Chavez appear even weaker.

"Hell, Chavez sure knows how to use the pump handle," said Red.

"He had to do something. The strikers are no match for the growers. The workers are getting frustrated. Things get violent ..." Mal left his sentence hanging.

"Billy knows how to work it, too, how to make things happen. Don't you forget it," said Webb.

Following Chavez was Dolores Huerta. Listening to her at the Farm Workers' Benefit at the Fillmore going on about the ills farmworkers suffered, Billy hadn't spotted anyone like him, a half-breed who as a kid toiled the backbreaking work in the fields alongside the Mexicans. Mostly, what he'd seen was a lost cause. If he ran for President and the Indian part of him was uncovered, he'd be just as defeated as the farmworkers were.

Chavez's wife wore a long, white veil hanging down her back, as if dressed for church. She and Huerta settled Chavez with a blanket over his legs. Kennedy sat on the other side of him. The priest stood at the microphone. Murmuring quieted. Then, the silence was complete.

"My name is Reverend Drake," said the man with the collar. "Cesar Chavez has asked me to read a letter to you."

As Reverend Drake thanked everyone, Billy thought about what it felt like to have someone believe in him like Webb did. Grandma used to tell him he would be a leader of men. But now that the girls were talking about him running for President, Billy couldn't register the idea of leading anyone.

When Billy turned his attention back to Reverend Drake, the crowd was fired up, cheering in agreement.

"To be a man is to suffer for others," said Drake, still reading from Chavez's letter. "God, help us to be men."

Billy hollered along with the rest of the crowd, but deep inside he didn't accept the message. Sacrificing in a nonviolent struggle for justice hadn't helped the Indians.

A little more than a month later, on April 4, 1968, Martin Luther King was assassinated, another non-violence failure. They shut off power to the factory in respect.

As they filed out, Billy spotted an off-line inspector sauntering toward Webb. Too late, Billy picked up what the inspector was singing under his breath. Something about goodbye blackbird. Blackbird bye, bye.

"Fucking, Klu Klux Klan Nazi," screamed Webb, and he jumped the inspector.

Alabama's guys jumped Webb.

"Mal," shouted Billy. "Red."

Alabama drew a blunt object from his pocket. As if in slow motion, Billy watched the knife blade discharge. Alabama flicked his wrist. Blood sprang from Webb's face.

Billy charged Alabama and head-butted him in the stomach. Alabama staggered backward. Billy yanked Alabama's arm. The switchblade skittered across the cement walkway. A closed fist came at Billy's face. He ducked too late and took it in the chin. Reeling, he shook his head in an attempt to clear his eyes.

After Billy, Red, Mal, and a bunch of the other guys finally had everyone off each other, Billy touched his jaw. He winced as a stab of pain shot up the side of his face.

Mal and Red, helped by the guards on their side, sent Alabama's guys out of the factory first.

With his jaw throbbing, Billy led Webb to the union office to wait for an all clear from Mal to bring him out. Wanting to give Webb time to get control, Billy offered his friend a beer. Webb was pissed. He was hurting, too.

Webb shook him off and paced the room. The fishbowl office, now surrounded in a deep darkness so unlike the normal light and chaos of the factory, was eerily quiet. The only sound was Webb's fist slamming into his hand like a baseball player with a mitt.

"Maybe there's always got to be a war going on," Webb muttered. "Maybe ain't none of this matters anyway."

The sound of fist against flesh struck in a steady rhythm, slow and cruel.

"Let's wait—" Pain stopped Billy. He clenched his teeth and tried again without opening his jaw. "Let's see what happens." He spotted Mal coming toward the office. "I want a doctor to take a look at that cut on your face, Webb."

Mal motioned them forward. Webb left by himself.

When Webb didn't come back the next day, Billy shifted from worried to frightened. He called Webb's apartment and found his telephone number disconnected. Billy drove by Webb's apartment and banged on his door. All the curtains were closed. No one answered.

Three weeks passed, and still Webb wasn't back.

As rioting raged all over the country in the wake of King's death, more and more guys on the line grumbled and complained about their jobs, the conditions, and each other. Johnson never would have signed the Civil Rights Act four years earlier, except for all the people standing up and demanding it. Now the battle for equal rights had turned into a free-for-all. The Negroes were getting theirs.

Farmworkers' theirs. Women theirs. Goddammit, autoworkers wanted theirs, too. There weren't many pacifists in the factory.

The deadline for names to be put forward for the election arrived, and still, no Webb. All of them in the Green Caucus congregated in the conference room at the union hall.

Old Skypiece surprised Billy by nominating him for president.

Buzzed from the mescaline he swallowed last night, Billy couldn't grasp this was really happening. As he balanced his way to the podium, the faces of his girls flashed in his eyes. Webb flashed in front of him, too. Billy hesitated.

"I promise to do my best to get us our fair share," Billy breathed into the microphone.

More than surprised, Billy was stunned when the vote came in as nearly unanimous for him as president under the Green Caucus. Mal was on the slate as sergeant at arms and Red the chairman of the bargaining committee. Webb still hadn't been heard from.

In the parking lot after the meeting, Red started in on Billy. "You can't lead the men. You're always tripping."

Red said it like he was joking, but Billy knew he was serious. Red had every right to be pissed. Billy had surprised himself, accepting like that.

"I didn't know Skypiece was putting up my name," Billy said.

Even so, he couldn't ignore the truth of Red's words. On his way home to watch the California presidential primary results between Kennedy and McCarthy, Billy imagined Webb hurt and blamed himself. Maybe Red was right. If Billy had been straight, he could've helped Webb better.

MR. EVANS

MAJA SQUARED HER SHOULDERS in front of Mr. Evans' apartment door. Freaked out and beating herself up for putting this off so late, Maja knocked. The sound echoed down the quiet of the corridor, and the door inched open. Making a face of regret, Maja didn't know whether to close the door—not wanting Mr. Evans to think she'd opened it—or just leave. Without breathing, she listened for his step. Nothing. His black Corvette Stingray was parked alone in a red zone opposite his building, so he had to be there.

When he didn't answer on the second knock, and the door opened further, Maja looked both ways and then peeked inside.

A red batik scarf draped over the lampshade cast her advisor's living room in a pink and shadowy light. The television was on without him. Maja held her breath. Over the sound of Walter Cronkite reporting that the California primary results were coming in, Maja heard snoring. Trembling, she rubbed her hands down her skirt, checked the hallway again, and slipped inside.

"Robert Francis Kennedy is leading," stated Walter Cronkite.

Buoyed with confidence at the news, Maja shuffled through unopened mail and overdue notices on Mr. Evans' kitchen table, one from the phone company with a demand for payment and threatening to disconnect his service. No sign of her folder.

As Walter Cronkite turned the coverage over to Roger Mudd, Maja went through stacks of newspapers cluttering the floor. Each crinkle colliding with the creepy sound of Mr. Evans snoring in breaks between the television broadcasting.

At the door to his bedroom, Maja's heart pounded so hard it beat against her eardrums. She'd written her report on deviant behavior to determine if she was in any real peril from Mr. Evans' seemingly obsessive attachment to her. Her statistical analysis confirmed what she most feared: if allowed to continue, deviant behavior never stayed unchanged. Deviant behavior always turned more deviant.

Asleep on his stomach in the middle of rumpled sheets, Mr. Evans appeared innocent. Maja wanted to slap herself across the face. What was she thinking, being here?

Rushing to the front door, she resolved to

rewrite the report. She'd ask for an extension so she could relocate the research and recalculate the statistics. It was a task that smelled like an old fish in the sun, but that was better than being where she shouldn't be.

"Who are you talking to?" Mr. Evans asked from behind her.

Maja whirled around, mortified she'd been whispering to herself, something she hadn't done for years. The sound of people whooping and hollering blended in with "When the Saints Go Marching In" playing in the background. The glow of the television screen lit her advisor's naked body, except for white briefs. Suddenly frightened, Maja slung her bag over her shoulder and pulled open the door.

"You're probably here for your report," Mr. Evans said, yawning. "Let me get it for you."

"What's the mood there?" asked Walter.

"Everyone is enthusiastic. They're singing and dancing in congo chains around the ballroom."

Maja stepped back inside.

When Mr. Evans didn't move to get her report, Maja squinted and fumbled with the doorknob. Then he shook his head as if remembering what he was doing.

"Your report is just over here," he said, motioning for her to follow him.

Reluctant to leave the door, Maja tried for a smile, attempting to make it look real. "Thank you," she said, without moving.

A flash came from the television. With his wife Ethel, Bobby Kennedy took the podium. The white light awakened something in Maja, a reminder she couldn't remember.

"We want Bobby. We want Bobby," the crowd chanted.

"Though it seems only fair that for you to get what you want," Mr. Evans said with a smile," I should get what I want."

"Thank you very much," started Bobby. "Can you hear this? Is there a working mic? Can you hear this?"

"Yeah." yelled the crowd.

Confused, Maja hesitated.

Mr. Evans snatched her wrist. She fought to shake loose. With a vice-grip on her, he pulled her back in his apartment, standing so near he folded his body to look into her face. He locked the door.

"Why, you're shivering," he said, his nostrils flaring. "Let me warm you up." He slid his hands under her top.

"I also want to thank my sisters and my mother and all the Kennedys who helped on my campaign," Bobby said.

Panicking, Maja pushed him away and fell backward on her long skirt.

"What's with girls like you?" said Mr. Evans. "I've tried being nice to you. Helped you with your schoolwork. But you think you're better than me, don't you?"

Maja muddied what he was saying with Bobby Kennedy speaking on the television and a nasty buzzing in her ears.

Mr. Evans shoved her against the door. She grunted at the force and avoided his mouth.

"No," he said sharply and yanked her hair so hard she moaned. He pulled again, wrenching her head back at a sharp angle.

Maja heard herself scream, and then grasped that screaming was coming from the television.

"What happened? Do you know?" someone said. "Please stay back. We're asking for your cooperation."

Maja stared into Mr. Evans' glassy eyes as he forced her head against the door.

"Girls like you always think you're too good for me. Treat me like I'm some kind of a loser." He pushed his hand past the elastic waistband of her skirt and down her belly.

"Stay back. We need a doctor. Any other doctors in the room? If not, please go get one."

Maja mumbled, unable to open her mouth wedged between his fingers. Blood pounded in her ears. She squirmed to get away.

"Still think I'm a loser?" Mr. Evans said. "Think again, sweetheart."

When he was finished, Maja scrambled for the door handle. Her fingers refused to work. After a couple of frantic tries, she burst out of his apartment building. The moon was dark, and the night smeared with stars. Maja ran into the middle of the street as he stumbled out the front door, zipping up a pair of jeans.

Maja ran with her heart flaying in her chest. Sure he was right behind her, she was too afraid to look back. Speeding faster, she didn't know if the sound of pounding feet came from her or from him closing in on her.

Out of breath, Maja stopped running. Instead of at home to scrub herself clean over and over again, she found herself in front of Raul's two-story apartment building. Light-headed, she bent over so as not to faint.

Light streamed out of all the windows. Voices and the radio blared through the opened door. Maja walked in one direction, and then turned, confused how to find her way home.

"Maja, is that you?" called Raul.

He trotted down the stairs from his apartment, wearing a felt hat with a crooked feather tucked in the band. His eyes were blurry and red.

"Come inside," Raul urged, gently leading her to the stairs.

Maja backed away, fumbling to pull her top around her and smooth down her long, peasant skirt, now torn. In the time she'd known Raul, Maja had been careful to only show him her earnest and hopeful side. She hated herself for shoving shame and her humiliation between them.

He put out his hands.

"Okay. Okay," he soothed, whispering. "Every-thing's okay. You're safe now."

"I've got to go," she mumbled.

"I'll drive you."

Even then she didn't appreciate how bad she looked until she peered at Raul through her eye slits and saw how still and chalky-white he stared at her.

"Let's get you cleaned up first," he said.

Maja gazed up the long, steep stairway. Wearing an encouraging smile, Raul motioned her forward. With a deep shuddering breath, she mounted the stairs. At the top, she leaned against the smooth stone pillar separating Raul's apartment from his neighbor's. Her jaw hurt, and her stomach felt brittle and raw. Her lip was bleeding. She followed with her fingertips the blood caked down her chin.

"Who did this to you?" Raul said, stepping toward her.

Shivering and nauseated, she backed away.

"Senator Kennedy. Is he—?" she asked, unable to say the word.

Overcome with filth, Maja turned away from Raul.

"Let me help you," he said, leading her into his apartment. "Let's see … KQED reports that Kennedy was shot. Large amounts of blood. Several gunshots. Another station says he's conscious with good color. The radio report said that the extent of his injuries is unknown."

Raul spoke calmly, and his voice soothed her.

"You're shaking," he said. "Should we go to the hospital?"

Maja shook her head and immediately turned dizzy. He offered her a red bandanna like the one he often wore around his forehead.

Inside, every chair was taken around the massive table in the front room. Paper lanterns hung from the ceiling and shone on a sleeping baby in the middle of the table next to the radio. Posters with brown fists and "Chicano Power" hung alongside black Aztec birds on a red background. A dog looked up and thumped its tail. A pregnant girl rocked back and forth, her bare feet solid and apart, a modern-day version of La Virgin de Guadalupe glowing from a poster behind her. Upon seeing Maja, the girl started toward her. Raul raised a hand, stopping her. Most of the people Maja recognized from Kennedy's campaign office. She stayed out of the light and averted her face.

"Hi, Maja," said Petrana.

Petrana, the girl Maja first saw at the Fillmore, and who was promised to Raul by their fathers, came out of his bedroom. After she met Petrana, Maja told her she wouldn't see Raul anymore if it bothered her. By Petrana's answer, Maja knew that unlike Raul, Petrana wanted to marry, and Maja backed off. Since then, things had been friendly between them.

Also a college student, Petrana's long black hair was parted down the middle. Beads hung around her neck. Seeing Maja in the light, Petrana gasped.

Raul shook his head. That one tiny gesture of his to Petrana spoke of an intimacy between them that turned Maja's legs weak. Raul helped her into the kitchen.

He touched her arm. "How about some coffee?"

"I should go," Maja said, fumbling with her top, knowing she had to do something and unable to think what.

"You just got here," Raul said, sitting her in front of someone's empty coffee cup, a thick oversized envelope, and a poster of Robert Kennedy.

As Raul tore a napkin in two and formed a filter in the coffee percolator basket, Maja squirmed in the chair, sore and uncomfortable and unable to ease the burning between her legs.

Raul handed her a wet hand towel.

Confused, Maja stared at cold water dripping off her hands and looked back at him. He lifted her hands, and she held the cool cloth to her fattened lip while he dumped three scoops of coffee beans into a grinder. The noise jarred her.

Caked blood gave way to the damp cloth. Maja remembered the apartment, the damp stench of unwashed laundry, her advisor slamming her against the door.

She must have cried out because Raul was asking questions again.

"Who did this to you?"

Maja knew he meant well, but talking about what had happened was unthinkable. She turned her head away. The perky bubbles of the coffee brewing died down.

As Raul handed her a cup, Maja felt him studying her as if searching for something to say.

"I dropped a class last semester," he said.

"So you could help with the oranges." Maja studied her calluses from helping him with the harvest.

"I'm ordered to the Oakland Inductiohn Center next week for a physical."

A quickening of understanding pulled Maja to the dusk of Raul's words. She looked up.

Raul took off his hat to reveal a sheer crew cut, just like Daddy's after the accident. Maja dropped her head and covered her face with both hands.

Somebody screamed. Maja leapt to her feet.

"He's dead," someone cried from the front room. "Robert Kenney is dead."

BRENDA

BILLY SHOT INTO HIS house, greeted by Sadie slamming her paws against his chest and nearly knocking him over. Boxes and suitcases were lined up at the front door; the sight of them kicked him in the gut. Winded, he pushed Sadie away and yelled for Brenda. Alternating between nosing him from behind and running ahead, Sadie led him to the bathroom.

Leaning against the doorjamb, Billy caught his breath. Trying to act natural, he scratched Sadie behind the ears, and her hind leg twitched.

As soon as he was able, Billy tried for a casual approach.

"What's happening?" he asked.

Brenda snatched the shampoo bottle from the shower and slapped it in a brand new toiletry bag on the sink.

"Shows how much you know about your own

family, now doesn't it?" she said.

A couple of deep breaths did nothing to slow down his heart. The air was so thick Billy wiped sweat from his face, ready to split inside out. He tried not to wheeze.

"I've sacrificed too much to run for President," he said, rolling the sleeves of his shirt up around his elbows. "I know that now. Me being president isn't going to change yours or your sisters' low opinion of the factory, the men, or of me."

Her sisters groaned from the kids' room where they were packing. He grimaced and banged the wall to back them off.

Brenda opened the medicine cabinet and closed it without removing anything. Taking hope, Billy stepped forward.

"I'm tired of doing this by myself, Billy," she said.

"So you pick today to leave?" Billy said. "Just give me a little time. I'm working my tail off for us."

"You've been drinking, haven't you?"

"The board election results are coming in any minute," he said, following her into their bedroom. "Sometimes a man gets himself an opportunity to make a difference. That's not something you can just turn away from."

"You have such a romantic view of yourself. Husband and father aren't good enough for Billy Wayman Wolfe. Oh, no. He's got to be the leader of men."

She swaggered across the bedroom with her hands on her hips. "Listen to me. I know everything."

"You're the one with the romantic views," Billy shot back. "Wanting to be something we're not. What's wrong with being an honest working-class family?"

As soon as the words were out of his mouth, he regretted them.

"We're only working-class because you want to be. Bob gave my sister a middle-class lifestyle. With a new station wagon and a few nice things, we're there, too."

Lowering her voice, Brenda added, "You're a lot smarter than Gene is, anyway."

Billy was silent. Brenda tossed the kids' plastic Tupperware toys in an empty suitcase.

"Well you are smart, Billy," she said, nodding. "Why do you think I married you? But you're stuck, and it's not the world holding you back or the factory or even me. It's you. You're not afraid of being poor again. The thought of being rich scares you half to death, and so you drink yourself silly. You take drugs. Even when you're here, you're either tripping or hung over. How much fun do you think it is for the rest of us?"

"There are more important things going on out in the big wide world than Tupperware parties. Wives aren't supposed to work anyway," Billy said. "And I'm good for a hell of a lot more than making a living so you can show off."

"Tupperware is the exclusive home-party sales company. Sarah says I'm a natural. She promises I'll make good money at it."

The house turned quiet, except for Billy's breathing. It was like they'd been talking from two separate planets that suddenly collided.

"Running for president of local is something I believe in, Bren, something I think you and the girls can be proud of me for."

"Why did you make all those promises to me before we were married anyway?" Brenda stood in front of the closet, yanking clothes from hangers.

"Why are you breaking up our family, Brenda? You can't just leave."

She brushed past him to the suitcase. He got there first and slammed the lid. She stared at his hand like she had all the time in the world, and there wasn't anything else in the room to see.

"The fine car," she said. "A grand house. Even a kidney-shaped aquamarine swimming pool, no less. You in a hat. Me wearing gloves. Our kids skipping to the candy store."

Billy frowned. "What are you talking about?"

An image from his childhood materialized outside a candy store in Oakland. He wasn't surprised to remember that the yellow-haired girl with the wide eyes stood at center stage in the memory—her father wearing a felt hat and driving a new Ford Fairlane, her mother wearing white gloves.

"Why'd you promise all those things when you

never even wanted to be a husband? Or a father either. Did you? I wouldn't mind you being gone from us all the time if I thought we were getting somewhere. But this? Your eyes are pointed in two directions at once. Can you see me, Billy? Can you hear me?"

Billy couldn't remember when he last thought about that old dream. All this time he'd been seeing a bright new future for him, for them, for the country, the world, and Brenda was stuck in a future from an earlier life and a different generation.

Lowering his voice so her sisters would have to work to hear, Billy tried not to hiss.

"The picture I had for us back then, that's not me. Not anymore. It was all a pipe dream anyway. What do I know about being a husband or father either? But I've been trying, Brenda. I have. That stuff? The car. The pool. They're just surface shit. Then, when we're all tied up trying to pay for them, the corporations steal everything that's not nailed down."

"Don't you dare bring your political garbage and your big-bad-they're-out-to-get-us nonsense into this," snapped Brenda.

"Daddy, Daddy," cried Melissa.

Billy whirled around and opened his arms to his little girl. Melissa jumped up, knocking the wind from him.

"Can we go to the beach again?" She picked at his collar and smoothed a hand against his cheek.

"Anytime you want, sweet pea."

"Oh, goodie," Melissa cried, jumping out of his arms and zooming out of the room. Sadie barked and chased her.

Tears pooled in Billy's eyes.

Brenda stuffed the bathroom bag in the suitcase. The suitcase snapped shut.

"Why are you taking away our kids," he said.

"It was your dream, Billy. You painted the words so pretty, I just followed right along beside you."

"You've never been beside me. You've always been ahead or behind. You've never been with me," he spit.

"Hi, Daddy."

Billy stopped talking and looked down. Squatting in front of Lisa, he gave her a big hug.

"Hi, baby doll."

"Where are we going, Mama?" Lisa asked.

"We're not going anywhere, baby doll," Billy said.

"To Grammy's house," Brenda said. "Pack three stuffed animals. Hurry now."

Lisa leaned her head sideways and hummed as if deciding if Billy looked different from that angle.

"You look like Jesus in the chapel," Lisa said.

"That's because his hair is so long," said Brenda. "Now, scat."

Lisa righted herself, smiled, and gave him a kiss on the cheek. On her way out the door, she was singing "An Itsy Bitsy Spider."

Without his family, he had nothing. An intolerable heat and crushing pressure surged through him.

"You believe I'm going to lose the election today, don't you?" he said.

"I'm quite sure you'll win. And with you as president, there's sure to be a strike. Standing still is hard enough. I'm not about to backslide again."

"If there is a strike, I'll be home a lot more. Isn't that what you want?"

"I think 6,000 grown men having a great big temper tantrum because they can't get what they want is disgraceful."

"Isn't that what you're doing, Brenda? Walking out on me so you can get what you want?"

"I don't intend to come back."

A sweet melody came from Lisa's room. All she did lately was sing. The more that went on between Brenda and him, the more his little girl sang. He lit a cigarette, knowing it was going to make him suffer while hoping that holding onto it would prevent him from throwing something. *What had I done? I'd risked everything, and for what?*

Billy wiped sweat off the side of his face. A chill passed down his neck. Dizzy, he held onto the doorframe.

"You're drunk." Brenda picked up her suitcase and stomped out of the room.

Her words pounded against him. He marched after her and plowed straight into the doorjamb.

Damn. She knew just how to club him over the head with his worthlessness and bludgeon him with his faults.

The front door slammed behind Brenda's sisters. *The Velveteen Rabbit* sat alone on the coffee table. He picked up the girls' favorite nighttime story. Would they abandon him like the boy tossed the rabbit in the story?

The house was quiet. Brenda put down her suitcase. Sadie curled up next to it as if to be sure she wasn't left behind.

Brenda straightened her purse.

"You're the one always going on about how workers need people like you to step up," she said. "But I also remember years of complaining about how the union was invented by management to control the masses. Isn't that why you're drunk all the time? Because now you're the one screwing the guys."

Billy tried to explain. "I'm not a politician. I do what I can for the guys, not for my own personal gain. I'm hoping to change the way the little guy is treated."

"You aren't the little guy anymore," Brenda said pointedly.

"This is something I got to do. Be patient. Please. Give me this one."

"You know, if I thought you could be a politician, I'd probably stick around to see what happens. But you're more pain than pleasure. More hurt than help."

"This could take me to International," he said. "You and the girls will have everything you want."

"You're a militant, Billy, a union activist. You're the first one they'll get rid of. When I met you, I never considered a life like this for myself. I couldn't believe my luck when you asked me to marry you." Brenda touched Billy's cheek. Her eyes were sad. "You and your stories and all your dreams, I didn't think I deserved any of it. Your vision of the future gave me a new vision for myself. It's all I could see."

Billy grabbed her hand. It wasn't her fault what was happening. Not Ma's or the guys, either. He'd done it to himself. He was the furthest away from his future he'd ever been.

Brenda picked up her suitcase and opened the front door.

Somber, Red stood with a fist raised to knock.

Sadie shot out to the car.

Brenda called Sadie back. "I'm leaving Sadie with you," she said, catching her by the collar. "I know how much you hate being alone."

She checked the front room and walked out the door.

"I can see this isn't a real good time," said Red.

Red's car sat at the curb with the engine running. Mal and Webb waited inside. Webb had come back from Death Valley a month ago, but something wasn't right with him anymore. In front of Red's car, Brenda's sister's car motor was running. From the

217

radio, Joni Mitchell blasted something about clouds getting in her way.

"Brenda, hold on," called Billy.

"Hell, Billy, they're ready with the results," interrupted Red.

Weakness pulled at Billy, and his knees wobbled. Brenda threw the suitcase in the rear of her sister's station wagon, all loaded up with bags and boxes. Lisa stuck her head out the window. She wasn't looking at him. She was more concerned with watching Mal. Summer and Melissa were laughing and playing in the backseat. Billy pushed past Red to stop Brenda before they pulled away.

1969

The Grandson and Wisaw are on a lonely and perilous journey to expand the limited view of themselves they've been raised to believe during a time when the whole world is off-kilter like a three-legged wolf or a broken wheel, a time wide open for change.

Too tame, Wisaw stagnates and grows fearful. I've tried to draw her out. Too often, new ideas sit untouched right beneath the surface of her consciousness.

The Grandson's addictions bog down the flow of change in his life. Without a balance between his wild spirit and the discovery of his true value, he will never succeed.

To provide them the time they need to develop and grow fully into their own power separately and master the tasks before them, I continue doing all I can to keep their identities secret from each other.

MR. REINGOR

THE MARLBORO MAN WINKED from a billboard that advertised cigarettes at Maja's Bay Bridge exit. His face and posture pulled Maja to the much younger man she'd kissed at the Fillmore. Back then, she was broken and unworthy. Her throat turned thick. Now, because of Mr. Evans, she was damaged beyond repair. At least she hadn't gotten pregnant.

She pressed down hard on the accelerator and the GTO zoomed onto 9th Avenue. Flashing lights with a piercing siren appeared in the rearview mirror. Maja pulled to the curb, her heart thrashing against her chest. She fumbled for what was left of the joint in the ashtray, ate it, and smoothed down her hair. She wondered how loaded she was.

A blur of red, black, and white screamed past her. She let out a stream of breath. Pulling back into traffic, her arms felt heavy. She was tired, tired of feeling so helpless and deficient, dirty and ashamed, worthless and alone. The sooner this photo shoot was over, the sooner she could tug the covers over her head and go back to sleep.

Up ahead on Market Street, Halloween cats hung in the windows of the old Crocker building. A catalog-shoot for next spring's bathing suit line on a drizzly October day made it difficult for her to stay related to the natural world. Her Native American history homework from last year, to connect with the rhythms of nature no matter what she was doing, was yet another example of how the new ideas she'd learned in school conflicted with the demands made of her in modeling. The two—school and modeling—had never been a good mix, and further confirmed that dropping out of college had been the right decision.

Besides, everything she'd learned in school came from a book written by a man and from a man's point of view. Male teachers gave every lecture she sat through. Men even dominated the entire fashion industry—models were expected to be blind, deaf, dumb, and beautiful.

The GTO purred like a new car down city streets slick with fog. Except for the gash in the bumper from sideswiping a mailbox after she learned of Daddy's accident nearly three years ago, no one would suspect the car was four years old. The GTO booked, maneuvering so smoothly she could drive, light a joint, and sing along to Aretha Franklin's

Respect all at the same time. Before long, doubts and insecurities melted from her mind.

Eric Burdon came on the radio, singing about warm San Franciscan nights. Maja's skin pulsated. The air felt electric. She slowed down to watch a mime in Union Square walk like a clown, every movement exaggerated. White-faced and blue-lipped, he braked with one knee bent to his chin and winked at her. Maja smiled for the first time in forever.

From this vantage point, the city was not a fantasy but a yearning. Wannabe hippies arrived more every day, looking for a world apart from the din of hypocrisy and the lies of the establishment. Here, they hoped to find a forgiving world. Maja recognized the futility. She on her way to help create more lies through photographs. Still, she loved the city no less for its imperfections.

Pulling into the studio lot, she parked in a far corner and appraised herself in the rearview mirror. Her eyes were puffy and her hair greasy—make-up and a stylist could fix all that. Maja liked how the outside reflected her internal feelings. She readjusted the wolf necklace.

Inside, a woman at the reception desk spoke on a telephone. The tinkle of bells on Maja's moccasin boots reminded her to stay focused and alert.

"Excuse me," she said.

The receptionist glanced up, the telephone still at her ear. Despite all Maja's measures to keep centered, she wasn't prepared for the stare she got.

Feeling judged and misunderstood, she ducked her head and readjusted her headband.

Jimmy trotted down a hallway of doors, wearing his trademark red.

"Maja, darling," he said.

A sagging roll of fat under Jimmy's chin hadn't been there when she first met him. He pulled in his elbows like chicken wings.

"You look a fright, my dear," he said. "Did you stick your head in a fan? Take off that horrid little thing." He flicked the wolf carving at her neck. "Hurry. Hurry. Off. Off. Off. Dag's on his way," he demanded.

Maja raised her chin in defiance. Jimmy caught her arm and turned her to a man with a ponytail striding toward them.

"This shoot is worth more than any shoot in Paris," he hissed.

Shorter than Maja by a foot, like the receptionist, Dag was still able to look down his nose at her.

"Dag, this is Maja." Jimmy crammed a cigarette into the lacquered red holder. "I have to apologize for her. She's at her absolute worst. Please tell me you think there's hope."

He lit his cigarette, his hands trembling.

"No, Jimmy," Maja said. "Don't apologize for me."

The word reverberated in Maja's mind. She hadn't commanded no to Mr. Evans, not that saying no would have stopped him. But she didn't speak up for herself. She didn't cry out for help. When did she first learn that by saying *no* to someone, anyone made her wrong and rude and a bad person? She didn't have to look any farther than the rules she and all the other little girls of her generation had been taught.

Lately, she was learning that the more verbal she became, the more visible she turned. She squared her shoulders and stood up straight.

Dag's eyes were serious, and she felt her insecurities returning as he moved around her.

Jimmy scuttled alongside Dag with his cigarette smoke bobbing behind them. An agent who still treated her like a child, when what she most needed was respect. Perhaps it was time she demanded it.

The two men reappeared in front of her.

"Great cheekbones," Jimmy said.

Jimmy had known Maja for as long as she could remember, and the one good thing he could say about her was that she had great cheekbones?

Feeling as if she were being watched, Maja checked over her shoulder. Seeing no one, she shook off prickles of fear. Then, she dropped her arms like a mannequin. She trained her eyes on a spot partway between the clear vision of solid reality and the world of make-believe. Her body relaxed. She moved from paranoid fashion dummy to inner visionary, or so her professor used to promise.

Dag tsked, his attention still on Maja's face. Then, he snapped his fingers and started down the hallway.

"Come," he commanded.

"Ever so good of you, my dear boy," said Jimmy with obvious relief in his voice. "Run along, Maja. Make these shots surpass even the last ones. Dag is the best there is. This is important."

Jimmy raised an eyebrow and squeezed her arm.

Rolling her eyes, Maja followed Dag. Somewhere in there was a compliment.

The camera stopped blinking. Dag would take his time checking proofs. Waiting to hear if he demanded retakes, Maja collapsed on a wicker table, grateful for the break.

Stiff white patent leather boots stuck to her sweaty calves. She hated these plastic possessions of a plastic society—the tubes of make-up, synthetic hairpieces, fake eyelashes, artificial jewelry, plastic bottles of shampoo, plastic toys, cups, glasses, plates, and utensils. Everything was turning plastic and all of it derived from oil, which meant more boys sent off to fight and die all in the name of boosting oil exports to fuel the war.

A clock on the wall read a minute past the last time she'd checked. Maja fashioned her outfit's matching hat into a pillow, splayed across the wicker table, and closed her eyes.

Above her spoke someone with a heavy Southern accent. "Jimmy said it's your favorite."

Opening her eyes to sticky fizz, the smell of artificial lemon and lime cleared Maja's nose. Self-conscious and blushing, she swung her legs off the table and sat up as the man finished pouring a bottle of Fresca into a jumble of ice. On the alert, Maja looked for the stylist and dresser and make-up man. Finding herself alone with the stranger, she rose to her feet and reluctantly accepted the glass he offered. Then, she distanced herself by a couple of feet and sized him up.

Tall and dark with light blue eyes, he smelled of Old Spice, Daddy's aftershave. As old as most of the university professors she'd had, this man's hair was styled, not short-cropped to be completely straight and not hippie-long either. A tanned face and wide shoulders made him appear athletic. He wore a turtleneck sweater and a Nehru jacket with its customary collar and no lapels.

The cleft in the stranger's chin deepened as he sat where she had been sitting. Lines fanned out from his eyes as he regarded her with what felt like an uncomfortable amount of interest.

"Alrighty then," the stranger said, clapping his hands together. "The instant Jimmy showed me your composite, I was hooked. No one else would do."

The stranger acted as if Maja should know him. She didn't and his unexpected presence irritated her. Angry that he didn't introduce or explain himself, she put the glass of Fresca beside him without drinking it.

"When you see Dag, please tell him I'm getting my things," she said curt and wary.

In the dressing room, she changed into her street clothes and poncho. Not bothering to wash off the make-up, she grabbed her things.

When Maja returned, the stranger was still perched on the wicker table with his legs spread and hands dangling between them.

"No Dag?" she asked.

The stranger shook his head. Maja hesitated, uncertain whether she should wait or just leave. She wiped an arm across her forehead. Flesh-colored make-up streaked the back of her hand.

"Why so tired?" the stranger asked.

Maja sensed the man was serious, as she dug for her keys at the bottom of her purse and started for the door. If he wanted something, he'd have to explain himself. Bells pinged from the buckskin fringe on her boots with every step.

"Where do you go to school?" the stranger asked.

Maja swung around. "I don't go to school."

The stranger put up both hands as if fending off a blow.

Satisfied with herself, Maja resumed walking. The stranger fell in step beside her. Determined to distance herself from him, she walked faster as they crossed the white-paper stage.

In the hallway, every other ceiling light was turned off. Her breathing turned shallow.

The stranger spoke slowly, his southern drawl almost homey. "Something has your attention.

You're much too serious for that to be a fellow. Am I right?"

"I was going to Berkeley," Maja said.

As soon as the words were out of her mouth, she crossed her arms and walked even faster, disgusted with herself for falling into his trap.

"Were going?"

"I'll return. Next year. No more than two."

Hearing her plan out-loud made the possibility sound reasonable and rational and attainable.

The stranger caught up with her.

"Then you're free to accept an exclusive contract," he said. "I'll pay you twice what you earn now."

Catching her breath, Maja stumbled. Flustered, she opened her mouth and then was at a loss for what to say.

"You emotionally connect to the camera like no other girl I've ever seen. I want you to be the next Reingor Girl."

Maja turned and stared at him. "Car dealerships and department stores."

"My grandfather started the dealerships. I opened the clothing stores."

"Would I have to walk in fashion shows?"

"We can work out details later. What do you say?"

Walking toward the back door, Maja considered his offer. One job. Money enough for Daddy. Was he serious? And, if he were?

"What does Jimmy say?" she asked.

"I haven't discussed this with Jimmy."

Again, Maja stopped walking, then started forward again.

"Thanks a lot for the Fresca, Mr. Reingor. Please tell Dag I waited as long as I could. I'm happy to come back for retakes if he needs me."

She pushed against the outside door. The door was locked. Her muscles tightened.

"I almost regret having to say this, but the proofs are flawless. If they weren't, I'd be sure to see you again."

Loki crouched in his tone, causing Maja to wonder yet again if she gave off some sort of scent only nasty men could smell. Since Mr. Evan's assault, she'd kept to herself.

Mr. Reingor took a set of keys from his pocket and unlocked the door.

Exasperated, Maja stepped outside. The sky drizzled on a line of little witches and princesses, cats and ballerinas, pirates and hobos skipping single file across the street toward a group of Black Panthers marching on the sidewalk wearing black ties, slacks, leather jackets, and berets.

"If you'd told me proofs were in earlier, I'd already be home," Maja said and walked away.

A week later, a scrub jay squawked from the maple tree outside Maja's bedroom window. She rolled her head across the pillow until the sun's feeble light hit her face through a break in the branches. An intoxicating scent tugged open her eyes. Long-stemmed red roses, posing on her nightstand, turned her throat rusty. She groaned and pulled the sheets over her head.

Yet another twisted method of intimidation, this time with roses no less. Mr. Evans must have discovered Dana's boyfriend Kevin had lied. Kevin had informed Maja's advisor that she'd moved out with no forwarding address and for him to leave them alone at the house. It must not have worked. No more excuses. It was time she moved home. All her things were packed. She'd resisted, terrified he'd follow her to Great Oaks. As much as she dreaded the thought, backing off Mr. Evans was her responsibility.

She tossed the roses out the window, pulled her stash from the drawer of her bedside table, and lowered the needle on the LP. A breeze sent crimson gold sunlight through the crystal vase, which broke the light into a rainbow of colors pirouetting across her bedroom walls. She rolled a joint while belting out "Blowin' in the Wind" with her favorite folk singer Joan Baez.

Maja held the smoke in her lungs as long as she could, feeling guilty about how much pot she was smoking. Getting high softened a harsh world, wiped out her negative feelings, and silenced the unrelenting criticism she flung at herself. Lately though—rather than bring peace and tranquility—the more she smoked, the more paranoid her thoughts grew.

Seeing the time, she pulled on the first clothes she found slung across the chair and grabbed her bag. She'd have to hurry if she wanted to call the UAW local office and still be on time for today's shoot. Rather than wait any longer to find enough time to drive to Fremont to ask about her mystery man, Maja decided calling was best. Humming with excitement for what she could learn about him, she vaulted down the stairs two at a time.

In the kitchen, the blender whirled. Kevin handed Dana a peeled banana for their morning smoothie. Her mouth dry with anticipation, Maja rooted in her bag for the union's telephone number she'd jotted down from the operator.

Dana shouted over the noise of the blender. "Your roses. Did you see her roses, Kevin? A vase of the longest stemmed roses."

"Yeah," Kevin said. "I answered the door. Remember?"

"How much do you think long-stemmed roses cost?" Dana asked.

"What? Are you writing a book?" Kevin's voice sounded sore.

Hurt that Dana would make light of anything that had to do with her academic advisor, nevertheless, Maja was grateful for both of them standing beside her at her darkest and most helpless time. Her roommates and their boyfriends blocked the door against Mr. Evans and stuck to their story that Maja was modeling in New York. Somehow, he'd gotten wise to their scheme.

She picked up the telephone. It had no dial tone.

"Who is Gerald Reingor?" asked Dana.

"Gerald Reingor?" Maja repeated, confused.

"I read the card."

A man's voice with a familiar southern drawl boomed through the receiver.

"Yes, Gerald Reingor here."

Maja took a step backward, nearly dropping the telephone. Behind her, Dana made a kissy face. Maja blushed and swatted at her friend.

"Is this Maja?"

"Is there a problem?" Maja asked.

"Only if you find my need to see you again a problem."

Maja sighed and pressed her fingers against her temple to stop the throbbing. The difference between the guys she'd known and Mr. Reingor was that he was willing to pay a lot of money to get in bed with her. Even if his job offer were real, her acceptance wouldn't make her any more of a tramp than she already was.

"I'm calling to inquire whether you are free for dinner tonight."

"I'm sorry—"

"Not tonight? Alrighty then, tomorrow night. Strictly business, you understand. By then you'll have had a chance to consider my proposition. You at least owe me that. Actually, you don't owe me anything. It would be decent of you to hear me out. I promise to get you home early. I'll send a car for you at six thirty How does that sound?"

"I won't—"

"Of course, I'll pick you up myself. Six thirty sharp tomorrow night. Right. I'll see you then."

The telephone clicked dead with Maja's hand tangled in the cord. Three months ago, a man had walked on the moon, and still she couldn't say no.

She left a message for Jimmy to call Mr. Reingor with her refusal. Then she dialed the UAW office in Fremont. The telephone rang without anyone picking up at the other end.

THE GRANDMOTHER

BILLY WAITED IN A gravel parking lot beside the tiny Diablo post office hung with Christmas lights. Drumming his fingertips on the steering wheel, he wondered what he expected to accomplish. Odds for getting directions to the Hawthorne residence were fixed against him. Ruffling Sadie's fur, he was grateful for her company.

When the postal clerk arrived for work, Billy left Sadie in the car and greeted her as she unlocked the door to the post office. Inside, a miniature Christmas tree sat on the counter circled with holly and red berries. The clerk was slow to remove the cardboard block in front of her enclosure. That bought Billy time. He ran over several approaches in his mind and rejected them all.

Finally, she was ready for him. Her glare momentarily threw him. He tried for a sincere smile.

The clerk folded her arms and frowned.

"I need your help," Billy started.

The clerk didn't answer. Behind her, rows of cubbyholes were filled with letters standing at a slant. Feeling a bit tilted himself, he grasped that his long hair was either disgusting or frightening the clerk. Either way, he didn't belong here.

"Let me get to the point," he said quickly. "I'm looking for the residence of a Mister Robert Hawthorne."

Her face closed up.

Billy spread open the paper where the factory's female clerical worker who helped him pin down the GTO buyer wrote the postal address.

"He bought an orange GTO several years back and—"

"I can't help you," the clerk said.

She replaced the cardboard and disappeared into the back room.

Billy waited until everyone left before he came out of hiding at the old Manteca graveyard, right up next to the railroad tracks. The bouquet he placed on the turned mound of dirt covering Grandma's coffin looked big compared to the others.

"You'd be proud of me, Grandma," he said. "I haven't had a drink in three months, two weeks and four days. I'm real sorry I never got you that big house like I promised."

Billy hunched his shoulders as he rifled through

recent memory for any accomplishment he could share about himself. All he could come up with were ten million ways he'd screwed up his life. He hadn't seen his girls since Brenda moved them out of state. Won't get to see them until she sent an address. He never figured Brenda to leave her mother and sisters. Showed how little he knew the woman, while the emptiness inside him kept growing bigger. At work, more and more of the guys were bitching about the shitty conditions and their shitty pay, and Billy was less and less able to accomplish much on anyone's behalf. He couldn't seem to do anything right.

"I lost the carving, but you probably already know that, don't you? I'm real hopeful I'll get it back soon. I haven't been able to get exact directions, but driving around the neighborhood, I'd say the wolf is living high on the hog and running with jet-setters."

"Where's your coat, Billy?" The hand Ma put on his shoulder was cold enough to send a chill through his shirt.

Startled, he lowered his shoulder. Her hand slipped away, and Billy regretted losing her touch. He'd found himself craving physical affection since Brenda left. He flicked his cigarette. A cold wind snatched the smoke. Red embers from the cigarette dulled to ashy gray.

"The service was real nice," Ma said. "Everyone was asking about you."

"I don't much like funerals."

The wind whipped Ma's cotton dress around her

calves and lifted yellow leaves littering the gravesite. Grandma would like that there was a tree nearby with leaves blowing. His throat tightened.

"I knew you were coming," Ma continued. "I told the boys they could say "hey" when you bring me back to your Aunt Ida's."

The white fur collar of Ma's black sweater was already smudged with suede-colored makeup. A gold cross hung at her neck, and she wore a plastic pin of Santa with Rudolph the Red-Nosed Reindeer.

Billy was twenty-five, a quarter century, which made Ma forty-two. That meant Grandma was fifty-eight when she died.

A train roared past the cemetery. Cattle cars brought with them the stench of manure and death. The train whistle faded in the distance.

Billy shook out a cigarette from the pack and pinched his lips around it.

"Hear about the Indians on Alcatraz?" Ma asked. "Now that takes some imagination. Seventy-five Indians taking over government land."

"Feds will have them rounded up and hauled out before you know it," Billy said, offering Ma a cigarette. He took a deep breath. "Brenda left me. Took the girls with her."

Ma held the cigarette to her lips for a light.

Billy lit his first. What with the wind, it took a couple of tries and getting real close before he could get Ma's going.

Ma took a drag off her cigarette and fiddled with

the bangs coiled like springs across her forehead.

"You don't seem particularly surprised she's gone," Ma said.

For his entire life, Billy had blamed Ma for everything that went wrong. Anymore he couldn't hide behind blaming others for anything. Brenda leaving wasn't Ma's fault, wasn't anyone's fault but his.

"You're right, Ma," he agreed.

"D'she give you fair warning?"

"Oh, so now it's all my fault?"

"You're awful high-spirited, Billy Wayman. You get that from me."

Ma offered Billy a flask from her purse. His mouth watered, imagining the feel of the cold metal against his lips. He tasted the high and shook his head no. He swore the swig she took burned down his throat, too. She wrapped an arm across her belly and rested her elbow with the cigarette real close to her face, making the distance to reach for a puff barely an inch.

"You sure do resemble your grandma with your hair long like that."

"You mean like an Indian?"

"Yeah. Like an Indian."

Billy looked at her more closely. "Are you crying?"

"Feeling a mite lonely without her."

Billy flicked his cigarette to the ground and crammed both hands in his pockets.

"Brenda warned me she'd walk out if I ran for president."

"Is that why you ran? So she'd leave you?"

"I don't know why I even try talking to you."

"That's a horrible thing to say to your own mother."

"You're right. I didn't come here to fight. Fighting never got me anywhere."

"Pray for forgiveness, son. God will take you and leave everyone else to deal with the devil. These are the Last Days. You know that, don't you, son?"

Billy shook his head; his mind fixated on the flask in her pocketbook.

"Well, it's true. You're saved if you know it in your heart. We had us some pretty good times together, you and me. D'you ever think of them days? Or you so goddamned poisoned against me, bad is all you got now?"

"I wasn't the one doing the poisoning, Ma. You took care of that all by yourself."

Billy said that, but in truth he wouldn't have traded growing up with Grandma for anything and, in the end, living with Ma hadn't turned out so bad.

Before Billy could apologize, Ma chimed in. "Until you forgive me, boy, you ain't never going to forgive yourself."

Billy didn't say anything to that. The wind sent leaves flying across the tight-fisted dirt.

"You think it's your God-given right to deserve something from me?" Ma continued. "Well, it ain't. I birthed you all right. Who's to say I owe you anything more than that?"

"A little love might've been nice."

"You can't say I ain't loved you your whole life now, Billy. Besides, the Bible don't say nothing about any one of us having something coming, except what we're able to scrabble together for ourselves. Now that I think of it, I do believe the fifth commandment says something about loving your mother."

"Why'd you have all of us?" he asked. "You certainly didn't want to raise us."

"People have babies for lots of reasons 'sides being a parent. Never having nothing wears a body down. I wanted excitement and fun. You know about excitement and fun, don't you, son? Having a little fun and making babies go together. Least in my day they did."

Another train whizzed by. Grandma was never going to get any rest.

"It's your life," Ma continued. "Just don't let all that pain and bitterness make you into someone you ain't."

"What the hell does that mean?"

"Always the smart-aleck. You got that from me—and your loud mouth and stubbornness and bull-headedness, too. Quick to temper."

Billy stopped listening. Damn. What he wouldn't give for Ma's flask.

"You and me, son? We did all right. I'm sorry I'm a disappointment to you. And I'm real sorry

241

about Brenda and the girls. I know they miss their daddy, and for that I'm truly sorry. Let me just ask you something, Billy. Seeing as we was talking about what a mother owes her son, I wonder what exactly does a father owe his girls?"

Ma moved out of the wind, and Billy flung his voice after her, trying to get the words out fast enough.

"We've given more money to the farmworkers than any other organization. We were the first to speak out against the war. The teamsters got in bed with Nixon after he let Hoffa off. Not us. I'm standing firm, making the world a better place for my kids. I want them to be proud of me. Someday, I hope they learn we changed things at the factory for the workers like they haven't been changed before. It's going to take everything I got. Someday my girls are going to know the good that came of my work."

DADDY

MAJA WALKED THROUGH THE mission cemetery of
the historic Nuestra Senora de la Soledad, or, as Raul
translated in English, Our Most Sorrowful Lady of
Solitude. She slipped into the back pew of the chapel
and gave herself up to the peace and quiet of the
church. She drew comfort that at least she didn't look
as miserable as the nearly life-sized statue of the most
sorrowful lady propped in the altar alcove. Or, so she
hoped.

The chapel smelled musty, reminding her of old
people and incense and spent wax. Though the room
was small, Raul and Petrana's vows didn't reach Maja
in the back. Raul spoke softly, and the veil covering
Petrana's face muffled her voice.

After Raul was drafted last year, he went absent
and hid in Mexico until his grandmother convinced
him to return. Since then, he'd been working toward

conscientious objector status based on his religious opposition to killing. The husband of Joan Baez recently went to jail for resisting the draft. Hoping to avoid the war *and* jail, Raul planned to propose to the draft board that he serve a two-year volunteer job at a halfway house in Berkeley for men recently released from Napa State Mental Hospital.

Noticing only family in attendance at Raul and Petrana's nuptials, and worried her presence might make Raul feel awkward or Petrana feel uncomfortable, Maja left before the service ended.

Stopping at a gas station to have the GTO filled up, on a whim, Maja checked the map. The El Camino Real would take her straight from Soledad to Fremont and the UAW union hall.

An hour and a half later, she pulled into the weedy parking lot of the hall, turned off the engine of the GTO, and then remained in the car. Finally, she opened the door, and then swung her leg back in the car and slammed the door. She smoothed her skirt. Twenty minutes later she got out.

"Hi," said the woman at the front desk. "May I help you?"

Well aware how out of place she was, Maja outlined seeing the UAW banner at the Fillmore for the farmworkers benefit.

"Yes, I remember," the woman said, nodding. "Last year the guys took the striking farmworkers a big check."

Pushing back a stray curl that escaped her upswept wedding-appropriate, friend-of-the-groom hairstyle, Maja started with the easy things first. She described the man who'd reminded her of Olle-the-Loyal.

With a curious stare, the woman blushed. "Malakaton," she said, fiddling with the silver clasp holding together the sweater thrown over her shoulders.

Maja raised her eyebrows and smiled. "That's his name?" she asked.

The woman nodded shyly.

Their connection fed Maja's confidence, and next she described Tjovik-the-Wise.

"Webb," said the woman, pressing her lips together and shaking her head.

Maja felt tears swelling in her eyes. She was so near. Swallowing hard to clear the lump in her throat, she began, hopeful.

"There … there … was a third man," she stuttered, at a loss how to describe his glow, his spark, his touch.

The woman looked toward the solid double doors leading into the union hall.

"Is he h—" Maja asked in a rush.

"Who wants to know?"

"He's someone special to me," Maja murmured, hoping to appeal to the woman's softer side and unable to come up with anything else.

"I'm sorry," the woman said. "That's confidential information."

Maja opened her mouth. Then she thanked the woman and left the building. She sat in her car and hoped that if he were there and the receptionist told him someone was asking about him that he might be curious and walk outside. By the woman's reaction, at least she knew her mystery man was real. While she waited, she surveyed the lot, wondering which car was his. She imagined herself storming through the double doors.

Minutes ticked by. After an hour, letting out the sob that had been waiting to escape, Maja gave up and cried all the way to Great Oaks.

From the musty smell of the chapel to the dusty smell of the union building, Maja lost herself in the stale and stuffy smell of Great Oaks east wing's third floor where old family antiques, jewelry, and first edition novels had been left as her great, great grandmother originally arranged them nearly one hundred years ago. The amount of money the heirlooms would bring at a major auction house—enough Maja hoped so she wouldn't have to travel—motivated her to inventory one room after another.

With the curtains swept back, the dark and forgotten ballroom transformed into a glowing, honeycombed expanse of light. Sitting on the floor with clipboard in hand, Maja glanced up at the high-beamed ceilings, sure she heard the echo of a string quartet, quiet laughter, the ping of crystal glasses and murmurings, as the swish of ladies' gowns swept across the floor. Concertos still permeating the room joined and contrasted with the music of her generation.

Returning to her work, Maja added a silver looking glass, part of a set, to her list. Steps, recognizable as Mother's, sounded on the stairs. At the sharp staccato her heels made crossing the hardwood floor, Maja braced herself for a tirade.

"Not that," Mother cried, lunging for the mirror.

"Sorry, Mother. We agreed—"

"If your father were better, he would not approve."

"Yes, he would," Maja answered, not backing down.

"I don't see why—"

"The funds will buy Daddy the best care."

"Thanks to you, he has been receiving the best care. And, until you fired them, most of the doctors said whatever he doesn't recover by year three, he likely never will. We are nearly at year three."

"How can you say that?" Maja exclaimed. "He's doing so much better."

Mother ran a hand across heavy velvet ceiling-to-floor draperies that protected the old hardwood flooring from sun damage. Satin, marble, crystal, stained glass, Shreve silver, ornate furniture, Persian rugs, gaslights, feathered fans, and Victorian gowns filled the closets—all of it valuable.

"It's time we transfer objects we don't use into the hands of people who will," said Maja.

"Don't part with anything without speaking to me first. I have someone to meet. Your father is with his speech therapist."

"Yes, Mother."

As soon as Mother's footsteps faded, Maja raced downstairs to work with Daddy.

"I'm glad you caught me," said Daddy's speech therapist, smiling when Maja entered her old bedroom.

Maja went to Daddy sitting at the desk Maja had set up. She gave him a kiss on the forehead and rested her hand on his shoulder. Deliberately setting up his therapy in her childhood bedroom, Maja was finally desensitized to the bad feelings the room used to bring up.

The therapist flipped through Daddy's file. "The work you're doing with your father is really helping. Isn't it, sir?"

Daddy nodded, and put his hand over Maja's.

"Your color-coded graph tracking his progress proves his improvement in a glance." The therapist pointed to the line that steadily rose.

"I hoped it would encourage him to keep trying," said Maja. When she started working with Daddy, therapy had primarily focused on helping him overcome his shame of not being able to speak.

"Very clever of you. When you're ready to go

back to school, I'm happy to write you a letter of recommendation."

Daddy twisted his neck and looked up at Maja. Together they grinned.

The therapist's words strengthened the slender ribbon that tied Maja to her dream of someday returning to school and continuing her work with autistic children. She was hopeful that by then she'd somehow have come up with a clever way to resolve the threat her academic advisor posed.

After the therapist instructed Maja on what to concentrate on during their session today, Maja pushed back the hanging beads she'd hung to Mother's chagrin in place of the sliding closet doors.

Maja grabbed her things from the file cabinet. Though her old bedroom no longer made her jittery, still, the closet represented secrets and pain. Her psych classes had taught that you moved on from the past by talking about it. More words.

She sat down across from Daddy and reached for his hands. He grinned. She grinned back. She'd always had more fun with him than with anyone else. Since his accident, she'd grown comfortable in their veil of shared silence.

His hands weighed less than air, lighter than the last time she'd tested. She'd kept on the couple of doctors who still held out hope for Daddy's sense of smell to return and reawaken his taste. She refused to hear that time for him to begin eating on his own was running out.

The setting sun flamed red through the window over his head. Dusk, the time between light and dark, made Maja uneasy.

Carmen soft-footed and smelling of lavender, stood in the doorway. "Excuse me, *por favor, Senoir* Hawthorne. *Mi hija.*"

"*Hola, mi abuelita,*" said Maja.

"Your mother asks you outside."

Maja gave Daddy a quick look. He shrugged.

"Mother is home?" asked Maja.

"*Sí.*"

At the French doors to the back garden, Carmen stepped aside. The grounds were awash in light. Maja wondered what was going on.

"Is someone here?" she asked.

Carmen nodded.

"*Cómo estás?*" asked Maja.

"*Bueno,*" said Carmen, answering in code that, in her opinion, the guest was okay, not great, just okay.

Carmen helped Daddy with the white, v-neck fisherman's sweater draped over his shoulders. Dressed in tennis whites, long pants in deference to the season, he looked much as he had at the height of his wealth. During the week, he still arose at six o'clock every morning and dressed like a business-man for work. On weekends, he wore tennis attire, although as far as she knew, he hadn't picked up a racket since the accident. Maja hadn't told him about all the country's turmoil and assumed no one else had either. Words and images were becoming clearer to him, though his world was still relatively small.

As the door closed behind them, her feet sank in the thick lawn. The nearer they came to the lilac-heavy gazebo, the more apprehensive Maja grew, and the slower she slogged through the evening dew.

Sitting at the wrought-iron table in a long blue chiffon dress, Mother spoke gaily to a stranger. Seeing who it was, Maja stopped, and then stepped back. Mr. Reingor wore a navy-blue, double-breasted suit, much like the clothes hanging in Daddy's closet. Mother threw her head back in laughter. Her face shone.

Mr. Reingor spotted Maja and Daddy and rose to his feet. Mother's head snapped, and her expression turned hard. The dragon awakened.

"I just met Mr. Reingor," said Mother. "He's been telling me some very interesting things."

Struggling to cool her face, Maja introduced Mr. Reingor to Daddy. She kept her tone curt. The two men shook hands.

"Nice to meet you," said Daddy.

Maja restrained herself from yelping for joy. Daddy had practiced that statement more times than he ever practiced his tennis swing. Mr. Reingor wouldn't even guess at the accident … unless Mother had told him all about her brave struggle.

Daddy's cheeks glowed. He was thin, too thin, but fit. His success gave Maja confidence.

"I called, looking for you," said Mr. Reingor. "Your mother asked to meet me and invited me here.

Forgive me, Maja. I mentioned your schooling situation. I had no idea your mother didn't know. I'm so sorry … for both of you."

Mr. Reingor glanced back and forth between mother and daughter, shaking his head. Maja glared at him and refused to face Mother.

"Sit down." Mother pointed to the wrought iron chair next to her.

Mr. Reingor sat in the seat on the opposite side. When he noticed Maja didn't sit down, he stood up again.

Maja turned to Mother and waited for her to speak. She was not going to be bullied. Mother said nothing. Maja felt like she was floating. The lies were gone.

Carmen carried a tray across the lawn, with the scent of Baltic herring and red onions. Maja helped Carmen lay out a *smorgasbord* of pickled herring and *crispbread* and *limpa*; soft and hard, yellow and orange cheeses; deviled eggs with caviar; olives; open-faced sandwiches of cucumber and shrimp; pickles; and a bowl of mixed nuts. The aroma of her childhood had been missing for so long, Maja had forgotten Mormor's favorites.

Arranged amongst the foodstuff sat four small glasses and a bottle of aquavit encased in ice. Green bottles of beer next to tall glasses were ready to chase down the potato-tasting Swedish vodka, an extravagant celebration.

With her head down arranging the display,

Carmen sent Maja a smile. Carmen's warmth calmed Maja. Ramon had quit the garden and hired-on at the nursery in town when Carmen learned about Maja paying the bills. Thanks to a promised high-paying assignment Jimmy set up that she wasn't looking forward to in Milan, Ramon was coming back early next month.

"If what Mister Reingor says is true, seems to me it would have been far easier if you'd just told me," said Mother.

"Gerald," Mr. Reingor murmured to Mother. "Please, call me Gerald."

Mr. Reingor turned an earnest face to Maja, and then switched his full attention back to Mother. Since he didn't even pretend to include Daddy, Maja knew that Mother had told him about the accident. Maja's chin rose. Now she knew the kind of man Mr. Reingor was.

Carmen gave Maja's hand a squeeze and left. As he wandered to the far side of the table, Maja kept an eye on Daddy.

"We have far greater issues to discuss than school." Mother raised an eyebrow like an exclamation mark.

Distracted, Maja watched Daddy lean toward the plate of deviled eggs. He closed his eyes and his chest swelled. He picked up an egg and sniffed it. His nostrils flared, and his face broke into a grin.

Maja's mouth dropped open. One simple breath and his sense of smell returned? She couldn't imagine what activated it. Could it be true? Maja held her breath, waiting to see if Daddy could taste now, too. Feeling Mother's eyes on her, she moved so she could see Daddy and keep him out of Mother's range of vision. Mr. Reingor had no business being part of such a milestone, and Maja knew to take her time with Mother.

"I see," Maja said, hoping it matched with whatever Mother had said.

Daddy bit into the egg and slowly chewed. His eyes closed against tears on his face.

"Gerald has delivered a very generous contract for you." Mother smiled up at the mogul. "Your father's attorney is on his way to take a look."

"What about Jimmy?" asked Maja.

"I'm prepared to reward your agent with a very handsome settlement," said Mr. Reingor.

"You don't need an agent anymore," said Mother. "Not with Gerald's offer."

Maja shook her head. She wanted to say, "I'm not here to be bought and sold." Tempted to reject Mr. Reingor's offer outright, Maja first had to shape the energy she'd need for the fight she'd get from Mother. Still, if she could negotiate on her terms …

Daddy's chewing sped up. He pushed an entire egg into his mouth and reached for a cracker. He looked stoned, devouring pickles and nuts and everything else in front of him. His act of complete abandon was innocent. His joy made Maja happy.

"Take all the time you need," Mr. Reingor said.

"I want you to approve every term."

"Yes, every term," Maja repeated, in a futile attempt to keep up her end of the conversation.

"We'll give Samuel a chance to review the contract, and then we'll celebrate with dinner," said Mother. "Gerald and Samuel have both accepted our invitation to stay."

Daddy pulled a slicer across the block of cheddar. He put the piece on his tongue and rolled it around in his mouth. Mother hadn't noticed his revelry. If Mr. Reingor did, he didn't show it.

"Maja," exclaimed Mother. "Mr. Reingor is speaking to you."

"A strict agreement guaranteeing nothing interfere with school—I plan to reapply immediately," Maja said, her attention still on Daddy. "No shows. No travel. With those terms, I'll sign."

BERKELEY

THE LATE AFTERNOON SUN squeezed Maja outdoors. In a snap of her fingers, she had a dream job and was back in school. Joyful at again living in Berkeley, she took a break from catching up on the coursework she'd missed: memorizing all the parts of the inner ear and the throat, transcribing phonetically recorded speeches from a cassette recorder, outlining normal language acquisition from infancy to adolescence, studying statistical analysis, cramming for tests and writing and rewriting papers.

She had just enough time to swing by school first before joining Raul and Petrana at their apartment, and then driving together to the Oakland Army Induction Center. Petrana had become a good friend, and Maja wanted to support the married couple.

Vines wrapped around the palm tree and engulfed her bicycle. Freeing it from the creepers proved harder than Maja expected. She hopped on, eager for exercise and the outdoors.

Keeping track of the time, she steered towards campus and fast-pedaled to the Philosophy Department. Winter turned her cheeks cold.

Maja heard shouting before she saw the crowd assembled in the quad. A woman stood on a make-shift stage leading a chant.

"Equality. The time is NOW."

Maja slowed down, and then stopped as she saw that the entire crowd was made up of women. Some of them held up signs: "Don't be a clown. Take Women Seriously." "Enough is Enough You Ignorant Men." "Justice." "Women Unite." "Equal Pay for Equal Jobs." "Out of the Kitchen and Into the World."

Scattered about were also signs against the war: "We're Not Fighting a Rich Man's War." "Drop Acid Not Bombs." "Love Not War."

Maja spotted the time on the clock tower. Wanting to learn more, she was reluctant to leave. She pushed her bike forward and slowly wound her way around the women.

When Maja had taken Professor Hicks' class as a sophomore, he'd stood tall and skinny. Now, hunched over his desk marking papers in red, he looked mousy and gray.

What sounded like President Nixon's inaugural address from last year replayed on the radio.

Where peace is fragile.

Make it strong.
Where peace is temporary.
Make it permanent.

"Excuse me. sir?" Maja's voice reflected her nervousness.

"What is it?" he said, without looking up.

Maja stepped inside the musty office. Dust motes streamed on a shaft of sunlight through a gap in the venetian blinds. Books filled dark ceiling-to-floor shelves, a bust of Plato sat on a pedestal between stacks of books, and a green-shaded lamp lit his desk. Everything looked ordinary and predictable and stuck in the past.

After a period of confrontation,
We are entering an era of negotiation.

Professor Hicks peered over reading glasses perched on the top of his head for class, and were now on his nose.

"I don't have all day." He held a red pen over a paper.

"I was in your philosophy class, sir," Maja said.

He flipped his grade book open and ran a finger down the list.

"No, no," she said, stepping forward to save him the effort. "A former student. Maja Hawthorne."

"Ah, yes." He turned down the radio and pushed his glasses on his head.

Frustrated, Maja refused to drop her eyes as he appraised her, something she'd grown accustomed to from men.

"If I remember correctly, you passed," he said as he put back on his glasses and returned to his reading.

The light outside faded. Well aware that her impatience was making her jittery, Maja spoke calmly.

"In class, you lectured about how before we can pass to the next stage of our lives, we first must slay the dragon of Thou Shalt. I looked in the library and I couldn't find where Nietzsche explains how one slays the dragon." She straightened her posture.

"Ah." Professor Hicks leaned back in his chair and rested his elbows on the arms. Forming a gun barrel with his fingers, he tapped them against his lips. Maja waited.

"As implied, to slay a dragon involves great risks," he said finally. "Not everyone is up to it, young lady."

Maja held his gaze.

"If one were so inclined, how would one go about it?"

"Slay the dragon?"

"The expectations of others." Her voice trailed off.

"Well, let me see. First you have to locate the dragon." He aimed his fingers' gun barrel at her and flung it in the air. "Then, you have to face it." He shot her again.

"And?" She leaned forward.

As the weight against her heart lifted, the less inhibited Maja felt. No longer reserved and shy, words bullied their way out her mouth and into the sky. Over time, rather than tumble out, speaking was becoming a graceful practice of spaciousness and light.

"There are as many ways to slay the dragon of Thou Shalt as there are people, Miss Hawthorne. That is a question only you can answer."

Maja sighed and turned to leave.

"Miss Hawthorne?" Professor Hicks called, posing his glasses halfway down his nose. "Before you face the dragon, you'd better have your sword and shield at the ready."

BILLY'S HEAD FILLED WITH the sweet, smoky smell of leather in downtown Berkeley. Brown roof shingles covered the inside walls of the shoe store, crowded from ceiling to floor with shoeboxes and psychedelic posters. Colored lights turned on and off a scrawny leftover Christmas tree.

A salesgirl carried a stack of boxes from the back room.

Red, his hair frizzy and long like a stoner, struck out a hand to the girl.

"Name's Red Harper. Perhaps you've heard of me."

The salesgirl's eyes grew wide.

"Why, no," she said. "I'm pleased to meet you. Did I happen to mention these boots are genuine alligator?"

Red settled back in the chair as if he were on a

social visit. Worried he'd forgotten to shut the closet
door in his new apartment, Billy gave Red a head-jerk.
It was time to leave. Last thing Billy wanted was to
come home to the other half of his boots gnawed and
shredded. Sadie hated being left alone.

Someone shouted from outside. Scrutinizing the
people swarming and demonstrating a changing time,
Billy spotted bare feet everywhere. By the look of
their clothes and the spring in their step, they weren't
barefooted because they couldn't walk in and afford
to buy them a pair of shoes. The pilgrimage from the
Midwest, and further points east, to Northern
California brought people intent on becoming flower
children and wearing second-hand clothes and ripped
jeans. Their fantasies of the place were changing the
heart and spirit of the Bay Area. No longer sleepy
little towns, they faced directly into the heat of the
ever-expanding war in Vietnam. Berkeley and San
Francisco now were places of revolution.

Sunlight caught the window across the way and
blinded Billy. Red slapped him on the shoulder.
Blinking and rubbing his eyes, Billy shook his head to
clear it.

Trying out the boots, Red spoke under his
breath and nodded toward the salesgirl with a click of
his tongue. "Snappy-looking girl."

Thinking that the salesgirl looked more like she'd
been dragged through a knothole, Billy kept his eyes
on the outdoors.

A guy wearing a hat and white bell-bottoms with

no shirt wound through the crowd, talking to himself. He was puffing on a joint in public and in broad daylight with a cop walking up the sidewalk.

Red strutted in front of a standing mirror, trying out the look and the fit of his boots.

Billy heard another shout. The joint-smoker was in handcuffs.

"Get a load of this," he said, directing Red's attention outside.

Red whistled low. "What the hell's going on?"

"A cop's in there," said Billy. "He's got that guy with the hat and long hair handcuffed."

"They've all got long hair," said Red.

The salesgirl joined them at the window. A crowd held back the cop from leading away the hippie.

"Wow. Dig all the beautiful freaks," the salesgirl exclaimed.

"If you plan on buying those boots, I suggest you pay the girl so we can get out of here while we still can." Billy wandered outside.

A FLASH OF WHITE light floated through a gap in the trees, as Maja sped down Telegraph Avenue with the wind in her face. Campus buildings and student housing turned into restaurants and storefronts. Worried about the time, having spent far too much of it with so little result, she pedaled hard toward Raul and Petrana's apartment. Maja admired Raul's decision—all wars would end if soldiers refused to fight—and had been helping him with the steps and procedures to register for conscientious objector status. Last month, his request was conditionally approved. This afternoon, he'd learn if his volunteer job at a halfway house in Berkeley qualified as service to his country.

Watching as their heads bent together over the paperwork, Maja had wondered if she'd ever find love. As much as she'd always dreamed of being with her mystery man, she knew it was a fantasy. She never knew when or where they would see one another. And, what if she'd been wrong all along and unlimited chances weren't a promise?

A car swerved in front of her, and she turned hard on her handlebars. With parked cars taking up the side of the road and the traffic building, Maja rode on the sidewalk instead. Nearing downtown, she approached a circle of chanting Hare Krishna dancers, gawking tourists in white tennis shoes and wrinkled clothes from the fifties, and a guy playing the polka on a tuba.

Wondering why so many people were congregated in her path and frustrated she couldn't get through, Maja hopped off and pushed her bicycle. The murmur of street musicians and the smell of incense competing with aromas from a nearby Chinese restaurant—all sensory details missing from a photo tableau. Passing through a cloud of the bluegrass scent of marijuana, she inhaled deeply.

"Good vibrations." A guy muttered the words as a foregone conclusion, not simply a desire.

The crowd thickened. Jostled, Maja knocked into a woman panhandling for change from a tourist.

"Sorry," Maja apologized.

"Nothing to be sorry about, darlin'. You didn't do anything wrong."

A guy wore a sign across his chest that read, "Take a hippie to lunch." Pushed and elbowed and shoved, Maja's frustration turned to apprehension. Hemmed in on all sides, she heard a shout. She gripped the handlebars of her bike for balance and tried moving to the street. The crowd had already spilled out, stopping traffic.

BILLY SPOTTED WISAW IN the crowd, pulling toward the cop and hippie. At the sight of her, without warning, a smile spread across his face. He shook his head, clearing it of marijuana fumes.

Like a high-pitched whistle only dogs hear, hundreds of hippies crossed between Billy and Wisaw. Guys strutted in bright shirts and giant Afros, girls in skimpy paisley tops, and mangy-looking white guys with scruffy beards and long hair.

Wisaw's eyes widened, and her head disappeared as if sucked underwater. Billy stepped forward. A car slowed in front of the shop. Within seconds, the car was surrounded. The driver got out and disappeared in the same mob as Wisaw.

265

A Beatles' song played in the background. Billy had found the girl with sunlight in her eyes. As always, she was gone.

A SHIFT IN ENERGY spread through the business district. A light flickered from the window across the street. Knocked from behind, Maja stumbled, feeling eyes on her. Her mystery man stared at her. The sense of inevitability made breathing difficult. A shiver spread across her shoulders.

Maja held his gaze as if floating above the mass of people. The look in his eyes was one of recognition and something like longing. Hemmed in by the people, Maja craned her neck. The wolf carving caressing her skin made her blood flow faster. A light and hopeful sensation ran from the top of her head to the tips of her toes. She smiled, unable to take her eyes from his, even as she found herself pinned in and drawn along with people surging forward.

She attempted to wade in the opposite direction toward the man. She didn't find it odd she was unafraid. Her future stood right in front of her. All she had to do was to hurl herself forward. Armed with her voice and words, Maja stepped out in good faith.

BILLY KEPT HIS EYES glued to Wisaw as she urged her way against a human tide with her bike. He started toward her, and then he stopped himself. What was the point? Meet her face-to-face in broad daylight? And, then what? He'd made a mess of his marriage. He'd lost his girls. What could he possibly hope to achieve by chasing a dream?

"It's going to be impossible to get out of here," Billy said, having lost the thread of conversation with Red.

"I vote we wait it out," said Red. "By the looks of it, things could get real messy. I don't want to get caught in the crossfire. Hell, this is the pair of boots for me, all right."

Billy lost sight of Wisaw again. When he finally caught a glimpse of her, using her bike as a shield, she no longer moved against the crowd toward him but rather toward the cop. She was tall enough that he could track her deliberate movement into the heat.

A guy in a purple vest worked his way to the cop on one side of the sidewalk. Wisaw was on the other.

The guy in the purple vest cupped his hands around his mouth. "Overthrow the pig."

The crowd heaved forward. Wisaw shouted something indistinguishable. Her face turned red, and she stood her ground. Billy would never forget that face. The crowd forced her and the cop and hippie backward.

Worried about her and unable to stop himself, he started forward. People blocked his way. Cornered, the cop climbed on a ledge against a display window and hauled the handcuffed guy beside him. Purple

Vest moved his lips, his words lost in the din of the mob. The cop shot out a hand. Purple Vest shoved him against the store window. The reflection of Wisaw in the window quivered, like in a light show. Billy stood on his toes for a better view.

"Back away," shouted the cop. "I'm taking off the cuffs."

Purple Vest lunged for the cop's gun.

Billy's eyes widened, and he glanced at Red. A gun was something he hadn't bargained for.

"Berkeley cops started carrying at the beginning of the year," said Red, slinging his arm around the salesgirl's waist.

Two guys appeared, blocking Wisaw from Billy's sight. Relieved to see Mal and Webb, Billy watched Mal snatch Purple Vest from behind and haul him off the cop. Webb protected Mal's back, facing the crowd, dressed in his old Marine fatigues and ready to fight.

A guy in front of Webb started spewing wrath and spat at him. Webb pushed aside the guy's face, so most of the spit landed on the sidewalk.

"How many babies did you kill?" the guy screamed.

Webb pushed him down the sidewalk. The guy stumbled. Before he could sling more, Webb pushed him again and then again, until the guy left yelling attacks at him.

Standing beside Mal, Webb folded his arms and scanned the mob. A fierce scowl dared someone to say something.

The hippie had thrust out both arms, and the cop stuck the key in the handcuffs. A shout went up from the crowd. People pointed for those who hadn't spotted the action. The cop's face was candy apple red. His eyes were hard as concrete.

The crowd turned quiet and even from where Billy stood, he heard the click of the lock.

Everyone cheered.

"That was so bitchin'," said the salesgirl.

"What's the world coming to?" Billy asked as a squad car arrived with lights flashing.

WHEN, RATHER THAN CONTINUING forward to meet her halfway, her mystery man had backed up, tears sprang in Maja's eyes. Confused, she stopped where she was and watched him turn away. A realization hit her. For her entire life, the only way she'd related to boys was through a fairytale-idealized version of true love. The time had come to stop fantasizing about the mystery man swooping in to save her. It was time she learned to save herself.

As the crowd dispersed, she hopped on her bicycle. When she was side-by-side the squad car and blinking red lights, she flashed a peace sign. Then, with the mystery man standing right in front of her, she winked.

"Hey," he shouted.

She rode straight past him and kept going.

STRIKE

WORD CAME DOWN THAT International was hitting General Motors with a nationwide strike. As ready for a strike as Billy was, the union's decision surprised him. In May, Walter Reuther died in a suspicious airplane accident. Without the activist to keep in line the UAW he'd built into one of the most progressive labor unions in America, the union had been moving to the right. A general strike did not qualify as a particularly conservative move—quite the opposite, though striking now was as good a time as any. The economy grew with American auto factories running full tilt and market increases steady. A strike would unite the rank and file, blacks and whites and Chicanos alike. If they stood together as a united front for better wages and improved working conditions, they'd win.

Skypiece told Billy what he thought of the union's decision.

"The UAW sat down against GM in the thirties. They changed American labor history forever. Sure, the corporation has the profits to pay a rate increase, but those fat cats aren't giving up their growth to guys like us. You saw the National Guard at the Democratic primaries. What Reagan did to those students at People's Park last Spring? Heck, look at what happened to the kids at Kent State. And then, there are the Indians on Alcatraz. They ain't seen nothing yet. Management isn't going to take a strike from us lying down. If they have to, they'll involve the government."

"Government can't act against us," Billy snorted.

"They got wiretapping now," Skypiece said.

"That's for organized crime."

"Don't be surprised."

Later that week, Red drove Webb and Mal and Billy in his green Impala to the strike ratification meeting at the union hall in the pouring rain. From the road separating the Hall and the assembly plant, the size difference between the two buildings was glaring, like Lisa standing beside Mal. Afternoon fog and rain and mist cut off the tail end of the factory, a giant freighter bearing down on a measly raft.

The hall's parking lot was already full of cars. Even with the nasty weather, guys had hung out here after work, drinking beer in their cars and smoking pot and waiting for them.

"Slow down, Red," Billy said, drawing his pea jacket around him, trying to contain his hyped-up buzzing energy. "Don't want to fire up the boys by coming in like Grant taking Richmond."

The vote today was mostly for show, but having all the factions in one room together—everyone suspicious of everyone else—made him edgy. They were all waiting for something to happen. Nothing you could put into words, but the guys were wound up tight enough to blow. Whichever way the meeting went today—peaceful or erupting into a nasty fight—would define the mood and tone of the real deal, the strike.

Billy tightened the band around his hair as Red drove through the front lot real slow, like out for a Sunday cruise. Careful to avoid mud puddles, Red swerved to miss a flooded patch. Guys honked and flashed their headlights, momentarily lifting the gloom. With a random peace sign thrown in here and there, everyone acted friendly enough.

Red told Billy his long hair was freaking out a lot of the guys.

"You got half an hour." Red peered at Billy in the rearview mirror.

Webb grinned over his shoulder from the front seat, wearing his military fatigues. His eyes were glassy, and with his Afro grown out at least six inches, no one from the old neighborhood would recognize him. When Martin Luther King was murdered, Webb said it was time to choose sides. He stayed with the caucus because, though he believed the war the Panthers waged was just, he was tired of fighting.

"And, Webb," said Red. "I don't understand why you wore your special forces' fatigues today of all days.

"I'm proud of the service I gave my country. I wear them to honor my brothers still on the battlefield."

Billy appreciated that Webb didn't want anyone taking his sacrifices from him. His current obsession, however, with his soul brother on account of their similarities—Indian grandmothers and service in the military—worried Billy. Jimi Hendrix skated on the edge of a razor blade.

"You ready for what's coming, Webb?" Billy asked, shaking out a cigarette.

"Let me put it this way, brother. There's a lot more to life than factory politics."

Hendrix came on the radio. Webb turned the song up full blast. Red parked the car and turned off the engine, wrapping them in the drumming rain.

Webb started singing about no one being able to hold him down. That he just had to keep moving.

"That so?" said Billy.

"Yeah, man," said Webb. "That so."

Inside the hall, Webb and the others unlocked the front doors and greeted the guys, everyone loud and shaking off the dreariness and the rain. Down the corridor in the opposite direction, past the bathrooms, Billy entered the meeting hall alone. Quiet and dark, the place felt like being in church. Windows sat up high. Outside, the rain continued.

Billy snapped on the lights. Chairs enough for an ordinary meeting were out, not nearly enough for everyone who would be crammed in here today. Many would have to stand, which could cause territorial misunderstandings, depending on who stood next to whom. He slung his drenched pea jacket on the chair back as guys entered by special-interest groups.

The Black Panthers, the Brown Berets and the hillbillies, the communists, the biker gangs, everyone had a buck knife folded in the sheath at their waist. Couldn't see the guns, but they were out there, slipped into shoulder straps under their shirts and calf belts hidden in cowboy boots.

They'd all witnessed Black Panther Party Chairman Bobby Seale on television at the Chicago Democratic convention, yelling at demonstrators to defend themselves by any means necessary. Most of the demonstrators were white middle-class guys with no thought of a weapon, so it didn't account for much. Guys in here were working men and fighting men. Grateful to be straight, Billy needed all his wits about him to prevent an outright war.

After Mal—as sergeant at arms—brought the meeting to order, Red read the long list of demands management had rejected. On the stage with the rest of the executive board, Billy breathed real slow and deliberate in air that was thick and sticky. With everyone soaked from the rain and the furnace turned up high, steam filled the room, making it smell like a giant sweat lodge. His chest tightened. He wheezed, panicked, and caught a breath.

Red was standing in front of him. Billy's turn now: time to bring the guys together as one. Leading these men into a nationwide strike was his purpose. Deep inside he knew this was Grandma's prophecy he'd been waiting and preparing for his entire life.

Guys clapped as Billy rose. Beaming, he thrust out his chest, moved aside the podium, and wheeled out a schoolroom blackboard from the side of the stage.

Chalk rolled off the ledge. He bent to pick it up, and his breathing turned shallow.

Taking a wide stance, his hands clasped behind his back, Billy looked out over the crowd of faces. By now, a blue cloud of cigarette smoke hung over the room with something big and vicious just beneath the mumbling, coughing, and scrapping. Most of the heavies holding the highest seniority sat up front. They were hard as iron and weren't about to let anyone or anything threaten their positions in the final-repair and final-paint inspections, material and handling departments, and as forklift drivers. Even the so-called cushy jobs weren't really so cushy, and they still didn't get paid enough or receive adequate benefits.

The longer Billy waited before speaking, the quieter the room became.

"Gentlemen, we are working men," he said. "We show up on time every day, walk five miles from the parking lot to inside, work an eight to ten hour-shift, and overtime when we can get it. Doing manual labor. For every two hours on, we get a twelve minute break. We stop the line for forty-two minutes for lunch. Why forty-two minutes exactly? Because six minutes is a tenth of an hour and that's how they calculate our lives—by the hour."

Without a power tool or oilcan, a punch tool or car part in hand, most of the guys fidgeted and looked awkward, glancing over their shoulders. In the factory, guards and supervisors and factory officials prowled the catwalks. Here, union members were on their own, stuck together like overcrowded sardines in a rusted tin can.

"And we do this, why?" Billy asked, raising his voice and pulling their attention away from each other to listen to him. "So we can buy new houses and cars, refrigerators and dryers. And that makes each of us keeping this country's economy rolling. Each of us making the rich get richer. As long as we working men are well compensated, we're happy. Dissatisfied, we wage a revolution."

Guys erupted out of their seats and onto their feet. Their speed and intensity surprised Billy as they whistled and clapped and shouted. His breathing was clear, and while he had everyone's attention, he drew a circle that covered most of the blackboard to make his point.

"This much goes for raw materials." He shouted over the chaos and marked out pie slices all the way around as he identified each one he'd researched. As the guys quieted and sat down, Billy lowered his voice.

"This much for overhead and rent. This big slice is for executive salaries. And this much for us—labor. We're here today, gentlemen, because we are not entirely satisfied with the way this pie is divided."

Billy went on to describe management executives with big college degrees playing golf together and their three martini lunches while the guys sweated, busting their humps inside the factory.

"They ain't worried about us," Billy continued. "Can't be. Too obsessed about pushing up profits in the next quarter so they can grab bigger bonuses and pay their shareholders bigger dividends. But all that greed has made them forget about us. We're the oil in the engine of this boom economy. We walk until we get our share. We walk. Now."

Grinning, Billy looked out over the men shouting and clapping each other on the back. His blood pumped like theirs. As he waited for the excitement to die down, he suddenly noticed how mean their eyes were, the set of their jaws, and the snarls across their lips.

A shiver hit between his shoulder blades. He should have chosen his words more carefully and written down a plan. Billy told himself off for speaking from his gut as usual. The country was coming apart at the seams. The last thing he wanted was the same thing happening to the guys.

Billy put out his hands.

Instead of dying down, their clapping grew, and Billy realized he'd already lost them. Two guys in the back broke into a fight. It was an outburst of raw energy, spilling over, looking for expression.

Billy's heart pounded. Rather than unite them around better wages and improved working conditions, he'd united them against management. He'd set the battle lines. All of the men unhesitatingly and boldly crossed over into enemy territory. Their boots stomped, shaking the stage.

Slow it down, the voice in his head screamed. Pull it back, and shut up. Trouble was there was no bringing them back now.

After the hall cleared, most of the guys stayed outside, milling around the parking lot. The rain had stopped, and bits of night sky showed through black storm clouds. The temperature had plunged. Standing in front with Webb, Billy thrust his fists into his pockets, buried his chin in his pea jacket, and lifted his shoulders, trying to get the collar to cover his ears.

The spotlight at the roof corner of the hall cast a dim glow on the parking lot turned into a swamp. Across the road, the factory that never closed looked eerily empty tonight. All the lights were on. Security guards smoked cigarettes, their eyes trained toward the union hall and the men outside it.

The workers egged each other on. Management

had screwed them. It was their turn now.

"I need your help," Billy said, aware of heat pouring from Webb. "We got to get a lid on the guys."

Webb smashed out his cigarette and stretched like he had something stuck between his shoulder blades. The bulb over their heads flickered and popped. The porch fell into shadows.

Webb stepped off the landing and strolled toward the darkened road. Billy caught up with him.

"All that talk of yours makes me feel mean," Webb said, talking like he was in a trance. "I've been trying to make it go away. I don't like feeling mean."

Webb was talking to Billy, but his attention was elsewhere.

"I know, man," said Billy. "It's all my fault. You know me and my big mouth. Thought I'd learned to control myself. It ain't easy, is it, Webb? Controlling our natures."

A group of about twenty guys fell in line behind Webb. Billy followed, too, tripping in a ditch and scrambling back to level ground.

"Don't it make you mad, Billy?" asked Webb. "All them things you were saying?"

"Sure it makes me mad," Billy said, his voice calm and steady. "That's why we're striking and not doing something crazy we'll regret later."

"I got blood on my hands, Billy. Blood on my hands."

Webb reached the road. The crowd behind

them, about thirty Panthers, made it hard for Billy to hear. He grabbed Webb by the arm. His friend's muscle turned rigid as steel. Billy felt himself falling into a deep, lonely pit where nothing made sense anymore. He clenched his teeth to prevent them from clattering and dropped his hand. Webb's gaunt ravaged face and rumpled hair scared him.

"You're a good and decent man, Webb. Come on. Let's go back."

"All those words of yours got me riled up inside. I'm sick of getting screwed. I can't just let it be anymore."

Tears streamed down Webb's cheeks. Swallowing hard, Billy leaned forward and spoke softly.

"That's right. And now we have us a chance to do something about it. We're young, and we're on strike. It's a brave thing we're doing, Webb. A powerful thing. Come back inside. Let's talk about this."

"No more talking," Webb said, his voice eerie and disconnected.

A shout came from inside the factory's chain-link fence.

"We changed things, brother," said Webb.

He grabbed Billy by the shoulders and, for the first time in years, looked Billy straight in the eye.

"Everything we've done has been for the good." Webb gave him a sad smile and started forward.

"Let's keep going," Billy said, trying to keep his voice from sounding desperate. "Let's focus on wages and conditions and change the way things are done on a fundamental level. I was wrong. Everything doesn't always have to be someone against someone else. One group against another. War. We don't have to be against management. Simply being for what we want is enough. Standing up for our rights is enough. We don't have to go up against anyone. Hold out for our due, and we'll get what we want."

A car whirred down the road. Billy held Webb back from it, but Webb pushed on. Billy stepped away, afraid of the man he'd known all his life.

Webb, along with the wave of men following him, disappeared into the dark. They reappeared in the light at the factory entrance, pushing through the security guards at the gates, and spreading out across the parking lot. Keeping Webb's Afro in his sights, Billy stayed fixed where he was.

Webb swerved left like he'd changed his mind after all. Billy let out his breath. But instead of coming back, Webb ended up at the garbage area. Men's shouts fired across the road, no words, just sounds.

Billy addressed guys crowding around him. "Remember guys. We're trying for non-violence here. Cesar Chavez. Martin Luther King."

The men weren't listening as they brushed past Billy. More and more of the guys he'd known and worked with and represented followed Webb's gang across the darkened street and into the factory parking lot.

There was a blast of light and an explosion. One

of the garbage trucks burst into flames. A roar went up from the workers. Red and white and blue flames curled in and out of billowing black smoke.

Lurching backward, Billy shouted, "Call the fire department."

His words were lost in the blast of another garbage truck, and then another. The sky lit up. The faces of the men glowed. Mean faces, frenzied and ready for a fight.

When the fire trucks arrived, a few men surrounding the garbage trucks refused to let the firefighters near enough to fight the fires. Immediately, more men joined the line of defense, operating as a unit with no prompting, automatically following the leadership and internal organization at work on the line.

Billy's view of Webb was obstructed as a truck barreled past. A painter darted into the road to catch up with the others.

"Get back. Get back," Billy shouted, running and waving his arms.

The road was dark. Tires screeched. Billy flinched as the painter's body thunked against the nose of the truck and was flung ten feet onto the pavement.

"Call an ambulance," Billy shouted.

With his ears echoing with the sound of two tons slamming against what he estimated could be no more than one hundred and fifty pounds, Billy ran into the road. The guy was ghastly white in the wash of headlight coming their way. Billy dragged him off the road.

Winded in the ditch, Billy doubled-over. His teeth chattered with cold. He rubbed his hands across his eyes. With a violent shudder, he wiped and rubbed faster and harder. The guy's eyes were looking at nothing; he was barely breathing and hemorrhaging badly.

"Hang in there, buddy," Billy whispered. "You're going be okay."

Flashing red lights announced the arrival of the ambulance. Before the emergency personnel could even open the doors, a wave of men lined up on one side of the ambulance. They began rocking it. Billy reeled backward.

"Stop, damn it," he shouted.

There were shouts and a crash as the vehicle toppled on its side.

Losing his balance, Billy stumbled through madness, keeping low in the weeds and mud. He'd drag the painter to safety until he could find him some help … that was it. Shaking and drenched in sweat, he found a dry spot under a bush and settled the painter as best he could.

"I'll be back with help," Billy said. "Hang in there just a little bit longer, buddy."

Still shaking his brain for the missing man's name, Billy turned to go and stepped into a pothole. His jaw crushed together at the unexpected drop. Billy found himself doing the splits, one leg lock-kneed straight in the freezing rain-filled hole, and the other stretched along the ground at an odd angle.

Unable to catch his breath, the shock of ice water numbed his submerged foot up to his knee. Groaning in pain, he shook his head to clear it. The movement widened the splits, causing his foot to slip further in the rain-soaked earth. Sweating, he hunched forward. Catching himself straight-armed in weeds smashed with mud and filth, he flinched as a flash of pain shot up his spine.

He searched the area for help. In the cockeyed lurid headlights of the ambulance, a riot raged. Billy heard war-cries and screams.

Breathing hard and sopping-wet, he dragged an arm across his forehead. A smearing of mud and blood and sweat and rain gushed into his eyes as he pulled himself to his hands and knees. He tasted blood and spit. Somewhere behind him, he heard a twig snap. Out of the pitch-black edges around him, Billy thought he spotted someone in the dark.

"Hey, I could use some help here," he called, twisting his upper body.

Everything went black.

THE DRIVE-BY

SITTING BACK ON THE couch with his foot on a chair in his apartment living room, Billy petted Sadie lying next to him. A white bandage wrapped around his head covered twenty-five stitches. The doctor warned Billy to keep his leg elevated and his head still, and he'd be fine. What wasn't so fine was that the deep gash and concussion came from the hand of one of his guys. Billy had a pretty good idea who it was.

Red and Mal watched the evening news with Billy. As the station broke for a commercial, Red got up to get a beer. The next news story covered the factory riot.

"You don't want to watch this," said Mal, getting to his feet.

"Don't turn it off," said Billy, leaning forward. Groggy, he spotted himself on television. "I don't remember cameras."

Pulling guys back. Blood smeared across his face. Yelling for calm in the middle of flames and violence and death. Billy kept waiting for the fog to lift and the nightmare to vanish. Wasn't going to happen.

The report ended with a news flash: Jimi Hendrix had died.

Billy fell back in the chair and covered his eyes.

"I'm going to look for Webb." He reached for the crutches next to the sofa and struggled to his feet.

"You've had a concussion, Billy," said Mal. "The doc said you're supposed to rest. Webb would want you to take care of yourself."

"I'm going." Billy leaned on the crutches to steady himself.

"People who don't want to be found generally aren't," said Red, but he and Mal went with Billy to the strike line.

None of the guys remembered seeing Webb. Hobbling on the crutches, Billy asked at their old neighborhood. An uncle of Webb's said he'd been hurting himself something awful, and there was a cloudiness in his eyes.

Billy kept looking. When he found himself dizzy and needing a break, he slowed down for some deep breathing.

Three days later, Webb's uncle gave him the address of a flophouse in the Haight.

Billy didn't have trouble finding the old Victorian. It sat next to a liquor store on one side and a boarded-up warehouse on the other. People milling around kept tripping over a guy sitting on a guitar case by a tree, moaning with his head in his hands. The sidewalk smelled of urine.

Unable to figure out how to use crutches on the front stairs, Billy leaned on the banister and gingerly mounted the steps. He rang the doorbell. Not hearing an actual bell, he knocked. Nothing. He knocked louder.

"All right, already," said the woman who answered the door. A dingy apron covered an equally dingy housedress.

"I'm looking for a buddy of mine," he said. "Webb Wolden. We've known each other since childhood."

"He paid for a month. I haven't seen him since. This way."

She unlocked a nondescript door and before it was all the way opened, Billy smelled death. The room was empty but for a soiled couch. Webb lay sprawled across it, dead with a needle in his arm. Billy wobbled, tears flooding his eyes. He thought of Jimi Hendrix. When he kissed the sky with his exotic spellbinding music, he must've known others would take seriously his invitation to hell. Webb's hope had turned to rage, and ultimately despair.

Webb couldn't go the distance. Billy could. He was determined to do whatever he had to for better working conditions and higher wages in his friend's name.

Every day, they posted strikers out front of the factory from six in the morning to nine at night. The longer they were out, the more cocaine and heroin started showing up. The Fillmore had closed its doors in the spring, marking the official end of the Flower Children. Hard drugs had finished it off long before that, as played out in the violence and death at the Altamont Festival. Guys were coming back to the factory from Vietnam with track marks on their arms. Unlike pot and psychedelics, cocaine and heroin cost money. The longer the strike went on, the harder it was to keep the guys focused on the long-term gains. All they wanted was to chase the almighty dollar and get high.

A week before Thanksgiving, Billy drafted a letter to International listing the progress he was making with management and requesting more financial help.

Red barged into the union office. "International settled."

"What?" exclaimed Billy.

"News just came down from the top."

"With no warning? No way."

And without notice, the fight ended. International settled the nationwide strike so quickly that the rank and file got not nearly enough.

Deceived and angry that he hadn't figured out the political motives before he went and caused so much damage, Billy fought back.

"Billy, I'm warning you," advised Red.

"International won't tolerate this kind of dissension."

"Eighteen-year-olds deserve better than slapping on tires knee-deep in oil and grime and factory chemicals. Fifty-five-year-olds driving forklifts and smoking cigarettes deserve better, too."

Billy convinced the guys to stay out longer.

International got wind and five reps from Solidarity House breezed in from Detroit.

"You're out," said the head guy to Billy.

"No way. We're making progress."

"Out."

The guy nodded and the others surrounded Billy.

"You can't do this." Billy shrugged out of their grasp.

"We just did."

At that, Billy was escorted from the union hall. He was locked out on his twenty-sixth birthday.

With Billy barred, the out-of-town reps, each one using a river of words—all of which were dried up and empty—explained things to the men. The workers followed their instructions. The plant started up without Billy.

From that one additional week Billy had convinced them to take, they got 100 percent of doctor and hospital bills, no dental, medical expenses for having babies—100 percent. In the end, a dollar an hour raise for a grand total of seventy-five dollars a week with some overtime just didn't cut it.

Billy complained to the International reps.

"Six thousand families. How many years do you

think it's going to take them to make back the money they lost during the strike? If I'd known you were going to just cave like that, I'd have fought against going out in the first place."

"They let you grow your hair long like that out here, huh?" commented the main negotiator, a polished slick guy with hair gel and shiny fingernails and a name Billy couldn't seem to remember, even after asking a bunch of times.

"He looks just like Charlie Manson, don't he, boys." Making a note in a thick binder, the guy shuddered along with all the men in his alliance.

Because of the likes of Manson and his cult, now everyone viewed anyone with long hair as a potential murderer. The convicted serial killer had long hair, but he wasn't a hippie. He was a five-foot-two conman, a mental midget, and sadistic maniac. Being lumped together with the likes of him shook Billy. He faced up to how deep the fear of long hair hippies ran in people.

THIRTY-TWO MILES NORTH of Fremont at Great Oaks, Maja was distracted and not much in the mood for work.

"You're working to heal yourself with the same intensity I remember as a child," she said to Daddy, gathering up the materials for a test the therapist had asked Maja to administer.

Like trying to have two conversations at once,

Maja spoke to Daddy and, at the same time, kept chiding herself for her cowardice. If she'd presented her idea to Mother months ago, as she should have, they'd be moving forward with her plan to convert the east wing of Great Oaks by now. Time she faced the fight she was getting herself into. Maja turned to Daddy.

"I'm sorry for taking what you did for us for granted. I won't ever again," she promised.

Her hands full, she motioned with her chin for him to sit so they could get started. Instead, he squeezed her by the shoulders, his reaction confusing her.

"I did ..." Daddy started.

"Yes, I know you did." Maja confirmed his words in her customary way of supporting him as he found his way to the words he wished to say.

Daddy squeezed harder. Maja squirmed to get away, sliding the testing materials across the desk before they spilled on the floor.

"I did. I did. I did," he repeated, the needle in his mind skipping.

Maja rested a hand over his, calming him.

"You did." She felt his hands relax on her shoulders. "You created all of this for us. You're learning to speak again. More than just want to. You're making it happen."

Daddy nodded his head yes and then no, and sighed. Usually Maja was able to figure out what he was trying to say. Now she was bewildered. She peeled back his grip on her shoulders.

"How about a spin in the Caddie?" she asked.

Daddy dropped his hands, grinning with guilty pleasure. Happy for a break, Maja replaced the test in the closet, arranging things in such a way that the next time she could determine if Mother had moved anything. After telling Mother about being accepted to graduate school, Maja often found Daddy's file moved or left open. Knowing that Mother was curious and rummaging through Maja's things, gave her an odd sense of comfort and hope that Mother would agree to her plan.

"COME ON. GET UP. Let's go support the Indians on Alcatraz," said Mal, yanking Billy to his feet.

Standing up too fast, Billy turned dizzy from the huge gash still healing on his head.

"Hell, helping them helps us, too," urged Red.

Billy glimpsed out a darkened window of his apartment, not at all ready to be alone, and sick to death of talking.

"The workers are struggling," he said, absently petting Sadie. "Last thing they want is to see their hard-earned money go to Indians."

"You'd be surprised," said Mal. "When a man gives something to someone else, it means he's got enough for himself. Gives a man dignity. And besides, everyone predicted the Indians would fail. Instead, they continue to control the island. Wouldn't hurt capitalizing on their success."

"It's no success," scoffed Billy. "Their spokes-man deserted the cause."

"More reason to go."

"Count me out." Billy grabbed his jacket and went outside, Sadie right on his heels.

"Hell, Billy—"

"I'm on ice, remember? Consider me a liability because I'm sure as hell not an asset." Billy opened the car door for Sadie.

Together, they headed toward the highway.

ON THEIR WAY TO the five-car garage, Maja and Daddy stopped to admire Daddy's rose garden. Now that Ramon was back, he helped, but most of the pruning and grooming of the neglected roses, Daddy did himself. A sea of color sent out an aroma of love and longing. He pushed back his favorite felt hat and dragged Maja to smell the red Abraham Lincoln. The pride on his face proved to Maja that anything was possible.

At the garage, he pinched the crease of his slacks and slid into his prized Cadillac. As she maneuvered the car onto the drive, he cranked down his window. Around the far side of the house, two mourning doves fluttered away.

Gravel crunched under the car tires as they slipped through the old oaks, past the vast lawns and the winding creek where a white mist clung to the surface, and into a shifting pattern of sunlight and shade. Maja pictured Kenny, and children like him, living on the grounds. Not running and jumping, they'd be rocking and pacing and twirling, resisting wading into the creek, stiff on horseback, eating Carmen's fragrant foods, and sleeping to the sound of crickets and frogs.

The master oak tree that tucked the butterfly house under its protective arms reached out to caress Maja. She eased the car onto the wooden bridge. Boards creaked beneath them. Totem poles on either side reminded her of when she was a captured Indian princess, and only the totem animals knew.

They drove into the late afternoon, a breeze tangling her hair. Daddy grinned. Maja grinned back.

Daddy hummed a wordless tune. "I did what I did. My life. Not yours."

Maja felt in her body, more than knew in her mind, how much time and effort he put into that simple declaration. Modeling wasn't her life. Maja was grateful he knew that. Still, she didn't have enough money to quit, not yet anyway. Her investments needed time to grow, not just for her parents, for the residential school she planned, too.

EXITING THE HIGHWAY WITH Sadie half out the window, her tongue hanging and ears plastered against her head, Billy turned east. Something drew him that way.

Passing newer homes, he veered south in search of the old estates. Poppies and lupine blanketed hillsides in sprawling patches of orange and blue. Red-winged blackbirds whistled from cattails swaying in the wind. The air smelled musty with last year's fallen oak leaves and acorns.

The truth was, Billy knew the GTO was Wisaw's. If, that was, she even still owned it. He'd spotted the wolf carving around her neck the day at the shoe store when she'd ridden past him.

Billy drove up and down on the off-chance he'd spot the GTO in the driveway of one of the estates. He often found himself doubled back on the same roads. Up ahead, a grove of towering eucalyptus trees crowned with buzzard nests became his compass. Grandma used buzzard feathers to clean away the past when she danced on the brink of the world.

Slowing down, Billy came upon an old sprawling home. Thick clay roof tiles and faded blue shutters spread out like a hacienda, with plenty of oak tree-studded land all the way around.

He took his time studying the house. No sign of the GTO. He moved to the next house. Trouble was, old-growth trees hid the houses set back from the road by long stately driveways, some behind wrought-iron gates. Billy didn't have a clue if he was in the right place or even if the car was still in service or what he'd say or do if he actually spotted it. Too many

ifs for his liking, but he had nothing else to do, and
Sadie looked the happiest he'd seen her since his girls
left.

Church bells chimed in the distance as cowboys
herded rust-colored cattle silhouetted against the
setting sun.

ON THE WAY HOME, Maja watched a slow-moving
car approach from the opposite direction. In front of
Clay's parents' estate, the car stopped. The house was
closed. Clay's parents were traveling in Africa, and
Clay was flying back and forth over the Mexican
border, smuggling in kilos of weed.

Maja passed the car, wondering if she should
offer her help, but the driver's head was turned, and
she doubted he even knew they were there—more
intent on searching for something.

A dog in the passenger seat leaped into the
driver's lap and lunged, taking up the entire window.

Maja laughed and pointed. Daddy joined in. The
dog's joy was irresistible.

Back home, Maja waved to Ramon, who'd
turned on the spotlight at the outside corner of the
garage. As Roman tended to a tower of broken tree
branches, he looked more hunched over than she
remembered, years stacked against bending and
reaching.

Maja gave Daddy a hug, something she learned
in encounter groups for her psychology classes. He

hugged her back, his warmth so unlike Mother's ironing-board body.

The drive settled Maja. She was ready to go into the fire for her dream. She was ready to face Mother.

A SAFE PLACE

MOTHER DARTED AROUND THE side of the garage, looking stricken.

"Maja. Richard. Where have you been?"

"What's wrong?" asked Maja.

She hadn't heard panic in Mother's voice like that since Daddy's accident. Now Daddy pulled Mother near, looking down at her, dashing and sincere. She sagged against him, the first show of need Maja had seen from Mother, perhaps ever.

Mother pulled away. "I'm fine. Just fine."

Daddy grasped her to him again. Rather than witness Mother turning rigid and pushing Daddy away, Maja watched Ramon dump a wheelbarrow of leaves on the pile of branches he'd arranged for a fire. The wide brim of Ramon's straw hat hid his eyes. Now, Maja told herself. Now was the perfect time to introduce her idea for Great Oaks to Mother.

"I don't want you getting a chill, Richard. Go inside and put on a sweater."

"Daddy is quite capable of knowing what's best for him"

Hearing her own words, Maja wondered why she'd never spoken them on her behalf. Just as quickly, she chastised herself. Now was not the time to irritate Mother. She needed her blessing if her plan was going to work.

"It's … okay, kiddo," said Daddy.

He gazed down at Mother, his eyes soft. Mother and Maja watched him leave around the garage, giving Maja the chance to introduce her idea.

"I want to talk to you abou—"

"Clay is dead," Mother said as if in a daze. "His mother telephoned from Cairo. He let go of a tree rope over a shallow spot in the Delta and broke his neck. Died instantly." Mother's held-back words gushed out in a rush.

Maja nodded her head even as her spine turned rigid, and a dark force awakened inside. She stamped her foot. Clay had died and robbed her of the chance to shift the burden of shame and guilt to him. Now she'd never be free of all the guys she'd slept with and hadn't loved, guys who had disrespected her because Clay had taught her to disrespect herself. Her skin felt on fire.

"I was so fond of that boy." Mother spoke with an intimacy that shook Maja into a state of alertness.

With her ears ringing, thinking perhaps she'd misunderstood, Maja spun around and tried to read Mother's face, but couldn't. Outrage broke through bottled-up depression and anxiety. A fierceness and power took over. Maja's breathing turned fast and hoarse.

"Are you going to tell Daddy?" she asked.

"It would break his heart."

Maja stepped back and shook her head. Daddy would mourn Clay's death and miss him. She hated him for that. Mostly, she hated Clay. Once upon a time, she'd also loved him.

In the distance, Ramon knotted braided strips of Mother's old paint rags. He dipped the rope in a pail of turpentine.

"Daddy is improving," said Maja as a bellow grew in her belly.

"Is that all you can say? Really, Maja. Clay is dead. He was your best friend."

Ramon uncoiled the patchwork cord. Maja watched as she herself uncoiled. Ramon buried one end deep in the three-foot teepee of kindling and branches and leaves.

"There's not much I can do about Clay," Maja said. "I can do something about Daddy."

Ramon lit the fuse.

"The funeral is planned for Friday." Mother's voice rose above the whirling fury. Flames shot into the darkening sky.

Maja stared at the blaze. Fire burned away the

shadow of the girl she'd been living. The finality of what was. The end.

"You should ask Gerald to take you." Mother fiddled with the loopy bow collar of her blouse. "He'd be more than happy to oblige."

"Let him take you," Maja said, no longer turned against herself.

Mother stared at her.

"I want to talk to you about converting Great Oaks into a home for autistic kids," declared Maja.

No longer complacent and intimidated, Maja stepped forward. Mother opened her mouth and closed it. Taking advantage of her uncharacteristic speechlessness, Maja positioned herself so they both were looking in the direction of the house.

"I have it all figured out," she spoke with authority. "I'll take the east wing. You'll never even know we're there."

She pointed to the far corner of the house.

"See how the kitchen blocks off the rest of the house? You and Daddy will have the entire main house and west wing. We'll live separately, though at first we'll share the kitchen until I can have one built."

As she waited in the silence, the smell of smoke teased out memories of Mormor's blazes and her singing at the turning of the seasons, and they warmed her.

"I have no idea what you're talking about," said Mother.

"Give it time," said Maja.

"You really should stop wasting your time at that psychobabble school," Mother said, her voice sharp. She marched toward the house.

"We're talking about kids who need a home," Maja said to Mother's back. "Daddy will love them."

Mother whirled around. "I worry about you when you're there. Berkeley is coming apart at the seams. Things are only going to get worse."

"Worse?" Maja put out a hand to stop Mother from going inside. "We're talking about a school. Giving children a safe place to thrive."

Mother lowered her voice. "Clay was on LSD when he let go of that rope." Her voice wavered. "He was such a special boy. Full of talents and dreams."

Maja snorted. "What about all the boys dying in Vietnam?" she snapped, unable to stop herself. "What about their dreams? They're all dead. And it's because of people like us. People who take more than we need."

Suddenly tired, Maja was ready to be alone. The definition of psychedelic floated into her mind. She'd learned from her Greek homework that psychedelic meant to reveal: soul made visible. Without words to explain, Maja understood that by the way he died, Clay's soul revealed itself in the end.

"I have to go to work," Maja said. "We'll talk about the school later. Oh, and the director of the speech clinic says to save April fourth."

"Your birthday," breathed Mother.

"I think I'm being honored for something. I

305

want Daddy there."

"That's impossible."

"I've already told him. He wants to come. He's delighted, really."

Mother went inside without another word.

The next morning, before going to the Reingor studio, Maja stopped off at the university police. With no sign of Mr. Evans since she'd moved back, she'd cautiously allowed herself to relax. Harder, she found, was pushing away the memories of her terror. Aberrant behavior turned more deviant over time; she worried about who he was hurting now.

Daring to direct her anger against the cruelty done to her, she walked into the office. Neither officer on duty looked up from reading the newspaper.

"Excuse me," Maja said, hating that she sounded weak and passive.

One of the officers lowered his paper. He slowly looked Maja up and down.

As her resolve to stay strong leaked from her, Maja used vague innuendoes about a friend of hers who'd been hurt by her academic advisor.

"Boys will be boys," the officer said, interrupting her with a sneer, as if she got what she deserved.

Hating him, Maja turned self-conscious in her Indian print sleeveless top and shorts. She wished she'd dressed more formally.

"Seeing as how the encounter occurred off

campus, and all," he said, going back to his reading. "Your friend needs to file a report about the incident with the Berkeley police."

"He's a university counselor," Maja cried. She knew her voice sounded desperate.

"Downtown. Can't miss it," he said, dismissing her.

In her dressing room after work, and with a scrubbed face, Maja pulled her hair into a ponytail. Mr. Reingor came in to discuss the month's sales figures for his department stores. Even after more than a year, still Maja felt awkward calling him Gerald. Tonight, his presence added to the pressure she felt against her chest, like a giant thumb pinning her down. He made her uncomfortable, but he didn't scare her. Clay had taught her fear. Now, he was gone. And still, the thumb pressed.

Nodding in front of the mirror, Maja retied the carving at her neck. She half-listened as Mr. Reingor thanked her for her part as the Reingor Girl.

Lately, his body postures and hand gestures, inflections and tone had begun to change. He liked to tell her what to do. Rather than connect, his words created distance and, more and more often, uncertainty. He narrated his thoughts and feelings. Maja often didn't understand what he meant.

"Is it old?" he asked.

Puzzled, she looked up. Mr. Reingor pointed to her carving.

"I'm not sure how old," she said. "I found it a long ti—"

"May I see it?"

Instinctively, she covered the carving with her hand. "I don't usually take it off." Her pulse raced.

"I'll give it back." He reached out a hand with a little nod.

She hesitated but could find no rational reason to deny his request. Pleased he was interested, she untied the rawhide cord.

"It looks very old."

She leaned in nearer to show him. "I think it's—"

"It doesn't belong around your neck," he said.

"Excuse me?"

"It's awfully crude."

Maja's face colored as Mr. Reingor handed the carving back to her. As much as she wanted to put it on her neck, she slipped the wolf in her pocket instead.

Exhausted from work, Maja found herself alone in the house she shared with her roommates. Hope blew in the opened window as twilight shadows skipped across a card stock envelope on the kitchen table. Addressed to Maja, the invitation was from Petrana. Raul would not be in attendance at his baby's christening. Due to a foul-up somewhere along the chain of command, he'd been denied conscientious objector status and shipped off. He went missing in action two days after he arrived in Vietnam.

Maja collapsed at the table. Over the sink, the window opened to the maple tree she also saw from her bedroom window. One limb, in infancy, had grown down instead of up. It formed a bench across the ground before righting itself like a beckoning finger. The air sighed and leaves shuddered. Mormor would instruct Maja to watch for the little ones—the elves and the fairies. Maja put her head in her hands. Kenny and Raul and his baby made fairies and elves silly and frivolous.

A shout came from outside, slung at her like a fist. She knew the voice and gagged. Slipping to the floor and keeping out of the light of the setting sun, she crawled to the edge of the window. Her advisor cruised past her house in his black Corvette. He flicked his lit cigarette in a shower of sparks.

Revving the engine, he shouted the same nasty abuse, as if all these months of thinking Mr. Evans had moved on, and she was safe, were part of his plan to torment her. His return made her eyelids sweat.

The Corvette's horsepower sparked his voice, inflated his grand view of himself, and bloated his delusions of power over her—just like Clay's privilege had done for him. Mr. Evans laughed a cruel laugh. The louder the car engine screamed, the louder and more sadistic the laugh.

Fantasies of retaliation overtook Maja. A bloodthirsty beast, she tore off his limbs. She sucked his blood. She held a knife … Aimed a gun … She felt possessed. Sure she was losing her mind. Maja covered her ears.

She lay on the cool kitchen tile, her cheek against the slick surface, wondering if she'd be sad to die. Instead, she fell asleep.

When she awoke, she knew what she had to do. She just hoped when the time came, she really could.

ALCATRAZ

On a cold still morning lost in fog, Billy and Sadie waited to board a boat called *Clearwater*, in honor of the fifteen thousand dollars the Creedence Clearwater Revival musicians had donated to the Indians from a benefit rock concert. Billy's head still ached, intensifying the hole left from losing Webb. First his family, then Webb, Billy wondered what next would be ripped from him.

Joining Billy, Mal, and Red were the captain and six other guys, all of whom were Indians. Their long, dark hair was parted down the middle.

They all held their breath as Mal boarded. Even with the UAW banner tucked under his arm, Mal made it just fine. From the Hawaiian tune he hummed, Mal was in pretty good spirits. Sadie leapt onboard behind him.

Red spoke to the captain. "We're from the UAW

East Bay executive board."

"Heard you were coming. Welcome aboard."

Everyone introduced each other as they handed down boxes of foodstuffs, clothes, and blankets they'd brought to support those on Alcatraz. One guy slurred his words, obviously drunk.

Billy picked up a box of his girl's outgrown clothing left behind at the house. As he did, he spotted someone marching down the pier, back-lit in the foggy morning light. Squinting, Billy raised a happy hand. Webb made it in time after all.

The shadow materialized into Janice and Remi with their latest convert in tow.

Webb was dead.

Billy turned to Red and demanded, "What are they doing here?"

"Hell, it can't hurt to hear them out."

"You know about this, Mal?" asked Billy.

Avoiding him, Mal held up the UAW banner he insisted they bring along for publicity.

"Anyone want to help me with this?" Mal asked.

A guy named Threefingers, a self-described *Anishinabe* with all of his fingers and a knit cap pulled down over his ears, followed Mal to the front of the boat.

Billy started to board. Remi shouted for him to wait up.

"Hell, Billy, I'm telling you," said Red. "Arm up with the girls, we win hands down."

Then the girls were upon them.

Janice motioned to Paul, a new assembler—young and rebellious and an easy mark—slouching next to her with a scowl on his face.

"You remember Paul, don't you, Billy?" Janice asked.

"Sure. Hey, Paul."

Paul nodded and yawned, like early morning wasn't his thing. Red helped the women into the cabin, without speaking much. With all the other women who'd been hired since the Civil Rights Act, Janice and Remi weren't such an oddity in the factory anymore.

SAILING ACROSS THE SAN Francisco Bay to Angel Island, Maja sat on one side of Gerald's yacht, still confused about which side was port and which was starboard. As the wind tugged the main sail, Maja slipped under a taut wire stretched in front of her. Holding tight to the cable, she leaned out over the water, becoming more liquid than solid form. Wind whistled with the sea. The cables cut into the palms of her hands.

In spots beyond the Golden Gate Bridge, the afternoon fog burned off where blue sky and water merged. Cold, brilliant sunshine glinted off a line of sea lions bobbing toward the city, like a string of shiny, black pearls. The skyline shimmered in blue shadows and white spines, as seagulls soared in the wake of the little boat trailing the yacht.

Gerald's voice rose from behind Maja and carried above the wind and the seals, as he joked at the wheel with his friend Charles and Charles's girlfriend, Clarissa. Gerald waved. Maja lifted a hand and quickly re-gripped the wire. When no one was watching, she leaned back. The boat sliced through the water and created a smooth swath. Seaspray wet her face. Salt formed on her lips.

With the ends of her hair trailing in the bay, the words to "You Don't Own Me" played in her head. Maja longed to live her life the way she wanted, say and do whatever she pleased, as the song said. For her own true liberation, first she had to act according to her own beliefs, most of which she found more and more stood in direct conflict with both Gerald's and Mother's expectations.

ON THE DECK OF the *Clearwater* with Sadie, Billy watched as fog drifted over the top half of the Bay Bridge. The expanse was clear all the way from San Francisco to the tip of the long, flat landmass of Treasure Island. From Treasure Island to Oakland, with the span locked in fog, sleek lines turned boxy and coarse.

Ma's old house hid high in the Oakland hills. The one time she'd ever seemed truly happy was the year or two they'd lived there. Grandma even came for a visit. Then Ray went and lost his license for drunk driving, and the bank foreclosed on them.

The bay was choppy. Puke-green caps sprayed Billy. Tugging up the collar of his pea jacket, he hunkered down. Still his cheeks froze, his ears turned numb, and his head wound throbbed.

Yellowdrum, the drunk of the group, leaned over the side railing. "We ain't Indians, you know?"

Hearing him speak, Sadie's tail thumped the deck.

"We've been here a whole lot longer than America, so we're not Native Americans neither." Yellowdrum lost it right in the bay.

Scratching Sadie behind the ears, Billy shook his head. Then he remembered visiting Billy Wolfe, who he was named after, with Grandma in San Quentin. Now Billy was on his way to another prison.

Janice poked her head out from the cabin below. "Come talk to us."

With the boat rocking so much, Billy didn't care to go below. Hoping for warmth, though, he clambered down the steps and peered into the cabin for a place to sit. The kid wedged in a booth between Janice and Remi gave a look that Billy wanted to flip off. The kid called himself a communist. Likely didn't even know what that was.

Red faced them on the opposite side of the table. Mal stood with his legs spread apart, and his arms braced against either wall. Sadie settled between the big man's feet as Billy slid in next to Red.

"Coffee?" asked Janice.

"Sure," Billy said.

Janice nudged Remi, who got to her feet and banged around at the tiny kitchen counter.

"It's never too early to talk about the next election," said Janice.

"Let's make things easy and negotiate right up front," Billy said.

Even as he spoke the words, Billy knew he wasn't a negotiator. Brenda was right. The essence of politics was negotiation and compromise. Billy had learned that the hard way. You gave things away, sometimes nearly everything, to gain one thing. If that didn't work, inflict pressure from the outside. Dissident factions he could unite, or so he once believed. Negotiation and compromise, though? Not his thing.

"Nobody gives a shit about the guys." Billy leaned forward. "Do you give a shit about the guys, Paul?"

"We're being asked to produce an inferior product in unsafe conditions with unfair pay," Paul said as if he were reciting in grade school. "There's no possibility for exportation or market increase. Consumers sure as hell aren't going to continue buying shitty cars and trucks. Management is making it so we'll eventually work ourselves out of a job."

Hearing the words from his strike speech, Billy leaned back. He warmed his hands on the coffee cup.

"Times have changed," said Janice. "A revolution is underway. The younger guys want in."

"You're wrong," Billy said. "The revolution is

over. And who the hell are you to tell me what to do anyway? Red and Mal and me? We're the only real deals here. We work to feed our families."

Paul rose up and leaned across the table. Red reached out a hand to back off the kid.

"I'm sure we can work something out." Red spoke easily.

Hating him, Billy looked at the kid and saw himself.

"You've moved to the right. The strike made you cynical," said Janice. "You need to step up, Billy. You have to show the guys you're still one of them."

"I'm done putting the guys on any more high balls."

"We don't need him," said the kid.

"Hell, I ain't doing this without Billy." Red rose to his feet.

Mal moved forward. Billy motioned Mal back and pulled Red down beside him. Their loyalty jarred his senses.

He'd lived his entire life on the turbulent surface of things, fueling and fighting the same misunderstandings, petty jealousies, and quarrels that hung in the cabin. He'd lost everything, including his own fear and ambition.

"The kid's right," Billy said. "You're a lot better off without me. The guys, too. You need Paul now. Not me."

STRIPED SPINNAKERS LEANED INTO the wind. White-caps stood out against the dark depths. The salty world of fish and rocks and seals lay hidden below. Maja, too, felt safely hidden away out here, a welcome break from the constant threat of Mr. Evans.

Alcatraz appeared upside down on Maja's left. She ducked under the wire. Studying the island, she smoothed her hair into a ponytail and squeezed out the water.

A tall narrow building next to a beige two-story, and even the land itself, looked hard and cold and dismal. A flock of water birds circled the dock where a few people huddled. Rocks climbed out of the sea, where an old stone retaining wall hugged the earth. An arched cement banister ran along the far side of the island, with tall grasses and yucca trees surround-ing a water tower with *Indian Land* printed in bold black letters.

To the left beyond the tower, fog faded from the Golden Gate Bridge. To the right stood Sausalito with its forest of ship masts. Angel Island appeared to be floating on a cloud. Alcatraz, the prison, stood stark in the midst of the surrounding beauty.

"Nixon called out the National Guard." Gerald held out his hands to Maja. "It's high time we storm the place and arrest the whole mess of them," he said.

Feeling chilled, Maja let him help her to her feet. "I wish we could stop. I'd love to see what's happening."

"When the Indians are gone, we'll make a day of it."

Maja and Gerald faced each other at the back of the boat, well out of reach of the boom. Maja opened her mouth, and then shook her head and sighed.

"I don't think so," she answered.

"Why you're trembling," he said. "You look absolutely wretched. What have you done to yourself?"

"I'm tired."

"You're sick."

She brushed off her windbreaker and low-slung cotton bell-bottom pants. "I came on the boat with you to discu—"

"Not now," Gerald said quickly. "We'll talk after a light dinner. I promise."

"On our way back, right after dinner." Maja reminded him of his promise to get her back before dark.

Having been unsuccessful at arranging a meeting at the studio and even at his office, when Gerald suggested this outing, Maja had seized the opportunity.

"There, there," Gerald said, patting her on the shoulder. "Go below. Take a nap. Go on now."

OUTSIDE, A BITTER WIND gusted. The sun had risen above the fog, but gave off no warmth. During the talk with the girls, for once in his life, Billy hadn't blurted out whatever words popped in his head. He'd kept back certain words and pushed away others.

Out of the mist, a desolate-looking water tower appeared. Big black letters covered the top.

Peace and Freedom
Welcome
Home of the Free
Indian Land

A lump formed in his throat, and his chest swelled. Billy took his first deep breath in years.

As the *Clearwater* approached the island, monster waves slammed against the rocks. A lone man huddled on a rocky crag with a tipi towering behind him. Beyond stood a mess of government-issued prison buildings, sterile, and as razor sharp as the factory.

Threefingers leaned up against the railing next to him at the bow of the boat.

"We have lookouts stationed on all sides of the island day and night." Threefingers pointed to the man at the tipi.

Billy nodded. The guy had pride in what they'd put together on Alcatraz.

The boat came around the island, where men stood on a flat cement dock atop piers and posts out over the water. Behind them emerged a four-story beige building with elongated red letters.

You are now on Indian land.

Looming over the building stood a burned-out lighthouse and a structure with no roof. Smudges like blackened flames on the walls outside the windows showed the direction the wind had been blowing during a fire. The stark reminder of what the island was, first and foremost, and always had been—a prison—turned his stomach queasy.

As the *Clearwater* slowed, everyone clustered on deck. Water crashed against gigantic landing posts. Billy spread his legs and clutched the boat railing.

"How do we get from here to there?" Janice pointed up at the six to ten feet to the dock landing.

An upsurge of water pitched the *Clearwater* five feet higher and dropped them into a ten-foot trough.

"The Feds confiscated all the landings." Three-fingers shouted over the wind.

Even in the aquatic roller coaster, they were able to tie the boat to the pier. Wind froze Billy's face and tightened his wound. Mist and fog seeped into his bones. From above, a couple of guys swung out a makeshift-landing platform that the wind tossed like a toy. Using a series of pulleys, the landing lowered inch by inch. All of them in the boat reached up in unison to keep the platform from smashing into them.

When it was his turn, Billy jumped from the boat to the platform with Sadie right beside him. He grabbed her collar and clutched the rebar pole.

Threefingers gestured to him and shouted. "Stay dead center."

Mal scrambled on. The landing platform tee-tered. Janice screamed. Sadie started to slide.

"Hell, straddle the middle, Mal," shouted Red.

Mal grabbed Billy's arm, his grip like a vise. The platform leveled.

Threefingers closed a little gate behind Mal, giving the big man something to grab hold of besides Billy, just as the wind flicked them forward. Billy clutched the railing and squatted low beside Sadie. Below them, Paul looked green, which pleased Billy to no end.

On the island, a woman with a headband pulled over her forehead, rode a bicycle through a puddle of water. The peace sign she flashed reminded Billy of Wisaw, and added to the gloom of the island.

When they were all standing on solid ground, Billy asked Threefingers, "What's it was like living in a place built for punishment?"

"No worse than living on the reservation," he answered. "Come on. Everyone's waiting at Cell Block 10."

Billy felt nauseous, but it wasn't seasickness. The cracked cement and falling plaster, a little girl with no shoes, and a boy without a coat, were all reminders of the poverty he'd lived with as a kid. His hands broke into a sweat even in the damp and fog.

Janice, Remi, and the kid went with the others from the boat up the hill. Mal, Red, and Billy followed more slowly with Threefingers, and Sadie racing ahead. Billy lagged behind. Mal's attention turned to the sound of kids' laughter. Out of shape, the big man puffed hard on the uphill walk.

"Urban kids have had little or no tribal contact," explained Threefingers. "We put them in art classes and a crafts' training center where they learn skills normally passed from one generation to the next. Beadwork, leatherwork, woodcarving, costume decoration, dance, like that."

The further they hiked, the harder it was for Billy to put one foot in front of the other. Every step, ghosts passed through him. They could have been convicts. To him, they felt tribal.

"Hippies wear headbands and want to be Indians," continued Threefingers. "Too many of us don't even know what that means, being Indian. The children know the occupation of this island, the fact that we defy the entire United States government, is for them, for the future of all tribes. Being here together is like coming home."

Red cupped his hands and blew them to keep warm.

"Is that why we don't see more people?" asked Mal. "Because of the cold?"

"Everyone's preparing for tonight's *pauwau*, or as white people pronounce it, a pow wow," said Threefingers. "You'll see more people as the day picks up. This is the one place Native Americans of all tribes can come together. Making a trip to Alcatraz has become a pilgrimage. After the first month or so, most of us moved out of the cells, too drafty and cold, and into the main block. Not much farther now."

Hearing they weren't going to the actual prison block, the weight of a full-sized Mac truck lifted from Billy's chest. Sadie rushed a yellow mutt running up to them with its ears plastered against its head. Threefingers introduced Many Moons. The two dogs took off up the hill.

"We have a live turkey, two ducks, several rabbits, chickens, and a couple dogs. What tribe are you?" asked Threefingers.

Billy shrugged at the looks of surprise Red and Mal shot him. Secretly he was pleased Threefingers picked it out in him.

"Your friends don't know," Threefingers said, nodding his head. "I'm not surprised. We get good at hiding it. I can always tell. You get real quiet when you first arrive here. You think it's the prison, but it's being on Indian land."

"*Bode'wadmi ndaw.* My mother's side," said Billy.

"No shit?" Mal looked hurt.

"People of the place of the fire," said Threefingers. "*Bozho.*"

"*Iwgwien,*" Billy replied, as a way of thanking Threefingers for his welcome. He hoped he said it right.

"Your people and my people are two of the traditional alliance of three known as the Council of Three Fires," said Threefingers.

Mal shook his head like he couldn't register that Billy was part Indian and never told him.

"Your people were moved from the Great Lakes

to Oklahoma during the Trail of Death?"

Billy nodded. After a moment of silence, he pointed to a craggy point where kids were fishing. Beyond them, whitecaps dotted the bay.

"What kind of fish?" he asked.

"Red snapper, bay perch, smelt," Threefingers answered. "They're snagging dinner for tonight's celebration."

"I thought a pow wow was something the white man made up," said Red.

"The old chiefs say the children need a *pauwau*. 'He who has revelations.' I think we all do," explained Threefingers. "Most of us who first arrived here were idealistic college students. The people coming now are older. Some of them are pretty screwed up, scarred from Vietnam, cynical, and some with serious addiction problems. The elders want to share what they can."

Threefingers stopped in front of the long low building. "Here we are. Hungry?"

He escorted them into a makeshift kitchen where three giant pots bubbled with something that made Billy's mouth water. His stomach turned weak. Groups of people laughed and talked. Janice waved from where she and Remi and Paul were headed to sit down.

Instead of joining the others, Billy sat across from Threefingers, next to an old woman who scooted over to make room for him. Being around so many Indians was rubbing off on him. There was a lost and lonely feeling deep inside he'd suffered from probably all his life. Now it didn't ache quite so bad.

AFTER AN EARLY DINNER of grilled halibut filets, salad, French bread—with Gerald and his friends drinking two bottles of white wine—Maja was upset when Charles yanked the starter line on the little boat. Rather than sail back now as promised, Gerald motored them to Angel Island. Maja wanted this to be over.

Beyond a small cove, an old deserted military building sat on a flat knoll. Behind it, rose a hill and deserted officers' housing.

At the beach, Maja and Clarissa disembarked while Gerald and Charles dragged the little boat onshore. Maja spotted a pure white sand dollar on the beach. Mermaid money washed up out of the deep from one of Mormor's fairy tales.

Gerald came up to her. She slipped the shell in her pocket.

"Alrighty, then," Gerald said, studying his watch. "Sunset at five-thirty. We motor back no later than six."

Charles and his girlfriend left to walk along the beach.

"We were supposed to sail back after dinner. What happened?" asked Maja.

Without answering, and carrying a brown paper bag, Gerald started up a narrow foot trail.

"I'd rather we talk here," she said, motioning to a picnic table.

When he didn't stop but kept walking, she

caught up to him leaning against a eucalyptus tree. The Golden Gate Bridge shone in the distance as if perched on his shoulder. A breeze carried the calming medicinal scent of eucalyptus.

"This will make you all better," he promised, sucking white powder up his nose. He offered her a tiny spoonful of what she recognized as cocaine.

Having struggled to finally quit smoking pot, she wasn't about to start something new. She shook her head no. He shrugged and snorted the spoonful himself.

Gerald kept on the dirt trail to the top of the hill. At the entrance to a three-story military building, he wagged his finger for her to follow him. Inside the abandoned building, Gerald handed Maja the bag he'd been carrying.

"The bottom steps are gone as part of the park's effort to disable all the old military buildings on what's now a defunct post."

Maja glanced in the bag and passed a hand over her forehead at the bottle of champagne. She sneezed and lost her breath. To Gerald, champagne meant victory and success.

He dragged a tree stump beneath an empty window frame. Using the windowsill as support, he scrambled up to what was now the bottom step. He leaned down, took the bottle of champagne first, and then gave Maja a hand-up.

At the top floor, she forgot all about Gerald as she moved from one empty window frame to the next. Around and around, the world she'd grown up in flashed through the openings.

AFTER EATING, BILLY PRESENTED Threefingers with a check from the UAW, and they all smoked pot together. Threefingers left and returned with an old man. Chief White Cloud wore beaded buckskin moccasins laced to the knees and fringed around the top, buckskin pants, and no shirt. The chief welcomed them and thanked them for coming.

"*Bozho nikan. Ahaw nciwe'nmoyan ewabmlman. Iwgwien 'ebyayen ms'ote*," he said.

Billy was surprised to hear the old man speaking Grandma's language. He returned the greeting.

"*Bozho nikan.*"

The chief offered a tour of the cellblock and the old, underground Army prison where military POW and deserters were housed during the Civil War.

Janice bowed out. "We'd love to stay, but it's getting late. We have work to get back to."

Paul looked relieved. No beer or alcohol was allowed on the island. Red and Mal wouldn't stay any longer than they had to either.

Outside, Sadie and Many Moons greeted them with tails wagging. Billy offered the bacon he'd stashed in his coat pocket. Each dog pulled back their mouth in giant grins.

Everyone said their goodbyes and took off for the docking area. Red huddled close to Janice and the kid. Red would secure their endorsement and be reelected just as he wanted. Mal had been recently chosen as the United Auto Workers' goodwill ambassador to China. In less than a month, he was leaving on a ninety-day tour of Chairman Mao's Cultural Revolution at a time when no one was allowed into Red China. Choosing Mal made sense, somewhere in the middle between Chicanos and Blacks and Whites.

Knowing his friends were going to be fine without him, Billy stayed behind. When Sadie saw he wasn't following the others, she barked. Mal turned around.

"Go on ahead," said Billy. "I'm sticking around."

Mal looked like he wanted to say something, and then decided against it. Billy nodded. He took a deep breath with no wheezing or coughing.

Threefingers went with the others down the hill to the boat landing. Chief White Cloud led Billy in the opposite direction.

"You feel it, don't you?"

"What?"

"Reconnecting with your grandmother," said the chief. "Knowing you come from a people. The feeling you belong for no other reason than part of you is Indian."

Not bothering to ask how he knew about Grandma, Billy admitted he felt it. And, for the first time, he truly did.

"I have to stick around to prepare for tonight. Many Moons will take you and your friend to join the others on the beach. Later, you'll be given a new name, new responsibilities, and privileges decided by the Council of the Clan Mothers' visions and sense of your destiny."

"Doesn't it make you mad?" asked Billy. "Living under a government that destroyed your way of life?"

Sadie trotted back to him and sat at his feet. Many Moons waited to guide them to the beach.

"We are, each tribe, a sovereign nation," said the chief. "They stripped us of everything sacred and tried to shatter us. And we're still standing. Ancient wisdom holds that when all the tribes come together as one people, peace will return to the earth. Young people demand we fight using the white man's way with guns and bullets and annihilation. The festival tonight is to remind them there's another way."

Billy nodded.

"You don't reek of the white man's poison," said the chief.

"Almost a year now."

"After tonight, it will be forever."

Chief White Cloud turned to go. Many Moons barked. The chief snapped his fingers and turned back.

"You were once given the name Running Wolf. I heard it on the wind."

Billy peered into the chief's eyes.

"What else do you know about me?" Billy asked.

The chief's face crinkled into a knowing smile. "You've learned the hard way to control your mouth.

That's good. Now it's time to listen to your heart and stay alert. A reward waits to reveal itself to you."

Billy watched the chief leave, his words echoing in his head. Then he trailed Sadie and Many Moons along a cement path and banister running along the water. In places, an arched support structure of stone was exposed.

Making their way around the island, Billy came to more than one place where the path had crumbled into waves lapping against the rocks. Many Moons showed him where to jump. Drums and rattles and laughter sounded from beyond the next bend.

Out here, where there wasn't a sign of the prison, he let the wind buffet him. He was homeless. Dylan's words played in his mind. Would he always be on his own and a rolling stone?

The wind picked up and was the only sound he heard. The sun had come out and, although he couldn't feel its heat, light rippled off the water.

In the distance, the outline of a sailboat reminded him of the dream vision Brenda went on about. Wisaw and her parents and grandmother at the candy store, a new Cadillac, shiny shoes, a full stomach—his inspiration for wealth and security and everything he'd failed to achieve. Still, off on his own, with the bay and the gulls and dogs for company, Billy felt strangely at peace.

Rubbing two coins together deep in his pocket made him ready to reclaim Grandma's carving. His eyes watered.

Spinning from one window to the next in the deserted military building, Maja stopped. A gigantic bonfire blazed at the tip of Alcatraz. A group of people circled a giant drum. As sparks flew, people on the beach danced one way around the fire and then back the way they had come. The solid and consistent beat spread a fire of certainty in her mind.

"Gerald, I—"

"When school is over," he interrupted. "I'll see to it that you never put yourself through this kind of torment again. It kills me to see you work so hard."

"I love the work I do with children," she said, annoyed.

Gerald moved behind her. Now that it was clear he wasn't going to make this easy for her—not that she expected him to—she was uncomfortable not being able to read his reaction. She was also relieved at not having him study her face as she went on speaking.

"I've been offered a position at a school for autistic kids in San Francisco." She tucked her hair behind her ears. "I move to the city next month."

She kept quiet about her plans for converting the east wing of Great Oaks into a school and home for autistic kids—he didn't need to know that.

A champagne pop came from behind her, just as a giant flame licked the sky, stoking history and lighting her ideas with success. A little way off from the drummers and dancers on the beach, a man faced the wind. He was too far away to make out his features, but Maja felt as if she recognized him. Two dogs sat on either side of him on the beach.

In that moment, Maja knew she was absolutely where she ought to be. Seeing the man and his dogs felt like a fitting end to this season of her life.

She turned. Gerald pushed a flute of champagne toward her. She put up a hand and shook her head no.

"Let's toast to school being a thing of the past," he said, nudging the glass at her until she took it.

Maja put the glass on a window ledge without taking a drink.

"Well, no, actually the past is me modeling for you," she said.

"In the meantime, this is so you won't be mad at me anymore." Gerald withdrew a long rectangular velvet box from his jacket.

"Mad?"

"I offended you about your necklace," he said. "I wanted the gold setting engraved, which is why it took me so long to make up for my insensitivity about your carving. Open it."

Maja hesitated. With his tongue tucked in his lower lip, Gerald lifted the lid himself. Moonlight flickered off a delicate gold linked chain with a solitary empire-cut diamond as big as a pea.

Maja gasped and looked away. Gerald lifted the necklace out of the box.

"It's as old or older than your carving," he said. "I know how much you loved your carving, and still you gave it up for me. This is my show of appreciation."

Maja unzipped her windbreaker and pulled out the wolf from under her turtleneck with cold, stiff fingers. "I wear the carving," she said, her voice distant and unemotional.

"Forget about that. Marry me."

Maja shook her head, weary from her own idiocy. Months ago she had sensed a change in him and, rather than deal with it, she'd ignored the warning.

Gerald took her face in both his hands. Maja's legs turned rubbery. The moment represented the kind of romance that made her ache with envy, and every inch of her long for true love.

"Say you'll marry me."

Maja backed up as the fire on Alcatraz grew larger. The drums beat louder. Lesley Gore's words came back to her: *You don't own me.* The words kept going round and round in her mind.

"I'm grateful for all you've done for me," Maja said, avoiding eye contact with him. "I never could have returned to school so quickly if not for you. The decisions you've made on my behalf have benefited me greatly."

He cut in front of her view. "I'll go right on making the right decisions for you. If you insist on working, you can move into the penthouse in San Francisco—"

Maja couldn't get the song's words out of her mind.

"I don't want you to make my decisions."

"Don't say no to me," Gerald said in a warning tone. "I've waited a long time for you."

Aware of a change in him, Maja edged toward the stairs. "I think you are—"

Gerald shot out an arm, snatched her by the wrist, and held her there. Maja turned rigid.

"I don't want you to think. You're not any good at it. I'll do the thinking for both of us. Marry me, and consider me your full-time job."

His words cut her. He acted as if he was still wired.

"No." The little two-letter word left Maja's lips and rebounded against her ears. She stood a bit taller.

"No," she said again and twisted from his grasp.

He took a swig of champagne and smashed the bottle against the concrete wall

Maja had never seen him angry. She ran down the stairs and jumped at the end to the bottom floor. Gerald followed her.

"Does your mother know about your plans?"

"She will. And, I'll tell her myself this time. It's time I learn how to talk to my own mother."

"You always make a mess of things with her," he said. "You know you will again."

Maja felt a growl rise in her throat.

"You're quite good at throwing my weaknesses at me, aren't you?" She trembled, not with fear but with anger. "It's time I take care of myself. And Gerald, when my contract is up in June, I'm done.

I'm a woman now. I'm finished with being the Reingor Girl."

"Now, just you wait a minute." Gerald practically shouted. "I have a great deal of money invested in you."

"And I thought you wanted me to be your wife," said Maja.

FREEDOM

UNABLE TO SLEEP ON the morning of the award ceremony, Maja dressed well before dawn. Before driving out to Great Oaks to pick up Daddy and Mother, she had a make a stop.

Having laid out the night before what she planned to wear, she took her time dressing—all in black. Stuffing her long blonde hair under a black knit cap, she surveyed herself in the mirror. Her pale face shone like a white light against the dark. She considered smudging black eyeliner across her cheeks but decided against it.

A darkened Shattuck Avenue was devoid of students with morning classes and the usual throngs of city commuters. She went through the steps for the ten billionth time—unknowns gnawed holes in her plan and left gaping caverns of anxiety dripping in her stomach—when something zipped out of the corner of her eye. Startled, she shook her head.

"Get a grip," she chastised herself and shivered.

A figure shot in front of the GTO. Maja slammed on her brakes. Whatever it was—human, part-human, beast—was clothed in dull trappings. One, or possibly even three, long, frayed, and paper-thin overcoats covered a bulky sweater and balloon-like pants. As Maja strained her eyes to determine what she was seeing, something bumped the rear of her car.

Confused, she looked both ways. Had a wrong turn landed her in this dark haunting world? She slowed at a blinking yellow light and locked her car door. Something stirred to her left. Twisting her head, before she could fix her eyes on what she was seeing, movement tracked in the opposite direction.

Faces wrapped in mufflers and shawls, people limped and sprinted, dashed and galloped, slunk and scooted—as silent as the night—like a shadow species, back and forth across the wide lanes. All shapes and sizes of people with full pockets and heavy bags. Grocery store shopping carts were swollen with bits of boxes and curious shapes of lost treasures.

Here, in the dark among the invisible, Maja's heart slowed. Whispers and betrayals and broken hearts, these vagabonds understood as she did the power of silence. They, as she, felt the urge to move ever away from the center—out from what was, far from judgment and ridicule, while expanding toward change, toward what could be.

Mr. Evans lived on the opposite side of campus in a three-story apartment building beside a line of identical buildings. The relief at seeing his black Stingray parked alone in the red zone caused her foot to slip from the gas. Flanking the far side of the walkway and framing his car stood a giant storage container. Beyond the container was a desolate-looking treeless field of weeds littered with old tires. Crags rose in the distance.

Her advisor's wing was dark, except for one solitary light burning in the front window of the third-floor apartment, two doors down from his. Someone was up and moving on the other side of sheer curtains. Mr. Evans wouldn't be awake this early; it was not his style. Still, she didn't like that someone else was up.

Maja parked the GTO two blocks away. The street was empty. She opened her car door and left it ajar, so as not to disturb the quiet. A wren heralded the brightening in the eastern foothills.

As she opened the trunk, a thick, low-hanging cloud of turpentine and paint crept out. Reeling at the smell, she questioned what she was doing. If she simply reported the car, no way could he manage the fee to get his car from the impound lot based on the unpaid bills she'd spotted in his apartment. His apartment. The stench of his breath. His sweat. The sound of his laughter at her pain.

She jerked on an old pair of Daddy's gardening gloves and snatched the short rope she'd braided with strips of Mother's painting rags.

Leaves fell around Maja as she marched toward the Stingray, her nose numb from the stench of fresh solvent. She tripped over a twig in her path. Her hand shook. Had she over-doused the rags? Within, she repeated over and over again:

My goal is to be safe. I deserve to be loved. I deserve to be safe.

She switched hands and untwisted the car's gas cap.

I am safe. I am safe. I am safe.

The wren fell silent.

She stuck the rags in the gas tank, leaving a tail hanging out. Her hand steady now, she slid back the top of the matchbox. Sparking a match against the flint, she broke the matchstick in two. The lit end snuffed itself out on the ground.

She fumbled for another, steeling her shoulders sure her advisor was right behind her. The matchstick blazed, burned her fingertips. She dropped it. Still burning, she picked up the match. Using both hands, she held it under the fuse.

The fire caught.

Maja walked away, then quickened her pace and ran.

Just as she reached the GTO, the explosion hit. The smell of smoke stank of gasoline and oil, cruelty and pain. Beneath the stench was something Maja decided tasted a lot like freedom.

Maja turned onto the wooden bridge to Great Oaks with the radio blasting, all the windows down, and a flapping heart. She belted out the words to Dolly Parton's "Just Because I'm a Woman" with more than a twinge of longing in her voice.

Stopping behind Gerald's Lamborghini, Maja left the engine idling and radio playing. The musty scent of her favorite oak tree floated dream murmurs from the days she hid from Clay, while painting rainbow colors around the boy that birds seemed to whisper in the tree's sheltering arms.

Gerald reached through the window and switched off the car. Silence breathed her name.

Mother motioned from the portico. "No more daydreaming, Maja. Come inside."

The same words Maja had heard as a child, calling her home, softened her heart and reminded her of who she was today.

Gerald opened the door and offered his hand. Maja emerged without his help.

"Mother invited you," she said, her voice hoarse from singing.

"What's that smell?" Gerald said, leaning in and sniffing at her. "Why do you smell of gasoline?"

Humming Parton's words, Maja walked toward the house where Mother stood framed in the big picture window overlooking the driveway. Her hair was parted down the middle with bangs and flipped up on the ends. She wore a coachman style V-necked dress with white piping and little white buttons running double-breasted down the front—Reingor's woman's line down to the white, fine-net stockings.

Inside, the Kingston Trio sang from the stereo about some folks being good and some being bad, and others just doing the best they could.

"I'll see if Daddy's ready," Maja said by way of a greeting to Mother.

Lines of irritation shattered the skin between Mother's eyes.

"Nurse Patricia is giving him a bite to eat. Then she's helping him shower and shave. I've asked Carmen to prepare a light lunch for Gerald and the two of us on the veranda. Nurse Patricia will have your father dressed and ready for the award ceremony. I promise."

That Mother would go to such trouble to eliminate any chance of her leaving softened Maja even more.

"I'll meet you outside in just a minute," she said, and walked into Daddy's deserted study.

She was relieved to find the curtains closed and room dark. Standing behind the desk Daddy no longer had any use for, Maja picked up the telephone and made a call to her attorney.

"Are you at your home number?" asked his secretary "He'll call you right back."

"It's important," said Maja.

After a short wait, Samuel came on the line.

"Hello, Maja," he said. "How can I help you?"

"A man has been posing as my academic advisor. I want you to have him arrested and prosecuted."

Then she gave Samuel Mr. Evans' name and address.

"How's that?"

"If you can't do it, hire someone who can."

Maja didn't need a woman at the academic center to tell her that the university didn't employ Mr. Evans. She had known in her bones he was an imposter and denied it since the day she met him.

"He hurt me. I want him punished."

"What happened?"

Just as she had never spoken about what Clay had done to her, Maja would never speak about what Mr. Evans had done. Knowing he had a criminal record would be enough for her.

"That isn't important," she said. "Get a restraining order. I'll check back with you later this afternoon."

With the telephone on the cradle, Maja fell into Daddy's chair. She put her head in her hands, and took long, deep breaths. Then she went out on the veranda. Mother and Gerald sat at the table overlooking the rolling hills. Gerald rose to his feet and pulled out a chair for Maja.

"You know how proud I am of you," said Mother, motioning for Maja to sit. "To receive an award for the work you've done with children is a great honor but—"

"I'm not so sure it's an award." Maja shook her head at Gerald and stayed on her feet.

"Well, I am." Mother smoothed the front of her skirt.

Mother's confidence surprised Maja.

"What's this I hear about you teaching in the city?" Mother asked.

Maja glanced at Gerald, her neck rigid.

"Your mother asked a direct question. I couldn't lie," he said.

That look had haunted Maja her entire life with the same horrid leer she knew meant ruin. His hands twisted, gleeful, and ready to shape her differently.

"When you and Gerald are married, you'll volunteer with the Junior League," said Mother. "You'll help so many more people that way."

So, Gerald had told Mother about Maja's school plans and remained silent about her refusal of marriage. Mother gushed about the wedding at the country club and whom to invite. Gerald agreed with everything she said.

"I'm not marrying Gerald," said Maja.

Mother and Gerald went on with their wedding plans as if she hadn't spoken.

Carmen smiled and served a luncheon of chicken salad and corn tortillas. Only then did Maja sit down.

"Gracias, mi abuelita," said Maja.

"De nada, mi hija."

Talking to Gerald, Mother looked like a peacock,

stuck in a prideful display around a wedding that would never be. Now that Maja knew the cost of speaking up, speaking out, and speaking back in life, she was willing to pay the price of freedom.

Mother dabbed her lips and folded the cloth napkin on her lap.

"Grace Cathedral is just the spot," said Mother. "Have I told you, Gerald? Maja sang in the church choir at Grace when she was a child."

Dolly Parton's words came back to her: She was glad she wasn't the woman they wanted her to be.

"I'm not getting married," said Maja. A sheen of sweat crept across her forehead and clung to her upper lip. With her throat burning, Maja went on. "Teaching in the city prepares me for the school I told you about starting here. When our plans are complet—"

Carmen emerged from the house carrying a tiny wedding cake complete with a tiny bride and a groom atop the second tier. Upon seeing the cake, Mother clasped her hands together and sighed.

Maja plucked the plastic couple off the cake top and tossed them on the table.

"I don't love Gerald," she said.

Gerald's complexion turned a few shades grayer. In that moment Maja saw him as an old man, keeping track of social connections, brunching with Mother on Sundays and bragging about his latest acquisitions, gossiping about so-called friends in a schedule that revolved around appointments to have his hair styled, nails buffed, new suits cut to order, keeping up with regular doctor visits. The same thing every day, never very happy, always striving, looking for more, always dull, predictable, and petty.

"Marriage of convenience was for your generation," Maja said, calmer as the tight tangle of emotions unraveled. "Lots of people my age want to make a difference for others. We want our actions and words to align with the truths we believe in.

"I've had Samuel set up a fund for you and Daddy," Maja continued. "I wouldn't be where I am now if you hadn't pushed me, Mother. Left to my own devices, I would have hidden away from the world. You threw me under the lights. In spite of myself, I flourished. I've made a great deal of money. I've also made a lot of mistakes. Along the way, I found something I love doing. Something I'd do for free. I never felt that way about modeling."

Maja looked over Mother's shoulder and grinned. Mother and Gerald turned.

Standing in the archway dressed in a three-piece suit, Daddy looked just as he always had, powerful and handsome and brave.

"Ready ... kiddo?"

Maja went to him and took his arm.

"I'm ready," she said.

1971

Generations ago, a young boy stumbled across a wounded timber wolf in the forest. The boy fed the wolf and nursed her wounds. Once healed, she returned to her pack. The boy often ventured deep into the woods to stay with her and play with her pups.

The males taught him strength and endurance, how to be part of the pack and still embody his own individual dreams and ideas.

The females taught him about loyalty and our deep desire for affection—all he needed to know in readiness for the "other".

As the boy grew into a man, he prepared to enter the civilized world by marrying. To bring honor to his beloved, he carved me from a piece of oak. The man and his wife lived happily together for many moons.

The time has come for the Grandson and Wisaw Ninsesen Kwe's last opportunity to reach the same spot at the same time. If they decide once and for all that the intersections of their lives were nothing more than chance encounters, they'll forever be out of step with the other. Or … they walk into their final test. The choice is theirs.

GOLDEN GATE PARK

UP BEFORE DAWN, MAJA skipped down the steps of her San Francisco apartment building. As the rest of the city slept, a rumbling blue newspaper truck idled as an old man filled a stand with stories of drug overdoses, the number of dead in Vietnam, and the ratification of the constitutional amendment giving eighteen-year-olds the right to vote.

Veils of dew dripped from overhead streetcar cables that shivered and moaned. Smoke from the chimney of a shabby Victorian mixed with the scent of the sea. On the sidewalk in front of her, a pile of battered cardboard boxes against a dry-cleaner's storefront collapsed as a straggly hippie emerged without a sound.

Hugging the architectural plans for the school for autistic children at Great Oaks, Maja stepped off the sidewalk and slipped into Golden Gate Park through a break in the crumbling rock wall. Full moon shadows cut through a protective stand of trees that blocked the unsteady stream of sleep-walking cars.

As a breeze promised warmth, her stomach pleaded for a hash-brown sandwich at Lou's Place. Maja hurried along the shortcut through the park.

BILLY STOOD ON THE flat cement dock along with most of the inhabitants of Alcatraz to bid him farewell.

"I send the blessings of the first people with you now and forever," said the young Cherokee woman who'd interviewed Billy in an effort to retrieve everything related to Grandma's native ways. She sprinkled water at his feet.

An older Lakota man who had dug deeper, bringing up recollections Billy had about Great Grandmother Martha Curly, held up the leather notebook where he'd transcribed Billy's earliest memories, and smiled.

Great Grandmother Martha Curly was still alive when Billy first went to live with Grandma, and he remembered how she used to stumble home drunk gobbling like a turkey. He laughed as he recounted her telling stories of a time when people cast their spirit into an eagle or a hawk and soared over the land. With how dead serious the Lakota scribbled notes in his notebook, Billy understood such an act was a sacred ability and not a laughing matter.

"Thank you, Running Wolf," said Chief White Cloud, clasping Billy's forearm.

Choked up and not wanting to embarrass himself or the others with a show of emotion, Billy bowed his head. Many Moons smiled up at him. Billy dropped to his knees and buried his face in the dog's fur.

After two months on Alcatraz teaching kids the lessons Grandma had taught him, Billy left the people who had become like family to him. With Sadie by his side, he boarded the makeshift-landing platform.

Scrambling onto the *Clearwater* below, he heard a shout and looked up. Chief White Cloud leaned over the side of the dock.

"She'll be riding a white owl," he shouted.

Confused as they motored away, Billy waved an arm goodbye.

As much as he'd needed to get lost in the old ways, he was glad when the boat landed, and he stepped on solid ground. Anyone who'd lived in poverty, thievery, drugs, alcohol, long hours and bone-breaking work wouldn't have it any other way. That wasn't to say he planned to ever go back to any of that. He was ready, however, for whatever disaster, risk, ruin, meaning, and success he was destined for.

An hour before the sun came up and reflected off skyscrapers on the other side of the city, Billy cut through Golden Gate Park. Lighting the way to his favorite all-night coffee shop was the first full moon of summer.

With his stomach grumbling, Billy picked up the pace, passing an old school bus covered with psychedelic designs parked and ticketed on Lincoln Way. He shook his head at all the cats who continued to pour into San Francisco, stuck flowers in their hair, and saw only their dreams of the place.

Thanks to Grandma believing in the tattered and passed-down story about an island of perfect peace and pure happiness on the western edge of the world, this was Billy's home. Grandma made up the part about the streets paved with gold. Even so, rocky shores and strange beasts guarding this place of freedom and acceptance for all who came, and all who dreamed of coming, was the ancestors' way.

After something to eat, Billy planned to call Ma to drive him to Brenda's mother in the East Bay. He wanted his girls to visit Alcatraz to learn about their great grandmother's ways.

A twig cracked. Sadie stuck her nose in the air. Billy sensed more than saw a movement. Someone approached from an adjoining trail. With a finger to his lips, he urged Sadie deeper into the darkness. Unless the person was up to no good, they'd eventually walk into the clearing.

KEEPING TO THE SHADOWS, Maja whispered.

Soon he will be here, for he is coming.

He is coming.

She smiled, remembering the chant from long

ago. Switching the permit papers and renderings of the changes to be made at Great Oaks from one arm to the other, Maja touched the carving hidden beneath a bulky turtleneck sweater. The wood seemed to vibrate with heat.

White flashed high in a redwood tree. An owl with a heart-shaped face stared out from a tree branch. Maja looked behind her and walked a little faster.

The owl swooped down. A dog barked.

BILLY SHUSHED SADIE. TOGETHER they walked into the light, Sadie running ahead.

Wisaw looked startled, and then smiled at the secret they shared.

The owl made a u-turn and circled them. Together, they stood motionless. The owl returned to the branch in the light of the full moon. Then Sadie ran ahead.

"She'll be riding a white owl," Billy said, repeating the words Chief White Cloud had shouted down to him.

Her Madonna smile grew into an all-out grin.

Sadie, with her ears plastered against her head, jumped against Wisaw. The girl stumbled. Billy gave her his hand. Papers floated from the pile in her arms, but she didn't move, seemingly content to hold hands with him forever. Billy waited to see if she'd bring his hands to her nose as she did as child. Or, if she'd bring him near and kiss him.

Instead, she bent to scoop up her papers. Sadie licked her face. Laughing, she pushed her away. Billy squatted beside her to help. Dew seeped into building permits, sticking the papers together.

Billy's arm jostled hers. They stood at the same time. She stumbled, and he caught her again.

Her face turned red. She didn't duck her head.

"I'm not usually so clumsy," she said.

"A tree root." Billy pointed out.

A frog croaked in the long grass just as a streetlight switched off.

"BREAKFAST AT LOU'S PLACE?" Maja said, running out of air at the end.

Smiling, he nodded. "Sure."

"My name's Maja. Maja Hawthorne."

"Billy. Billy Wayman Wolfe."

"It's nice to meet you, Billy Wayman Wolfe." Her toes tingled.

"Likewise, Maja Hawthorne."

As the sun came up, Maja grabbed his hand and pulled him with her. With Sadie leading the way, together, they moved into high spring grass toward a hole in the brush, reached the sidewalk, and leaned into a warm westerly off the bay as if following a plan they'd both decided on a long, long time ago.

The dawning of a brand new day.

EVER AFTER

Running Wolf and Wisaw have succeeded at replacing loneliness with power, expanded their limited views, and learned to listen to the small still voice within— my voice. As they each transformed from small to becoming great, I've guarded them the best I could—sometimes gently, often harshly—and always with great love.

Now it's up to them to prove they are equal to each other in heart and spirit, have learned to keep hold of their individual sovereignty, and are ready to spend the rest of their tomorrows together, having earned entrance to real love.

I'm not going anywhere. I plan to stick around and bear witness to their future …

ACKNOWLEDGMENTS

The idea for this novel started years ago when my husband and I discovered how many of the same places and events we'd both been to at the same time, though separately and long before our first meeting. Thankfully, he has a bottomless store of memories and is a gifted storyteller. It has taken me years of patience, determination, and great perseverance to complete this novel. I couldn't have done it without him, and without the support and love of others.

Thank you editor extraordinaire, Peter Archer, for your help, insight, and support.

Special thanks to Hallee Adelman for sharing your fond treasure and for your friendship and many kindnesses, one of which was sharing my novel with the generous women in your writing group—Eve, Valerie, Heather, Ann, Sharon, Anita. Thank you for your feedback and encouragement.

To my earliest writing group, thank you for your patience and love. Your belief in me as a fiction writer helped me believe in myself—Cyn, Becky, Lee, Beth, and Jackie.

My heartfelt gratitude and appreciation to each of you early readers—Sandra Foster and Linda Woods, Luisa Adams and Teresa Jade LeYung, and Lynn Gordon—for offering your time, comments, and unwavering support along the way to making *PARALLEL LIVES A 60's Love Story* a better novel.

And thank you Paula and Linda for miraculously stepping in at the last minute and lending your expertise.

Last but not least to Bobby for sharing your heart and life and stories with me through thick and thin, and for always believing in me.

Having completed this book, I finally own my own story and have healed my spirit.

ABOUT THE AUTHOR

Born in San Francisco, a fifth-generation Californian, Martha Alderson grew up in the Bay Area in the 50's and 60's, non-verbal and dyslexic. She modeled for a time and then became a speech pathologist. Now as the author of the best-selling *The Plot Whisperer* and *Boundless Creativity: A Spiritual Guide for Overcoming Self-Doubt, Emotional Traps, and Other Creative Blocks*, she takes readers and writers beyond the words into the very heart of the Universal Story, and deep into the creative process. She invites you to visit MarthaAlderson.com and is happy to meet virtually with book groups and writing groups.

ABOUT THE CONTRIBUTOR

Just as World War II ended, Bobby Ray Alderson at three years old traveled by troop train from Oklahoma to California with his Potawatomi Grandmother Ethel Wolfe and uncle Billy Wayman. They settled in Delano where Bobby became a fruit tramp, picking peaches, apricots, and cherries with his grandfather, uncles, and cousins. At nineteen years old, he started working on the assembly line as a proud member of the United Auto Workers. Two years later, he won his first union election and went on to hold office for ten years. He is a member of the Potawatomi Citizen Band in Shawnee, Oklahoma.

Martha and Bobby have been married for nearly forty years. Today, they live in Santa Cruz, each with their own beach bungalow linked together by a secret garden.

Dear Reader,

Thank you so much for reading *PARALLEL LIVES A 60's Love Story*.

If you'd like to support me in achieving my dream of getting my novel into the hands of readers who will enjoy the story, here are four ways you can help.

1) If you feel so moved, I'd love you to post your impressions of the story in a review on Amazon and / or Goodreads. Lots of readers rely on reviews when deciding which novel next to read. Also, reviews drive sales and are one of the metrics Amazon uses when ranking books.

2) Recommend *PARALLEL LIVES A 60's Love Story* to your friends and family.

3) Gift the novel to anyone you believe will enjoy the story.

4) Share your impressions and the cover of the book on social media.

I appreciate any help you choose to offer. Thank you.

Wishing you well on your spiritual and creative journey,

Martha

Martha Alderson
MarthaAlderson.com